Wine in my Sippy Cup

Deborah Dove

WINE IN MY SIPPY CUP

For Ally, Hayden, and Caroline
who know my heart better than anyone else.
Always know how much you are loved.

And for Robert for stitching the quilt with me, crooked seams and all.

Chapter One

Monday, September 29th, 7:05 p.m.

If you'd told me fifteen years ago that one day I'd be sitting in someone's living room examining sex toys with twenty women I barely knew, I would have called you a liar. But to be fair, fifteen years ago I was a different person. Not literally, of course. I didn't witness a murder and get assigned a new identity in the witness protection program or anything. I was still Elizabeth Cartwright. Actually, no I wasn't. Fifteen years ago I was Elizabeth Moore, so I guess I actually was a different person.

Fifteen years ago, Lizzie Moore had a crisp diploma with the ink barely dry on it from Duke University and a job as the media coordinator for McMillan hotels. She was slim and fit and wore stylishly hip outfits (size 6) from stores such as Harold's and Ann Taylor and J Crew. She was fun and witty and spontaneous, and drove a sporty candy apple red Fiat convertible. Her smart apartment in fashionable uptown was furnished with Pottery Barn furniture, framed photographs from trips to Milan, London and Paris, with nothing but a couple of expired cartons of yogurt and a bottle of Evian in the refrigerator because Liz Moore was too busy going out every night to need anything as mundane as groceries.

Today, Liz Cartwright (nee Lizzie Moore) is the wife of Scott Cartwright, corporate attorney, and mother to Isabella (age 6), Will (age 4) and Daisy, who's eighteen months old. Unlike my former self, I am now a size 12 with a rounded tummy that has never quite bounced back from carrying three children and I wear an assortment of jeans, yoga pants and t-shirts impulsively grabbed off the racks at Target while running in with three kids in tow for toilet paper. Looking good today means I actually left the house in a shirt without spit up down the back or a blob of carrots on the front. A baby blue Honda minivan with sliding doors and a flip down DVD player has taken the place of the candy apple red convertible, and instead of a smart apartment in the city, I now live in suburbia in a brick two story McMansion that looks just like every other house on the street, but with longer grass and more weeds in the flower bed. My frig is now well stocked with organic milk, Yo Baby yogurt, last night's leftover macaroni and cheese, several half started ketchup bottles, and a secret stash of fun size Milky Ways. I'm still fun and witty, although not many of the uber moms in suburbia always get my jokes. Thankfully, I have a few good friends that do. Thanks to one of those so called good friends, I am sitting here in someone named Jennifer's immaculate living room while Julie, a perky blond, tells me how to bring the romance back into my life.

"This small bottle," she says confidentially, holding up a tiny red bottle, "will change your life. This is a fun little lubricant that goes on COLD, becomes WARM when you rub it in and ON FIRE when you blow on it!" She adds the last with a triumphant little squeal that makes me jump.

Julie looks quite pleased with the prospect of the magical lubricant, but I can't help but wonder if you really want to feel like you're on fire at any time, much less when you're naked. Julie has been urging us to "hold" the products and "feel" the products – "this is a fun girl's night out!" she enthuses. Across the room, a small cluster of giggling women have taken her at her word and have disappeared into the bathroom together with the bottle of lubricant and a handful of Q-tips.

I glance over at my friend Angie, who knows Jennifer from her neighborhood bunko group and was the one who coerced me into coming. We've been friends ever since our daughters met in preschool. We bonded almost instantly over the fact that we were both transplants (she from California, me from Pennsylvania) and career women at heart who had reluctantly put our careers on hold for the sake of our daughters, whom we adored more than life itself. However, I quickly realize that knowing someone well enough to help yourself to their Motrin without asking doesn't mean you know whether they are the sort of woman who might go into the bathroom with another woman to experiment with a "fun" lubricant. My misgivings must show on my face because Angie takes one look at me, laughs and says, "As if!"

Relieved, I lean over to whisper to her, "Does Richard know you're here?"

"Oh, yes," she whispers back. "This is the one home party he doesn't give me a budget for or complain about keeping the kids for. I always buy a lot of sex toys. Then every time I want to go out for happy hour or just to Target by myself, I tell him I'm going to a Playful Passion party and pull something out of my secret stash to show him that I 'bought' when I get home."

"Wow," I say, impressed. This is one of the reasons I'm friends with Angie. She is devious in ways I can only aspire to.

I don't get the opportunity to say anything else because Julie has now whipped out a translucent blue phallus-shaped object that has several whirling parts. I sit there transfixed and more than a little befuddled. Since I resolutely became familiar with my own body with a hand mirror and a tampon at the ripe age of 17 (no thanks to my mom, who still refers to her own vagina as a whispered "down there"), I feel fairly in touch with the makeup of the female anatomy, but I can't for the life of me figure out what you'd possibly need *three* motorized parts for.

"What's the third part for?" I whisper to Angie.

"The backdoor, honey," she whispers back.

Julie clears her throat to get our attention, which in my opinion is pretty unnecessary. When you turn a vibrator on in a room full of women, you pretty much have everyone's attention.

"This is our most popular vibrator, the Blue Love Bunny," Julie announces. I can't help it. A giggle slips out. Julie looks knowingly in my direction.

"Many of us have husbands that work a lot," she says. "They spend a lot of time at the office, and when they come home they need to unwind."

Uh huh. I can see where this is going. In fact, I could probably give her sales pitch. Your husband works hard, blah, blah, blah. You can help him unwind with a little sex, help him blow off steam (ha ha —maybe I *could* sell this stuff).

"Let's be honest," she says. "Some of us just don't get sex as often as we want it."

Huh?

"My husband Mark was so glad when I purchased the Love Bunny," she continues confidentially. "If we do it two or three times a week he's happy. Me? I need a little more. Now, thanks to this little blue guy, we're both happy and Mark can get some sleep."

Obviously I've been plopped down in an alternative universe where the women want sex and the men have headaches. Julie looks human, but she can't possibly be. I mean, what American woman wants sex all the time? We're way too tired. On a typical evening, by the time I give Daisy and Will a bath, oversee Isabella's shower and blow dry and braid her long hair, make sure everyone has brushed their teeth, rock Daisy to sleep, read Will and Bella books, say prayers and sing songs with Will, say prayers and sing songs with Bella, feed the dog, make lunches for the next day, take something out of the freezer to defrost for dinner tomorrow, check Bella's school papers and start the dishwasher, I'm exhausted. Of course, Scott is usually just getting home about then, so I fix him a plate to eat and sit with him and hear about his day. By the time we're finished talking, I just want to crawl into bed in an oversized comfy t-shirt with a good book and spend fifteen minutes without anyone touching me, talking to me or needing anything from me. So yeah, I'm thinking I could live without the Blue Love Bunny. Most of my friends feel exactly the same, so I can't explain Julie's oddly voracious appetite for sex. Unless....

"Do you have any kids?" I ask, certain I have hit upon her secret. I have very vague but pleasant memories of great sex, and lots of it, before Bella was born.

"Oh yes, I have four," she says. "And three of them have been conceived since I began selling Playful Passion products," she adds with a wink. "Do you have any of our products already?"

Oh crap, I groan inwardly. Way to go and attract attention to myself.

"Ummm, no," I say apologetically. "I don't really have a place to keep, uh, these kinds of products." This is true. Nothing is sacred in my house. In fact, yesterday Will raided my lingerie drawer and was using my bra as a slingshot to shoot bouncy balls at Bella. Apparently Will was David and Bella was Goliath.

"We have just the solution for that," says the ever perky Julie. She turns to the table behind her where all of the products are displayed and selects a small pink satin pillow. "It's the Hide Away Pillow. You just slide your product in this hidden zippered compartment on the side like so and there you go!" She expertly zips the pillow closed around the Blue Love Bunny. "Your toy is hidden in plain sight."

That would be just great until Bella grabbed the vibrator pillow during a pillow fight and clunked Will in the head with it. I can just imagine explaining that one in the emergency room.

After Julie has demonstrated a few more products, we all meander around nibbling at the spread Jennifer has provided, drinking wine and looking at all the products.

"What are you getting, the Blue Love Bunny?" Angie says, smiling wickedly as she comes over to where I'm half-heartedly inspecting massage oils.

"Uggh, do I have to get anything?"

"Yes, you know the rules. You go to a party, you have to buy something. In fact, even if you don't go to the party you have to buy something. It's in the rule book." She holds out her arms, which are loaded with stuff. "I'm getting some Lickety Split - it's an edible lubricant that tastes like a banana split, a strip tease card game, a book on erotic massage, and Mr. Pickle." She waves a bumpy, green dildo at me.

"You've got to be joking!" We both look at Mr. Pickle and burst out laughing.

"Seriously Liz," she says a few minutes later when we have finally stopped laughing. "Not all of us have a perfect marriage like you and Scott. I have to work to keep Richard interested."

Although I seriously doubt gorgeous, ballsy Angie has to work at keeping her husband interested, Scott and I do have a pretty good marriage. We met at the beginning of our last year of college in what is still one of the most embarrassing moments of my life. My friend Amber and I were headed to the Cosmic Cantina, a local watering hole near campus, for margaritas the weekend before fall classes started. Amber had picked me up in her roommate's car, something white and economical, and at her insistence, we'd stopped at a 7-Eleven to get some condoms ("just in case" she said). Amber stayed in the car while I ran in and bought the condoms, chuckling to myself as I picked out a box of Trojan Magnum Extra Larges for her. I figured if she was going to dream, she might as well dream big. After I paid for the condoms I came out of the store, got back into the passenger side of the car, shut the door, looked over at Amber and said, "Alright. I got you some huge condoms. Let's go." Only it wasn't Amber. I looked past the cute guy sitting in the driver's seat to the other white car parked one space over just in time to see Amber's head hit the steering wheel, her shoulders shaking with laughter. I scrambled out of the car as fast as humanly possible, got into the right car and threatened to strangle Amber with the straps of her brand new backpack if she didn't get the hell out of there.

Three days later, classes started and on Tuesday morning I walked into my Media Law and Ethics class and sat down in the only available seat. As the professor passed out the syllabus, I surreptitiously glanced around the room to see if anyone I knew was taking the same class. There were several girls and a guy I knew who had been in some of my other classes, but most of the faces were unfamiliar. Except for the guy sitting next to me. He looked vaguely familiar, with his golden, curly hair and piercing blue eyes, but I couldn't quite place how I knew him. I'd about given up trying to figure it out when the class dismissed. He leaned over and said in voice so low that only I could hear, "Still got those huge condoms?"

After turning as red as my shiny new spiral notebook, I did a very poor job of trying to explain why I had bought extra large condoms, Scott started laughing, and we ended up spending the next two hours together. He asked me out for the next weekend and the weekend after that, and we were pretty much a couple from then on. After we both graduated, Scott attended law school and I established myself as the head media coordinator for McMillan Hotels and we continued to date. The day after Scott's graduation from law school, he proposed with a beautiful one carat marquise diamond solitaire hidden in the tip of a Trojan Magnum extra large condom. He got a job at a prestigious Dallas law firm and I applied for and got a transfer to McMillan's Dallas branch. A year later we got married, moved in together, took frequent jaunts to Europe during the summer (staying at McMillan Hotels for free, of course), and met our friends for drinks and dinner at the newest trendy restaurants and clubs after work. Then, three days short of our third anniversary, I peed on a stick, watching as the window turned from lilac to dark purple before leaving behind two distinct lines, changing our lives forever.

Although we could have continued to live in our apartment in the city, Scott and I both agreed it wasn't the best place to raise a baby. Catering to upwardly mobile professionals like ourselves, our apartment complex featured a pool where the beer flowed and the music blasted on the weekends, a sophisticated fitness room, a putting green and sand volleyball court and two single guys who lived above us who frequently had loud parties, which had never really bothered us since we were usually at the parties. What our apartment didn't have was a second bedroom, a backyard, or even a nearby playground.

Six months pregnant and big enough to be incubating a large land mammal instead of a little human the size of a peanut (my doctor had double checked to make sure I wasn't having twins at my five month check up), Scott and I spent our weekends in the backseat of an enormous black Lincoln Town Car with Gladys the Ultimate Dallasite Realtor, who had unnaturally bleached blond hair teased so high her hair pins got scared and a vast collection of gaudy jewelry that she felt compelled to wear all at the same time. We finally settled on the upscale suburb of Westfield, thirty miles northwest of Dallas, population 50,000. We built our dream home in a subdivision called Twin Oaks, complete with granite countertops, hand scraped hardwood floors, a sweeping fairytale staircase, a three car garage, and a study with built in bookshelves filled with Scott's hard bound law journals and my first edition collection of books by Anna Quinlan. In short, we settled into life in suburbia.

Although I sometimes miss the hum and excitement of the city and being able to walk to shops or to get a coffee, it's a nice neighborhood, especially for families. All of the streets are named after trees (ours is Weeping Willow Lane), there's a community swimming pool, two parks, and the elementary school Bella attends is in walking distance. There is a Homeowner's Association that organizes garage sales and Halloween parties and progressive dinners, in addition to telling you what color you can paint your front door, how many shrubs you can plant in your front yard and what color Christmas lights you can put on your house.

Soon after we moved in, Isabella was born and together, Scott and I slowly morphed from trendy, stylish, professional globetrotters into parents, although my morphing was much more dramatic than Scott's.

I have not always been a stay at home mom; I did go back to work for awhile after Isabella was born. I have always considered myself to be a career woman, and I loved my job. I loved writing press releases and articles and coordinating events for the hotel. I loved that I could travel just about anywhere in the world and stay at a McMillan Hotel for free. And in those days of Bella's infancy, there were days that I loved that I could walk into work and talk to my friend Laura about the shoe sale at Nordstrom's instead of how many times the baby had pooped and what it looked like. But as much as I loved my job, I loved being with Isabella more. I quickly grew tired of leaving her each day, breast pump inconspicuously concealed in a black briefcase as breastfeeding became incorporated in my professional persona, to be accomplished quickly and efficiently in the sterility of my office instead of in the rocking chair in front of a sunny window with Bella's warm little body tucked next to mine as one chubby hand reached up to play with my hair. I dreaded the day that my babysitter Carla would tell me that Bella laughed for the first time, or finally rolled over, or took her first steps, while I was on the phone in an office overlooking the freeway arranging for the hotel to be featured in an article on the best places to have a wedding.

I began to don a mantle of guilt which I wore to work each day like an old aunt's favorite cardigan. Guilt over not spending enough time with Isabella, over not being the one to comfort her when a loud noise made her cry, over not being there to rock her to sleep. About six months after I went back to work, Scott found me crying in the kitchen over a loaf of bread.

"What's wrong?" he had asked, concerned that his once sane wife had once again dissolved into a mess of hormonal tears.

"I can't cut sandwiches into fun shapes for Bella," I said through my sobs.

"Sandwiches! Honey, she's six months old. She doesn't even have teeth."

"I know," I said with a big hiccup. "But one day she will and I'll be late for work 'cause I'm always late for work and I won't have time to cut the crusts off or make teddy bear shapes and she'll have to eat those horrible lunchable things every day for the rest of her life until she's old enough to make a peanut butter and jelly sandwich for herself."

Okay, so it wasn't my sanest moment, but it's hard to be sane when you're operating on four hours sleep (not necessarily in a row), padding your bra when you're not even wearing a low cut top or going to a club, and being so scattered from trying to give 100 percent at work and 100 percent at home that you end up cleaning the bathrooms with spray starch (true story). Scott suggested that I trying staying at home with Isabella for awhile and I agreed, but I was adamant that it was only until Bella was in school. It was to be a hiatus; I was too much of an independent woman to give up my career entirely. Of course here I am, six years, three kids and twenty pounds later. Scott has been a trooper about it, and I will always be grateful to him for making it possible for me to stay at home with our kids. And overall, we do have a pretty good marriage. But perfect? Not hardly. Of course, Scott is usually charming when he is around my friends so they all think he's great, which he usually is. But he can also be moody, uncommunicative, unreasonable and downright grumpy, especially when he's working on a big case and stressed out from work. He's also hardly ever home since he became a partner two years ago, and when he is home he's constantly checking his phone or logging onto his work laptop to review a case.

Hmmm, maybe we do need to spice up our sex life a little. I check out the product table again and end up buying a book called *52 Weeks of Spice: One Year to a Sexier Relationship.* I know, I know. It's not Mr. Pickle, but it's a start.

Chapter Two

Tuesday, October 7th

It's my birthday, and I'm not having a good day. It all started this morning when I got home from walking Bella to school. I noticed the powder room toilet smelled a little funky, but that isn't really anything out of the ordinary with a four year old boy in the house. Will insists on peeing standing up "like Daddy," but he has the attention span of a housefly so any distraction – a crack on the ceiling, the phone ringing, the sudden need to check and see if the bug bite from last week is gone – and his little willy is like one of those sprinkler toys that gyrate and wiggle every which way, spraying everything in a 360 degree radius.

Thinking this was the cause of the funky smell, I scoured the toilet, scrubbed the walls and tile around the toilet and sprayed Febreeze all around it for the third time in as many days. That was an hour ago; now the toilet has started belching.

"Will!" I yell up the stairs to the playroom where he is playing. "Have you lost any of your Power Rangers in the potty?"

This isn't as crazy as it sounds. Will adores action figures and plays with them constantly, even when he's sitting on the toilet. On more than one occasion I, outfitted with rubber gloves and sheer resolve, have reached into an unflushed toilet to fish out an action figure. The kids usually crowd around the toilet to watch me perform this task with a mix of horror and gleeful fascination.

"I'm never going to be a mom," Bella usually says with disgust once I have triumphantly brandished the retrieved toy. "You have to do too much gross stuff."

Although Will assures me he hasn't dropped anyone in the toilet lately, on accident or on purpose, I'm thinking it's quite possible that one of his Red Rangers has been surfing the sewer line and the toilet gods are about to spew him back. So I do what every smart, educated woman would do in this situation. I call my husband. His secretary, Connie, answers.

"Hi Liz," she says brightly. Connie is a very sweet woman of about fifty five and I adore her. Competent, briskly efficient but easy going, she is the perfect assistant for Scott, who can get a little intense, especially when it comes to work. Connie is great at helping him get what he needs without putting up with his bullshit. Kind of like me, but in an older, Naturalizer shoe wearing sort of way that makes me fairly confident I will never walk into Scott's office to find him bending the secretary over the water cooler. Well…at least not his own secretary.

"Sorry Liz, he's in a partner meeting," Connie says. "Are you at home? I'll have him call you back when he gets out."

Scott hates partner meetings. Last month they spent two hours discussing how to make their meetings more efficient. Leave it to a bunch of lawyers! "Actually it's kind of an emergency," I say, certain he will welcome the interruption. "Can you get him now?"

"Sure Liz. Just a minute."

A good three minutes later, Scott picks up the phone.

"What is it Liz?" He sounds impatient and short tempered.

"Sorry to interrupt your partner meeting but the toilet is kind of belching and it smells like rotten eggs and I think it's about to overflow. I tried using the plunger thing and I poured Drano down it, but it didn't help. What should I do?"

"Jeez Liz," he sounds exasperated. "One of the reasons you stay at home is to deal with this kind of stuff so I don't have

13

to. I don't know. Call a plumber!"

O-kay. Someone got up on the wrong side of the conference table. After I hang up the phone, I look over at Daisy, who is busily pulling all of the scotch tape out of the dispenser. "Looks like it's up to you and me," I say in a happy, cheerful voice, as if fixing the toilet on my birthday will be just wonderful – almost as good the spa day gift certificate I was hoping for (but hey, it's still early). She smiles at me, a toothy grin that I can't help but smile back at. With the baby balanced on my hip, I look through the file cabinet and finally locate the plumber's business card.

After parking Daisy in front of a Wiggles DVD with a cup of Cheerios to ensure I will actually be able to carry on a five minute telephone conversation (Will is still deeply engrossed in whatever he's playing upstairs), I call the plumber. He says that although he could come out, it would be day after tomorrow before he could fit me in and I would end up paying a $175 service call for something my husband could just as easily do himself. He says it's probably a stopped up line and suggests that I get something called a toilet snake. I snicker, wondering if this is some kind of deviant plumber joke. Surely there isn't really a tool called that.

He goes on to tell me that if that doesn't work, the problem may be with the outside line to the street and I should get something called a rubber bladder at the hardware store, attach it to a garden hose and use the water pressure to force out whatever is stopping up the line. I think I might have better luck performing brain surgery or solving the national health crisis.

"You got kids?" he asks.

"Yes, three," I say.

"That's it, then," he says triumphantly. "They're always throwing stuff down the toilet. Get your husband to put his snake down the hole until he gets past the resistance. If that fails, then he can just blow it and fix the problem."

Spoken just like a man! I hang up the phone and check the number to make sure I didn't just call 1-900-PLUMBER-PORN.

Although this sounds way out of my league as far as home repairs go, Scott was so pissy on the phone that I am determined to fix the toilet myself. No way will I ask for his help again! Besides, I tell myself, I am a smart, independent woman who can take care of herself. I can do this!

After much pleading and cajoling, I lure Will away from the elaborate battle he has staged between the Star Wars action figures and the Power Rangers action figures with the promise of playing "I Spy" all the way to and from the store, and the kids and I head to Home Depot. I feel like a chain smoker at a pulmonologists convention walking into a suburban Home Depot on a weekday morning with two small kids.

Unlike when I go to Super Target, where I am perfectly content to wander each aisle looking for that one specific item I need (okay, okay, so I know the exact layout of the Target store and never actually have to wander looking for anything, and I never get just one thing), when we get to Home Depot I go straight to the first guy I see in an orange vest and tell him what I'm looking for. There is just no joy in browsing at Home Depot. He calls over another sales associate, who has to flag down yet another sales guy, who finally directs me to the plumbing parts aisle. Whatever idiot decided the plumbing aisle should be directly across from the riding lawnmowers should be shot. Although to be fair, probably not many women toting kids shop the plumbing aisle with any regularity.

Of course, Will begs to sit on all of them, and being a good Mommy I oblige him. Daisy, who thinks she should do everything Will does, starts to wail and wave her arms so I extricate her from the shopping cart and put her on one of the tractors also. Will is definitely my most imaginative child, and he immediately starts making race car noises. He whips the steering wheel around and jumps up and down in the seat, all the while narrating the close

NASCAR tractor race he is apparently winning. I hope whoever buys the display tractors gets a really good deal. People are stopping to stare. I give Will the one minute warning, and as he is dismounting from the winning tractor, an older gentleman in a Home Depot vest smiles at us and shakes his head.

"You sure do have your hands full," he says.

"Yes," I say brightly. "But I can't tell you how much easier it is with my other five at school."

I go back to the plumbing section, finally locate the part I'm looking for (huh, there really is something called a toilet snake) and leave the store. One Happy Meal and a Big Mac combo later (I really was going to get a salad, but I had to get French fries to share with Daisy), we're back home. Daisy is napping and I'm trying to figure out how the heck to use the toilet snake. Will is bouncing around the bathroom, keeping up a running commentary of questions and remarks that I could happily do without. "Why's it called a snake mommy? Cause' it doesn't even have eyes or fangs. How old do I have to be to have a snake?" "Can I try? I can fit my hand up that hole. I know, 'cause one time Bella dropped a Polly Pocket shoe in there and I got it out for her." "Where does the poop go when it's flushed down the potty? Danny says it gets cycled and comes out your sink. I bet that's why we drink bottled water."

I finally give up and go get Bella from school. Once we're back home and I've given everyone a snack, I put PBS cartoons on with strict instructions for Bella to watch Daisy while I go back into the bathroom. Things don't look good. There's no longer any water left in the toilet and it smells even worse than before. I concede defeat. Pissy or not, Scott is going to have to fix this one. Luckily, since it's my birthday, he's planning to be home early so he and the kids can take me out to dinner.

He texts me at 4:00 p.m. *"Off 2 client meeting, then home for big bday celebration. Where do u want to go for dinner?"*

16

Although somewhere dimly lit, with candles on the table, linen tablecloths, an attentive waiter and an extensive wine menu would be nice, I will have to settle for what's doable with three small children – the ubiquitous family friendly restaurant. This means there will be sticky tables and floors, lots of noise, crayons, and unlimited self-serve ice cream. It also means that I will spend my meal performing like a well-trained athlete trying to complete a sprint before the clock runs out. Hurry and cut three plates of meat into tiny bite sized pieces, unwrap three straws and insert in cups, hand out drinks, squirt ketchup, flag down the waiter and ask him to bring Ranch, take someone to the bathroom, hurry back, take the other child who now has to go to bathroom, then come back and shovel my own (now cold) food in before Daisy has finished her meal and starts wailing to get down, or worse, entertaining herself by trying to remove her diaper, spitting milk out of her mouth, or playing drums on the table with knives she managed to swipe from somewhere despite the fact that we always put them out of her reach. I do, however, draw the line at spending my birthday anywhere there is someone dressed up as an overgrown rodent.

"How about Joe's?"

At least they have a playground where the kids can play while Scott and I enjoy a drink.

"Gr8. C U soon".

Scott calls at 6:45.

"I'm so sorry," he says. "My client meeting ran late. I'm on my way home now. Why don't you fix the kids something quick, and then after they go to bed I can go pick up something for us or I'll make you dinner."

Although I am a little annoyed (after all, everyone has had a bath and is all dressed and waiting for Daddy to come home and I don't want to actually cook anything on my birthday), there is a certain appeal to his suggestion. We can enjoy a nice quiet dinner, maybe on the patio, and some unhurried conversation before he presents me with my spa gift certificate or maybe even something better. Hmmm, can't think of anything better. He better stick with the spa day.

Amid much disappointed protest, I explain to the kids that Daddy is running late and we will all go out to celebrate my birthday on the weekend, and then I make them macaroni and cheese and peas. Scott walks through the door at 7:45 with kisses and hugs for the kids and a bouquet of flowers for me.

"Happy birthday," he says with a kiss. "Sorry I'm late."

"You can make it up to me," I say. "Why don't you make me your famous bacon and tomato linguine?"

Although he rarely does it anymore, Scott is quite a good cook and used to make dinner a lot. I simply love his linguine; he makes it with a delicious homemade light cream sauce with spinach, bacon and tomato. It's so good I sometimes fantasize about it when we make love. Actually, in the fantasy he cleans the house, does the laundry, and then makes the linguine in a pair of tight Levis and nothing else, but you get the point. The linguine is an integral part.

"But first," I say. "Remember the toilet problem I called you about? I can't fix it. I bought a toilet snake," I waggle my eyebrows at him. "But it didn't work. Why don't you take a look at it while I'm putting the kids to bed? Then we can have dinner."

He agrees and I take Daisy upstairs, put her pajamas on, read her books, turn on the musical aquarium that she can't fall asleep without, and tuck her into her crib. When I come back downstairs to corral Will and Bella to bed, Bella informs me that Daddy has gone to the hardware store.

"Now?" I say with surprise. It's almost 8:30.

"He said to tell you he'd be right back," she says. "He was on the phone with a plumber and said he had to go get something."

"Okay. It's time for bed," I say.

"Mommy, wait," Bella says. "Close your eyes." She leads me over to the kitchen table and pulls out a chair for me. "No peeking!" she orders. I hear much giggling, whispering, a rustle of wrappers, and then, "Open your eyes, Mommy."

The lights have been turned out, and I see that my sweet little girl has arranged four Little Debbie cosmic brownies on a plate surrounding a battery operated tea light.

"I know it's not a real candle but you won't let me use matches," she says apologetically.

I have a sudden lump in my throat. "This is perfect," I say truthfully. The two of them sing Happy Birthday to me, and then produce cards they have made.

"This is you and me Mommy," says Bella, showing me her card on which she has drawn meticulous pictures of our stick figure family beneath a rainbow and a smiling sun.

"Look at mine," says Will, bouncing up and down and pointing to the red and brown circular scribbles on his card. "This is the inside of a ladybug."

"We'll help Daisy draw one for you tomorrow," Bella adds. "We just didn't think of doing it 'til now."

"I am a very lucky mommy," I say, giving each one of them a big hug. "I love my cards and I love you! Thank you for making my birthday so special!"

I make a wish, turn off the tea light, and pour milk for the three of us, which we drink while we eat our brownies. A battery operated tea light and a plate of manufactured-tasting brownies with candy sprinkles is a far cry from a fancy, dimly lit restaurant with a great wine menu, but I wouldn't trade it for anything.

I give both Bella and Will piggyback rides up stairs, then time them as they race to put on their pjs and brush their teeth before we all hop into Bella's bed, me in the middle with a child snuggled under each of my arms. We read three books, then I piggy back Will to his room, playing our nightly game of "is this your room?," where I try to put him to bed in Bella's room, the playroom, and the bathroom, and he tells me why each won't work.

"Too girly," he says with a giggle. Then, "No toys," and finally, "No bed." When we finally make it to his room ("yes, this one Mommy"), I tuck him in, and then go back to Bella's room. She wants no part of such childish games, thank you very much, so I climb under her quilt with her and she reads a chapter of Junie B. Jones to me. I sing her the lullaby I have been singing to her since she was born, tuck her in, and then go back downstairs.

I find Scott outside in a flower bed in front of the house with a flashlight tucked under his chin and an assortment of tools spread out around him.

"What are you doing?" I ask curiously.

"The plumber told me the problem is with our line to the street and if we don't get it taken care of as soon as possible, it could flood our house. He said if I got this bladder thing and hooked it up to our garden hose, the water pressure would blow out whatever was blocking the pipe."

"Did he tell you that a good blow will solve all your problems?"

"What?" Scott looks up in confusion.

"Never mind," I say. "Want me to hold the flashlight?"

We stand in the flower bed for the next thirty minutes, me holding the flashlight while Scott tries to work the rubber bladder down into the drain.

"I got it," he finally says triumphantly. "I'm going to go turn the hose on. Tell me if anything happens."

Scott walks around to the side of the house and turns the water on.

"Anything happening?" he yells.

"No," I yell back. I can hear the water rushing through the hose as he turns it on full blast.

"Now?" he asks.

"I don't hear anything," I call back. "I think it's clear."

Scott turns the water off and comes back to the flower bed.

I keep the flashlight trained on the hole as he carefully pulls the hose out. He turns to go into the garage and, tired of standing, I sit down in the flower bed and peer into the hole to see if I can see anything.

Suddenly, whoosh! I am hit square in the face by an explosion of backed up sewage. Scott turns around in time to see a clump of toilet paper whack me in the forehead.

"Humph," he says. "I guess it wasn't clear." He looks in bewilderment at the drain, which is pouring brownish water (I don't even want to think about it) and toilet paper into the flower bed.

Uggh! I run inside and take a thirty minute shower, washing my hair and body three times. Finally clean and dry in comfy sweat pants and an old t-shirt, I go in search of Scott. He's still in the flower bed, shoveling the last of the toilet paper into a trash bag.

"I called the plumber," he says without looking up. I have a sneaking suspicion it's because he's afraid he might start laughing if he looks me in the eye. "He said it must be blocked pretty good. When we poured the water in, it had no place to go but back out, taking with it all of the sewage that has accumulated since it got blocked."

"We?" I ask incredulously.

He looks up at me. "He said he can come out tomorrow," he adds helpfully.

"Great!" I say. "That's just great. I'm going inside to make myself a bologna sandwich."

As I turn to go inside, he calls after me, "Sorry you've had a crappy birthday!" I swear I can hear him laughing as I close the door.

Chapter Three

Friday, October 10th

Now this is a birthday celebration! I'm sitting on Kate's patio with a glass of red wine in my hand, surrounded by my three closest friends. Usually we go to a restaurant to celebrate each other's birthdays, but Kate's husband is out of town and her babysitter fell through, so we're at her house. However, Kate's house is just as good, if not better than, any restaurant we could afford.

Kate is my perfect friend. And I don't just mean she's a great friend, although she is that too. She is, after all, the one of the four of us who always remembers to mail birthday cards (which are always the perfect blend of sophisticated and sweet and arrive exactly on time in brightly colored envelopes which she has festively embellished with a paint pen). Unlike me, Kate would never send an off humor card grabbed off the 99 cent rack at Wal-Mart and stuck in the mailbox three days late. Before our neighborhood was finished, we were considered to be on a rural route and had a mail carrier who delivered mail in a regular car. Once, his car caught on fire and we got a letter from the post office telling us that any or all of our mail could have been burned in the fire. Now that I know this is a real possibility, any time I mail something late I feign surprise when the recipient doesn't get it on time.

"Wow, maybe the mail carrier's car caught on fire," I suggest. "You know, it happened to me once!"

Of course, you can really only use that excuse with someone once (and actually, as it turns out, never when it comes to an overdue credit card payment), and I exhausted it pretty early on with Kate, Angie and Meg. But they all know me well enough now that it doesn't matter.

But our Kate, she's not like that at all. In addition to being the perfect friend, she has the perfect life. And you can't even hate her for it because she's so genuinely nice. In addition to being smart, thoughtful, slim, petite and pretty, she has a gorgeous husband who adores her, one perfect child, Chloe (a beautiful little girl Bella's age who dresses in the perfectly coordinated outfits Kate lays out for her, attends private school and never fails to compliment me on my hair or outfit when she has play dates at our house), and a house that looks like it was just featured in *Southern Living* magazine. Actually, come to think of it, Kate's house actually was once featured in *Southern Living*.

The first time I walked into Kate's house, I went home and cried. Seriously! Will was four months old at the time, and the shock of going from her beautiful house, which was so tidy and clean and organized to my house, with it's piles of laundry, Bella's Barbie's strewn across the floor which hadn't been vacuumed in a week and dishes piled in the sink because there was never enough time to actually get them all put away between feedings, was too much too bear. Overwhelmed with the demands of a new baby and a toddler, I would have given anything to be transported to the calm beauty of Kate's house.

When I explained my outburst to Scott that evening, he had looked almost joyful. "I know exactly what you mean," he said excitedly. "I've been thinking our house looks like a wreck too! I'm so glad to know you feel the same way. But I think you could fix it if you have a little more structure to your day!"

I'm pretty sure that if I had strangled him with the cord of my electric breast pump (it was the closest weapon I had at the time) a jury of women would have acquitted me. We hired a housekeeper a week later. We could barely afford it so I only had her come for six months, but I figured it was cheaper than marriage counseling.

So anyway, here we are sitting on perfect Kate's perfect patio, while her perfect child is inside doing something quiet and good (perhaps cross stitching the Lord's Prayer on a linen pillowcase?). As you might imagine, Kate's patio is gorgeous. There are white wicker patio chairs sporting brightly covered cushions, a porch swing piled high with comfy pillows, and a variety of potted plants and flowers clustered around the edges of the patio – an oasis of sophisticated calm in the suburbs. The trill of birds from the feeders located in her heavily treed back yard and the cascade of water from a water fountain in one of the flower beds create soothing background music, although that's not really necessary since classical music (Kate's favorite) is softly wafting from the speakers subtly tucked under the eaves of the porch. Several citronella candles in sherbet shades of light orange, lime green and a pale lemon yellow are lit to keep the mosquitoes at bay, although since it is early October, we don't have to worry about them too much. A low, iron table holds three gaily wrapped packages (yay, presents!), and I'm pretty sure I caught sight of a chocolate frosted cake under a pretty glass cake server in the kitchen. This is one of the nice things about having girlfriends. Girlfriends know how to celebrate your birthday!

"This is so nice," I sigh as I lean my head back against a comfy floral pillow. "So where's Hugh?"

"He's in New York," says Kate. "Chloe and I were going to meet him for the weekend but I have a job."

Did I mention that in addition to everything else perfect in her life, Kate also has the perfect job? She calls it her jobette because it's part time, but the rest of us are jealous. She's a freelance writer for several local magazines and newspapers, and although a lot of times her assignments involve boring stuff like interviewing mayors and arguing the merits of zoning proposals, every once in while she gets to do something fun.

"What is it?" Angie asks. "It had better be good if you're giving up a weekend with Mr. Hunk for it."

"Forget Mr. Hunk," Meg chimes in. "She's giving up a week in New York City."

"Good point," I say. "How can you possibly give up New York in the fall? Think about the leaves in Central Park, shopping, SoHo, shopping, taking a taxi everywhere, shopping..."

"Room service," adds Meg.

"Broadway shows," I interject.

Everyone starts laughing.

"What?" I say. "Angie, I know you like Broadway shows just as much as I do. Remember Mamma Mia?"

"Liz, you said Broadway shoes," Angie says.

"I did not."

"Yes, you did. I swear you need a shoe twelve step program."

"Well, whatever," I say with sniff. "Shoes are important. No matter how much weight you gain, you can always fit into your shoes. And New York does have the best shoe shopping. When I was there before Bella was born..." I start.

"We know, we know," Angie says with a groan. "You got that pair of fabulous Manolo suede ankle boots on sale for $500. I still covet those."

I stop and sigh. As a stay at home mom, I can't fathom spending $500 dollars on a pair of shoes anymore (no matter how fabulous they are, and let me tell you those boots are pretty fabulous). Five hundred dollars is a month's worth of groceries, almost half of what we manage to put away each year for the kids' college, or about thirty pairs of shoes from Payless if they're doing that "buy one, get one" deal.

"My point is that New York is major," I say. "So c'mon Kate, this had better be good."

"Well," Kate says with a small smile. "It's an article on dating services and whether they can really match people up with their perfect soul mate. I have an interview with the founder of Web of Love Saturday afternoon."

"Nope," says Meg decisively. "People always lie on those things and you find out that 'values family relationships' means he still lives at home with his parents."

"Yeah," I add with a laugh. "And 'self aware' means he masturbates."

"Wait a minute," Angie says seriously. "I really think dating services can work. It's the one time you can list the qualities you want in a partner without reservation and actually ask for them. Why wouldn't you be honest? "

"Oh my gosh," I say with a dawning realization. "I think that's the dating service Scott's dad uses."

"Eeew," Meg says.

My friends have heard all about Scott's dad, who seems to be in the throes of a midlife crisis. Three months ago, he told Candace, Scott's mom and his wife of forty years, that he didn't really think their marriage was working anymore and he wanted to be free. Two weeks later he had signed a contract with an online dating service. Now he is dating a woman named Ruth who according to Scott's sister Elise looks just like Candace, but about fifteen years younger. The whole thing drives Scott nuts. Me, I can't get over the fact that thirty years ago, Ruth wouldn't have been old enough to baby-sit Scott. Not that I share that little tidbit with him.

"Really?" Kate says with interest. "Do you think he'd tell me about it? Is it love?"

"How can you be in love with someone you just met through a dating service?" I scoff.

"My college roommate met her husband on the Date Connection and they couldn't be more perfect for each other," Angie chimes in.

Seriously," she adds as she sees our skeptical looks. "They're like Liz and Scott."

"Really?" I say with a smile. "Did he spend her birthday shoveling excrement out of the flower bed and laughing about the fact that it hit her in the face?"

"Oh, sweetie," Kate says as she wraps an arm around my shoulder. "What happened?"

See what I mean about Kate being the perfect friend? Angie, on the other hand, just snorted wine out of her nose.

I tell them the whole story amid many quite satisfactory murmurs of sympathy and outrage and some comforting pats on the back. Okay, and a few laughs too. It's much easier to see the humor in the situation after a few glasses of wine and a proper birthday celebration. Plus, Scott has promised me linguine tomorrow. I'm trying to figure out how to get him to clean the house first.

"Sweetie, you need to open some presents," Meg says, reaching across the table to pour me some more wine.

Well, you don't have to ask me twice. I love presents. I open Kate's present first. I know it's Kate's because of the thick, glossy, cream colored paper, beautiful pink organza bow, and handmade card. Inside is a gorgeous Brighton silver charm bracelet. It's fabulous and totally me. I thank her profusely and put it on, admiring how the assortment of silver crosses (my favorite) dangle.

Next is Meg's. Of the four of us, Meg struggles the most financially. As a result, she tends to put more thought and personality than money into her gifts, and they are always unique and creative, like the pink papier-mâché scrapbook she gave me when Daisy was born, or the decoupaged clipboard in a funky pink and orange print she gave me for my birthday last year. I love Meg's gifts. I open the gift bag excitedly. Inside the tissue paper is a pretty brown wicker tote bag. Inside Meg has packed the components for a perfect picnic. There is a fleece blanket Meg has hand knotted, a glass candle holder with a lavender votive candle, a frou frou box of crackers, a bar of dark chocolate, a round of brie, a disposable camera, and a four pack of Three Thieves pinot grigio single serving packs that resemble elongated juice boxes.

"Oooh, yummy," I say.

"Aren't they cute?" Meg says, pointing to the wine boxes. "They're perfect for a picnic! And environmentally conscious too, so I knew you would love it."

"It's perfect," I say, and it is. Especially since I am on a mission to improve my love life.

"Look, look," Meg says, waving an envelope. "There's a card too."

Inside the card is a printed coupon for an afternoon of free babysitting.

"You're the best," I say, giving Meg a hug. "Thank you so much. I love it. And I am so dumping my kids on you next weekend."

"Absolutely!" Meg says. "Now Angie's." She hands me the last package, which is actually two packages wrapped in red Spiderman paper.

"Sorry," Angie says apologetically. "It's the only paper I had."

I rip open the paper of the first box. It's a plain brown box. I open the box and squeal with laughter. "Oh my gosh!" I exclaim. "You did not!"

Angie starts laughing. Meg and Kate are craning their necks, trying to see what's in the box. Angie and I can't stop laughing.

"What is it?" Kate asks.

"Yeah, c'mon," Meg says. "What's so funny?"

I remove Angie's gift from the box and dramatically hold it up for them to see.

"This," I say dramatically, "is the Blue Love Bunny."

"Is that a, uh…" Kate's voice trails off.

"Yes, it is an uh…." Angie says with a laugh. "I knew you really wanted it at the party," she says teasingly to me. "You were just too embarrassed to buy it."

"Yeah, right!" I say sarcastically.

"Open the other one."

A little afraid, I open the second package to more peals of laughter.

"I knew I couldn't give you the bunny without giving you that too," Angie says as I brandish the pink satin pillow.

Still laughing, I hug her.

"You'll be sorry you gave me this when I keep canceling our play dates."

"I'll take my chances," she says.

Chapter Four

Wednesday, October 15th

    It's 6:15 a.m., and although my alarm isn't set to go off for another fifteen minutes I am awakened by Will, who has climbed into bed with me. Still warm and sleepy, he scoots himself over until he is pressed as close to me as possible, his little batman pajama clad body fitting perfectly into the curves of mine, as if his body remembers the contours of my womb. Will has been like this since he was born. When I would nurse him in bed in the middle of the night, he'd wriggle as close as possible to me and we'd often fall asleep that way. As a toddler, he'd wake up way earlier than I was ready to get up, so I'd plop him in bed with me and Scott and like a little heat seeking missile, he'd snuggle up close to one of us (usually me, as Scott would get disgusted with his space being invaded and get up). Now that he's old enough to get up by himself, he comes downstairs almost every morning with his bedraggled and much loved blue bear tucked under his little arm and still climbs into bed with me for our morning cuddle.

    This is one of the compensations for mothers like me floundering in that unknown territory known as raising boys. I knew what I was getting into when I had Bella. When I gazed into her newborn face, I could envision my future as the mother of a little girl. I imagined cute outfits with coordinating shoes and hair bows, afternoons spent playing Barbies, princess dress up clothes and a cabinet full of art supplies.

When Will was born two years later, his precious scrunched up face, although achingly familiar, held an aura of mystery. Sure, I grew up with two brothers and am familiar enough with the male species to actually live somewhat peacefully with one, but what did I know about parenting a boy? Would I know how to play whatever boys played? Would I be able to handle a boy, who in my little girl filled world, appeared to all be wild little heathens who tied up their babysitters? Would I know what to buy him for Christmas or would that become Scott's exclusive domain?

Of course four years later, I have found many of my fears to be unfounded. I have discovered that tiny grey crew socks and mini athletic shorts can be almost as adorable as a pink dress with coordinating accessories and that super hero capes and fireman hats are equally at home in the dress up trunk. Will and I spend afternoons playing Power Rangers, which is pretty much the same thing as playing Barbies, just with transformer parts and weapons instead of stylish outfits. Furthermore, I have developed what must be a God given ability to know just what he will like because there is just no other reasonable explanation for my innate knowledge of Lego sets, Rescue Heroes and action figures. As far as I know, Will has never tied up the babysitter, although he once convinced one to eat Play-doh by telling her it was a cookie. And he loves the cabinet of art supplies just as much as Bella does.

I will say that having Will has made me realize that boys and girls are as different as night and day, no matter how equally you treat them. For example, if I give Will and Bella a few inanimate objects, say a package of sponges or plastic spoons, Bella will inevitably pretend they are a mommy, a daddy and a baby while Will turns them into weapons of mass destruction. When he was two, Will begged for a doll stroller like Bella's and, despite Scott's purely male chauvinist protests, my parents got him one for Christmas. I was congratulating myself on raising a boy who was not afraid to be nurturing when he started loading his Matchbox cars into it and ramming it into the wall.

Burping is another example. Will recently learned (with no outside instruction) how to make himself burp. And like most little boys, he finds burps incredibly funny. Come to think of it so does Bella, but I'm proof that she will outgrow it, whereas Scott is proof that no matter how old a male gets burps will always be funny.

I've also learned that like their daddies, little boys are equipped with an abundance of love that humbles me. Rarely a day goes by without Will saying to me, completely out of the blue, "Mommy, I love you." And just a few months ago when we were riding our bikes to the playground, he suddenly slammed on his brakes, hopped off his bike, and raced over to pick a dandelion which he proudly presented to me before calmly climbing back on his bike. Now carefully pressed inside a book, what was once a weed in someone's yard will always be a precious reminder to me of the simple abundance of my little boy's love.

So I wrap my arm around Will's warm little body, content to snuggle him until he grows too old to want to anymore. I must have turned off my alarm clock because when the sound of Daisy babbling over the monitor wakes me again, it is 7:30. Oh, crap. Bella has to be at school in twenty minutes. She already has three tardies this year (all of them my fault) and after the last one I got a very official letter in the mail informing me that my daughter was going to be considered truant if she had two more tardies. As if she has been skipping first grade to go smoke under the swing set!

I fly out of bed and up to Bella's room, nudging her awake and telling her to hurry and get dressed. I make a mental note (again) to get Scott to wake me up before he leaves for the office at 6:00. Back in the kitchen, I hastily pack her lunch (a Lunchable, which, ironically, she adores and I keep on hand for days just such as this), a banana, a granola bar and a juice box. Bella arrives in the kitchen just in time for me to hand her a cereal bar while I go rouse Will and pluck Daisy out of her crib and into the double stroller, still in her footy pajamas and soggy diaper, with a sippy cup of milk. We speed walk to school, Will and Daisy sucking away at their sippy cups like mini crack addicts and Bella skipping along beside me while keeping a running commentary on what she wants for Christmas (a new American Girl doll to go with her other four American Girl dolls), where her best friend Madison sat at lunch yesterday (next to Michael, who is so gross because he puts chocolate pudding on his hamburger), what she plans to do after school (organize her pencil case), and why purple is so much better than pink (I'm still not sure about that one).

When I get back home, I change Daisy's diaper, dress her and then make her and Will breakfast. I spend the next two hours racing around tidying up the house, which is like trying to bail water out of a boat with a sieve with an eighteen month old around. While I am unloading the dishwasher, Daisy is busy unloading the DVD cabinet. While I hastily put the DVDs away, she moves on to the shoe basket by the front door, trying on everyone's shoes and wearing them around the house before discarding them in obscure places (one of Bella's flip flops in the bathroom linen closet, Scott's yard shoes in the pantry and one of my sneakers in the trash can). Imelda Marcos has nothing on Daisy Cartwright, who is her mother's girl when it comes to her love of shoes.

The phone rings while I'm running the vacuum cleaner over the carpet. I run to get it before the answering machine picks up, certain it's Meg, who is coming over with her boys in thirty minutes.

Except it's not Meg. It's Harry, Scott's dad.

"How's my favorite daughter-in-law?" he booms over the phone. I'm pretty sure he says that because I'm his only daughter in law, but I've never asked about it, just in case. No point in bringing more skeletons out of the closet unnecessarily. I'm pretty sure the only reason he likes me at all is because I have given him three grandchildren. Scott's sister Elise, who has MS, and her husband Mike have decided not to have children because of her health issues, so Bella, Will and Daisy are the only grandchildren he is likely to have. Not that he really likes them all that much; the

34

reality of them is far too loud and chaotic for him. He just likes the idea of grandchildren and the continuation of the Cartwright line. In fact, in the hospital room when Bella was less than twenty-four hours old, he told Elise and me that he would give fifty bucks to the first one who had a boy. He's subtle like that.

"Do you and Scott have plans this weekend?" he asks.

"Um…not really" I stammer. What do I say? We're planning to play a game or two of strip Scrabble (suggestion number four in *52 Weeks of Spice*)?

"Good," he says. "Why don't you guys come to lunch on Sunday?"

"Um, okay," I agree reluctantly. Scott's going to kill me. So far, he's been successfully avoiding his dad ever since he split up with his mom. He is angry with his dad for hurting his mother and for ruining his ability to take for granted the fact that his parents would be together forever, a wish that every child has, whether they are four or forty. Me, I'm angry that because of him, my best (not to mention cheapest) babysitter now lives in Florida and we're stuck with Harry, who would barely edge out a crack dealer on my list of preferred babysitters. Once he told Candace it was over, she moved to Jacksonville to live near her sister and "find herself." I can't really blame her though; I don't particularly want to witness Harry's midlife crisis either. Unfortunately, thanks to my slow-witted thinking, we now have a front row seat.

About ten minutes later, the doorbell rings. This time, it's Meg with Chase, who's five, and Ryan, who's three. The boys immediately race up the stairs to find Will and I sigh. Although I love Meg and her daughter Ellie, who is friends with Bella, is okay, her boys are a nightmare. To say they are a handful is like saying Brad Pitt is attractive. I used to think that they only acted the way they did because of Meg and her parenting style. A self-described Prozac Mom, as long as she has her happy pill (as she calls it), nothing really fazes her. As the boys pummel each other, a regular occurrence, she says gently, "Now boys, use your words." Then she looks at us, shakes her head and says, "They just don't listen to me." When Ryan stomps on her foot and screams, "I hate you," she smiles and says, "I can see you're angry. Mommy will just go put some ice on her foot until you feel happier." And when Chase tried to drive her Suburban through Angie's dining room, she calmly pulled him out of the car and said, "Do you think that was a good choice or a bad choice, Chase?" Surely, I thought to myself, with a few firm but friendly rules that were consistently enforced, her boys would behave just fine.

I realized the error of my thinking, as well as how deluded and judgmental I was being, the first time I kept them for her when she had a root canal. Within fifteen minutes, I was searching the diaper bag just in case Meg kept a back up bottle of happy pills. The boys were masters at the game, and I quickly realized I was a neophyte. They played quietly together for about five minutes, lulling me into a false sense of complacency. Then Chase and Will decided they wanted to go outside. Ryan, however, adamantly refused to go outside; he wanted to play with the toys upstairs. By the time I realized he wasn't budging, Chase and Will were already outside and of course they didn't want to come back in. I ran upstairs to check on Ryan, who was playing with Will's Rescue Heroes, then back downstairs and outside where the other two boys were playing on the swing set. I went back inside to check on Ryan, who had disappeared. After several long minutes of frantic searching, I found him on the floor of the pantry with a sleeve of Girl Scout Thin Mints (my favorite), one bite taken out of each cookie. Of course he didn't touch the Lemon Crèmes. I drug him out of the pantry, and then glanced out the window in time to see Chase scaling the roof of the play fort, a good fourteen feet off the ground. I raced outside and cajoled him down with the promise of a Popsicle. "Let's just clean up first," I said, then realized I was talking to myself. The boys had already dashed inside. I quickly gathered up the amazing quantity of balls and other outside toys the boys had managed to strew about the yard in record time then headed for the door. This, I quickly discovered, was locked. I looked up to see Chase on the other side of the plate glass window, laughing.

"Will, you open the door this minute!" I yelled through the glass at my son, who was looking at Chase with a mixture of awe and confusion. Luckily, he decided not to cross over to the dark side and unlocked the door for me. Of course the boys still come over (usually with Meg, who actually has more control over them than I obviously did), but now I know to be prepared, which is why I have put the wine boxes she gave me for my birthday in the refrigerator.

Despite our differences in child-rearing, Meg and I definitely bond over the fact that we each have three children, which seems like so many *more* than Angie's two kids, and an absolute mob compared to Kate's well-behaved Chloe. Of course, sometimes I look at Meg's kids and think to myself, "Oh, my gosh, are my kids like that and I just don't see it?" As mothers of three, we also share our worries about our middle children. I worry about Will because he's my middle child, not the oldest who does everything first as her parents dotingly hang on her every word and endeavor, and not the youngest, who everyone caters to and fusses over and marvels over how cute she is. I try to ensure he gets equal attention and time, but like most middle children, Will is my easygoing child, quick to make friends, adaptable, resourceful about figuring out ways to do things for himself. Sometimes he gets lost in the shuffle because he doesn't demand that he be noticed. I think about the time we were at an Easter egg hunt at the park with my college roommate Heather and her family and we accidentally left Maggie, her middle child, behind as we moved over to the egg hunt area. Heather thought she was with her husband Mike, and Mike had thought she was with Heather. After a few moments, we realized Maggie wasn't with Mike or Heather and we all began frantically looking for her. We found her sitting patiently at the picnic table where we'd left our coolers.

"I knew you'd come back for the coolers," she said solemnly.

If this can happen to Heather, who is one of the best moms I know, who knows what grave mistakes I'll make with Will. That's why I worry about Will. Meg worries about Chase because he's the devil's spawn.

Meg and I chat, referee squabbles and organize a fundraiser for the girls' soccer team, which is why Meg has come over in the first place. Kate arrives about thirty minutes later to help and we work diligently and amicably, comfortable in each other's company. The doorbell rings and I am surprised to see Angie on my doorstep.

"Hey!" I say, opening the door for her to come inside. "I didn't think you were going to make it." Her oldest daughter Hannah is also on the team, but Angie had to take her mom to a doctor's appointment.

"I had to come," she says dramatically. Angie has always been a bit of a drama queen. She walks into the kitchen, where we are all working around the table, and collapses into a chair. "What is the worst possible thing that could happen to me?"

"Oh my gosh, Richard is having an affair!" I shout. She shoots me a puzzled look.

"Oh honey, are you sick? Is it something serious? Oh my gosh! Is it cancer?" Kate asks with concern. We all look up, our hearts in our throats, but Angie is waving her hand dismissively.

"No, no, nothing like that," she says. "It has to do with sex."

"Well, doesn't it always," Meg laughs with relief. "Is Richard a sprinter instead of a marathoner?"

"Do you want to borrow the bunny?" I ask wickedly.

"Ewww," says Kate.

"I think I'm pregnant," Angie says.

The rest of us are speechless. I find my voice first.

"I'm guessing by your reaction that this wasn't planned, but it's not the end of the world." I'm secretly thrilled. I'd love for Daisy, the youngest in our little group, to have a friend. Plus, I'm secretly worried that next year when Angie's youngest goes to school she'll go back to work and then I'll only see her once or twice a year for dinner and drinks on our birthdays. This is what happens when moms go back to work. There's simply not enough time for kids, husband, home, work and friends.

"I know it's terrible, but I don't want a baby," she wails. "I like sleeping through the night. I don't want to change diapers again. Next year, both of my kids will be in school and I'll actually be able to go to the bathroom by myself. I was really looking forward to that!"

"Oh honey," Kate says soothingly. "It will be okay. It may take a while to get used to the idea, but after he or she arrives you won't be able to imagine not having him or her."

At that moment, Daisy goes streaking by, totally naked, gripping Will's favorite Power Ranger tightly in her chubby hand, laughing her big belly laugh as Will, Chase and Ryan follow in hot pursuit.

"No offense," she says, "but I don't think I can handle three."

"It's a little crazy sometimes, I admit," I say truthfully. "But in a wonderful, my cup runs over kind of way. I wouldn't want it any other way. I'm going to be devastated when they grow up and the house is quiet and tidy and my to-do list is caught up. You'll be okay. You just have to embrace the chaos."

"When did you take the pregnancy test?" Meg asks.

"I haven't taken one yet," Angie says.

"Then how do you know you're pregnant?"

"I just know," Angie says. "My boobs are sore, my period's late, and I had a dream about a dragonfly, which is an image of fertility."

I roll my eyes. "Come on!" I say, grabbing Angie's arm and pulling her back to my bedroom. "Don't freak out until you know for sure. I have an extra EPT test. Maybe you're not even pregnant."

"I know I am," she says dolefully.

I rummage through the medicine cabinet until I find the test. I thrust it into her hands and say, "Just do it!"

A few minutes later, she emerges from the bathroom, pregnancy test in hand.

"Well?" asks Meg.

Angie sets it gingerly on the table. "Three minutes," she says.

We all hover over the little white stick, holding our breath as the purple dye moves through the window. Well, we all hover except for Angie, who refuses to look.

"Okay, tell me," she says with resignation.

"Honey, you're not pregnant," I say.

"What?" she grabs the stick off the table and looks at it. "Huh. I'm not pregnant."

Then, jubilantly, "I'm not pregnant!"

She grabs Kate and dances her around the kitchen, singing, "I'm not pregnant, I'm not pregnant."

They dance into the living room, where Angie ends with a twirl, then falls onto the sofa.

"How could you have thought you were pregnant?" I ask. "Didn't Richard get a vasectomy?"

"Nope," says Angie. "He went in for the consultation, but then he chickened out. They made him watch a DVD," she explains.

We all nod knowingly and roll our eyes at the idea of a doctor coming up with such a crazy idea. Everyone knows men are complete babies about stuff like that, especially when it involves their manhood. Never mind what we go through having babies. Actually showing them the process would be a deal breaker for even the bravest man.

"Scott's the same," I confess.

"Hugh just keeps putting it off," Kate adds.

"Just tell him that until he gets the vasectomy, the teddies stay in the drawer," Meg says. I remember that John did actually keep the appointment Meg made for him and had a vasectomy last Christmas. Scott took him a care package consisting of a cooler packed with ice, a six pack of beer and a box of blue Christmas ornaments ("blue balls," Scott laughingly explained).

"I'd have to actually have teddies to make that threat," I say.

"Yeah. As I pull on my sweat pants, Hugh jokes that how many clothes I wear to bed is directly proportionate to how many years we've been married. He already says I look like I'm in training to be a bee keeper," Kate adds.

"Me too. In my house, the teddies stay in the playroom with the other stuffed animals."

We all groan at Angie's joke.

"This calls for a celebration," I say decisively. I go to the refrigerator to get the wine boxes.

"Oh crap," I say. There on the middle shelf where last night there were four wine boxes are now three wine boxes, plus the apple juice box that was supposed to have gone in Bella's lunch box.

Later, after I have rushed up to the school, cajoled the receptionist into letting me into the cafeteria, slipped the cafeteria worker a twenty to switch out the wine box for the apple juice box, and convinced her that it was an innocent mistake and I am not an

41

unfit mother, we all agree to never speak of it again. But by the way Angie's eyes are dancing, I'm not sure that's going to happen.

Chapter Five

Saturday, October 25th

It's a gorgeous October afternoon, smack in the middle of that glorious three week period known as fall in Texas, an all too short season sandwiched in between five months of stiflingly hot, one hundred degree summer days when you don't want to go outside and five months of drearily cold, soulless winter days when you don't want to go outside. I love fall. There's just something in the crispness of the air makes the sky seem bluer, the colors around you sharper, your step lighter and everything right with your world. In the fall, I feel like just about anything, even happiness, is possible.

I am sitting in the passenger seat of Scott's car with the window down and my hand out the window, air surfing. I love Scott's car. It's not anything that special, not like a Porsche or a convertible or anything. But it's not a minivan, and it hasn't been "mommed," which means there aren't Cheerios in the cracks of the seats, melted crayons in the cup holders, a funky smell from a forgotten sippy cup forgotten under a seat, or a Wiggles CD in the stereo. When I'm in Scott's car, which still has a faint new car smell even though it's three years old, I feel like a passenger in life, not just the chauffer. I love that it's a five speed, which is way more fun to drive than an automatic but completely impractical with kids since you always have to keep one hand free to pick up a dropped pacifier, hand back a toy, take someone's trash, put on

43

some lipstick so you don't look like you just crawled out of bed after four hours of interrupted sleep, or just call time and temperature on your cell phone to hear another adult voice. Scott's car makes me feel young and cool again. Not that he ever really lets me drive it. He's still hung up on that time I forgot to put the trunk hatch down and tried to drive out of the garage, taking the door frame with me. Plus, he thinks I'm responsible for all the random dings and dents that keep mysteriously appearing on my minivan.

But that's okay because it is a beautiful day and I am out on a date with the man I love. Best of all, my kids are at home with a sitter that I don't have to shell out a quarter of my grocery money for because my parents drove their Airstream into town yesterday and offered to keep the kids for a few hours. We are going to play tennis. Scott looked at me a little funny when I suggested tennis – I'm not exactly what you'd call a gifted athlete and he didn't even know I owned a tennis racket (I did have to look through seventeen boxes in the attic before I found it), much less knew how to use one (I don't, really) – but he went along with it. I think he's pretty much afraid of me right now and will go along with anything I suggest because he knows I'm still mad that he got me nothing for my birthday. He didn't even try to cover and say he left it at the office or he had to special order it and it hadn't come in yet or he was mugged by Jehovah's Witnesses or anything. I would have happily bought just about any excuse rather than believe he forgot, or just didn't care, about my birthday. He's never been much on birthdays, but there's never been a year he hasn't gotten me anything! But no, he just said that my birthday falls at a bad time of year for him, as if I had a choice in the matter, and he didn't have time to go shopping. Even worse, when I made a big deal about him not getting me anything he said, "What's the big deal? You're turning thirty-five, not ten. If it's that important to you just go buy yourself something you want. We have the money for it."

He obviously doesn't get the whole point of birthdays.

That exchange happened after Scott got home last Saturday night at 10:00 p.m. after going into the office all day to work on an appeal that had to be filed on Monday. By that point, I had given up on him making me a piece of toast, much less linguine. He's probably hoping I'm not luring him out to the tennis courts to bash him in the head with my tennis racket. Not that the idea has crossed my mind or anything......

Actually, playing tennis with your significant other is suggestion number nine in my book on how to spice up your love life. Since my parents' unexpected arrival and willingness to baby-sit, I decided to save strip Scrabble for another time and take advantage of the fact that we could go out. Scott won't know what hit him. (No, I don't mean my tennis racket!) Scott doesn't know this yet, but we probably won't be playing a lot of tennis. I'm wearing a cute little tennis outfit I just bought last week, which has a short, flippy little skirt. Only, as the book suggested, I'm not wearing any underwear! We're playing at a nearby elementary school (not Isabella's – that would be weird) that has tennis courts. We pull into the parking lot and I hop out of the car quickly. Not only am I ready to play, but it was getting kind of uncomfortable sitting au natural on leather seats.

Scott is just a wee bit competitive. He usually won't play sports with me because he says he has to hold back too much and go "too easy" when he plays with women. I bet after today he'll be begging me to play sports with him.

As we walk over to the courts Scott says, "I never knew you liked to play tennis."

"Just because you've known me for fourteen years doesn't mean you know everything about me," I say. "Prepare for defeat!"

"We'll see about that," he laughs.

We warm up by volleying a few balls back and forth. I miss a few, which I just let roll to the side, but I'm not doing so bad. Hmmm, maybe I should take up tennis. Tennis instructors are usually pretty hot. Of course, it's doubtful a hot tennis instructor would feel anything for me but pity, or at best, disdain. When you show up with three kids in tow no one really sees you as a sex object anymore, which is probably why couples have problems keeping their marriage exciting after kids. Of course they don't have my secret weapon – *52 Weeks of Spice.*

I'm ready to implement phase one. "Let's play a game," I call to Scott over the net. He smiles and gives me the thumbs up. He's having so much fun actually playing tennis I almost hate to ruin it for him.

I serve the ball and unbelievably, he misses it. Woo hoo. This is fun. Time for phase two. My plan is to lob a few balls back and forth, then "accidentally" miss one, which won't be too hard since the last time I played tennis I wore acid washed jeans. I'll bend over to pick up the ball and….you can figure out what happens next. I'm about to serve the ball again when I'm distracted by the commotion on the court next us. What?! In three years I have never seen anyone actually play tennis on these courts, and the one day I pick to seduce my husband the Swiss Family Robinson shows up to play? Yep. There's mom, dad, and four boys ranging in age from about twelve to four bouncing around whacking each other in the head with their rackets.

"C'mon, serve the ball already," Scott calls.

Now would be a good time to find my inner Serena Williams because there is no way in hell I'm going to be able to bend over to pick up a ball now. I close my eyes, say a quick prayer and smack the ball over the net. Scott returns it and using an inner reserve of speed borne out of desperation and six years of chasing toddlers, I race across the court and manage to thwack it back to Scott's side. Effortlessly, he returns the ball and again I race to hit it. I manage to make contact, but it's not pretty. The ball goes flying to the side, landing on the court next to Scott where one of the boys and the mom are playing. As the boy throws the tennis ball to Scott, I heave a sigh of relief. I can miss balls; I just have to

46

make sure they land in the opposite court so someone else has to pick them up.

I grasp the fallacy of this plan as soon as I realize I don't have a ball to serve.

"Hit me that ball," I call to Scott.

"It's still your serve," he says, tossing the ball towards the fence.

Great. I slowly walk over to the fence on my side where half a dozen balls are lying. I am suddenly very conscious of just how short this tennis skirt is. There's no way I can bend over from the waist without mooning the Robinsons. I try a plié, but I quickly realize that's even worse because it makes my skirt ride up in the front. I'm like a parched sailor surrounded by the ocean. There are balls everywhere, but I can't pick up a single one of them. I'm trying to figure out how to casually kick one over to the bench when I hear a booming, "Cartwright, is that you?"

I look over and see Scott walking over to Mr. Robinson. "Clay!" he exclaims warmly, slapping him on the back in the way that men do. He gestures to me to come over.

"This is my wife Liz," he says. I smile non-commitally, unsure who this guy is who is crashing my tennis court seduction and how he knows Scott. "Liz, this is Clay Anderson. Or I should say Judge Anderson." Both men laugh. "Clay was elected to the 290th district court last year," he explains to me. Turning back to the man, whom I can't stop thinking of as Mr. Robinson, he says, "Who would have guessed when we were going head to head over the Pickens case that one day you would be a judge."

I vaguely remember Scott working on the Pickens case when I was pregnant with Daisy. Although I certainly don't remember him mentioning this Clay guy, I do remember he spent the better part of a month in Houston, working on the case during the day and going out with the attorneys on both sides of the case in the evenings. I also remember being just the tiniest bit jealous that he got to travel, even if it was on business, and wishing he would just once plan a trip for the two of us (or even a family vacation) with the enthusiasm with which he planned his business trips.

"I saw your name as council of record on my docket next week," says Mr. Robinson. "Any chance of that case settling?"

I groan inwardly. Work, work, work. I can't seem to separate Scott from his job, not even when I'm standing on an elementary school tennis court with the wind blowing on my privates. I tune out the men's conversation, instead watching the two younger boys try to hit out one of the lights with a tennis ball.

I tune back in just in time to hear, "You and Liz want to play some doubles?"

"Oh no," I say quickly. "I'm not very good."

"That's okay," Mr. Robinson says with smile. "Neither is Rita. C'mon," he says with a nod towards his sons. "Let's show them how the old folks can still do it."

Ew. Although I had hoped to do it, I have no intention of letting his sons or anyone else watch (although that is suggestion number twenty-eight).

Scott is looking at me questioningly, but I can read the unspoken message in his eyes. This guy is important to his career and he will never forgive me if I don't agree to play tennis with him and his wife.

"Sure," I say with resignation.

As Scott and I walk over to our side of the court, I lean close to him and say emphatically, "You have to pick up every single ball, do you understand?"

Scott looks at me in bewilderment. "Why?"

"Just do it," I say bitingly. "You owe me one."

Somehow, I make it through an excruciating three sets of tennis, which I officially suck at, since I'm afraid to run, jump or otherwise exert myself for fear of mooning a judge. Several times I have to glare at Scott until he remembers he has to pick up the balls, which he does with increasing irritation.

"That one was right next to you," he mutters under his breath at one point. "Judge Anderson is going to think I'm some kind of lap dog."

When we finally finish the game, we walk over to the Andersons.

"Great game," Judge Anderson booms. "Why don't you join us for some pizza and a pitcher?"

"No!" I say emphatically. "I mean, my mom just got into town and is keeping the kids so we really need to get back." Seeing Scott's obvious disappointment I say to him, "But you can go if you want."

"You sure you don't mind?" he says eagerly.

Well yes, of course I mind, but he's supposed to know that. Just because I said he could go doesn't mean he can go. But I can't very explain that to him right now, so I force a smile and say, "Sure."

"The boys and I have some errands to run too, so why don't you two just go grab a beer," says Rita. "I know you guys just want to talk shop anyway," she says indulgently.

It is quickly agreed that Judge Anderson will catch a ride with Scott so Rita and their kids can use their Suburban and the men will drop me off at home on their way to the sports bar. As we approach Scott's car, I am silently cursing everything about it that I found so fabulous just two hours ago. Now I would give my secret stash of chocolate for my minivan, with its wide sliding doors and roomy back seat. Instead, I have to figure out how to climb into the cramped backseat of Scott's two door coupe without exposing myself. I can't exactly ask the Judge, who is a burly man of at least six feet tall, to sit in the back. In a moment of inspired genius I drop my racket as I'm getting in the car and as Judge

Anderson bends over to retrieve it for me, I quickly climb into the car.

I am silent on the way home, alternately fuming and on the verge of tears. The men, happily reliving the glory days of the Pickens case, don't seem to notice. Scott drops me off at our house and promises to be home in a few hours. Luckily, I discover it's much easier to ease your way out of a car and keep your skirt down than it is to get into one.

I let myself in the house and can hear the kids upstairs playing with my mom. Glad for the reprieve, I slip into the bedroom and change clothes (putting on one of my oldest pairs of cotton granny panties that Scott hates and that I usually reserve for "that time of the month" as a kind of keep out signal just in case he somehow misses the point that I am totally pissed off at him) before going upstairs. The irony of the situation – going from no panties to granny panties – is not lost on me.

My dad is sitting on the floor playing Trouble with Bella and Will. It's always entertaining to watch my dad play with my kids. He's a quiet man, steady as a rock but definitely the calm and silent type, and seeing him gleefully send Will back home makes me smile.

"Where's Mom?" I ask.

"Oh, hi," he says mildly, looking up. "She's in there with Daisy." He nods towards Daisy's room before popping the Trouble dice button. "Watch and learn!" he says to the kids.

Shaking my head, I walk into Daisy's room. My mom is sitting in the rocking chair.

She looks up in surprise. "I didn't expect you and Scott home for another few hours," she says. She looks behind me. "Is Scott downstairs?"

"No," I say with a sigh. "He went out to have a drink with some judge he knows that we ran into at the tennis courts."

Mom makes a frown. Between the two of my parents, she is definitely the one that wears the pants in the family and she can never quite figure out how I haven't managed to train Scott better after ten years of marriage. Or, for that matter, why I had three kids when I already had a boy and girl, why my children weren't potty trained at eighteen months ("I had you and your brothers out of diapers by fifteen months," she likes to remind me) and how I can keep my house anything less than spotless ("It's so nice that you are a relaxed mother and don't have to keep everything neat and tidy all of the time like I did."). And I'm sure she certainly can't fathom why Scott would go anywhere without me, as my dad and mom go everywhere together. While I think they carry it to the extreme sometimes, it is kind of sweet, especially in light of the fact that my own husband just ditched me during a date.

"It's a long story," I say finally. I'm about to explain when I glance over to see what Daisy, who is being unusually quiet, is playing with. Generally when she is this quiet it's because she is engrossed with something she's not supposed to play with, like calculator batteries, or my cell phone, or my eyeliner and lipstick. In the past this has translated into a trip to the ER, a visit from the local police (along with a stern warning about false 911 calls), and my baby looking like a war victim.

"Uh, mom, what is she playing with?"

"Oh, Bella gave it to her. I think it's something from her doll set,"

I look over to where Bella's dolls have been lovingly put to bed in Daisy's crib, tucked in with an assortment of blankets. Her favorite doll Coco is resting her head on a pink satin pillow that looks suspiciously familiar.

Horrified I turn back to Daisy, who is holding my vibrator in her chubby little hand, mesmerized at all three parts which are whirling around rhythmically. Every once in a while, she sticks out her tongue and tries to lick it as if it's a tasty blue lollipop. My first thought is thank goodness I never used it. My second thought is too bad I never used it because I sure as hell will never be able to now.

"Mom, do you have any idea what that is?" I ask in exasperation. But of course she doesn't. This is the same woman who handed me a book called "Your Body and You" when I was twelve and then never brought the subject up again until I was twenty-four when she asked, out loud at the checkout register at Nordstrom's, "By the way, dear, what on earth is a blow job?"

I pry the bunny out of Daisy's fingers and she promptly starts crying, reaching up and saying emphatically, "Mine! Mine!"

"Poor baby," Mom says, scooping her up and patting her back. "Why can't you just let her play with it? She'll get tired of it in a minute."

Thinking quickly I say, "It was really expensive." Which is not a lie. I remember being amazed at the party that someone would actually shell out forty bucks for a sex toy when you could buy a pair of boots, get a really fantastic pedicure, or buy an armload of books for that.

"Really?" my mom says with interest, inspecting the bunny a little closer. "What is it?"

"It's an, umm, egg beater," I say desperately. "It makes great meringue."

"Really! Do you mind if I borrow it?"

"Well, I was planning to make some meringue pie for Scott's office party on Wednesday, so maybe another time," I say. I fervently hope there really is such a thing as meringue pie.

"Oh, don't worry. I'll just try it out tonight and bring it back to you on Monday," she says, slipping the blue bunny into her pocket. I can just picture my dad's face as mom whips out a vibrator and starts whipping egg whites with it, but I can't for the life of me figure out how to get it back. Bella saves the day by pulling it out of Grandma's pocket and running off with it as they are leaving.

After I put the kids to bed (Scott calls at six to let me know he and Clay are going to stay and watch the Cowboy game," if I don't mind"), I pick up the book that got me into this mess and idly flip through the pages. I randomly open to suggestion twenty-one, which says to kiss for twenty minutes.

"Whatever," I mutter to myself. "That's two good loads of laundry."

Disgusted, I shove the book into the back of a drawer and go start the washing machine.

Chapter Six

Sunday, October 26th

Scott and I are barely speaking to each other, which makes the forty-five minute drive to Scott's dad's house in the mid-cities area between Dallas and Fort Worth seem interminable. The kids love it because it means mommy is free to play "I Spy" and "Guess the Animal" instead of shushing them and saying, "I'm trying to talk to Daddy."

In addition to the tension created by yesterday's tennis seduction gone awry and Scott's subsequent spontaneous boys' night out, we're both apprehensive about meeting Ruth, my father-in-law's current paramour, although how anyone could find him attractive with his greasy gray comb-over and argyle socks with shorts and sandals look, is beyond me. I find out as soon as we pull into the apartment complex where Harry now lives and Harry comes out to meet us. At least I think it's Harry. I can't be completely sure because although this man is built like Harry and talks like Harry, he doesn't really look like Harry. This man is nicely dressed in khaki Dockers, a polo shirt and sneakers that bear a logo I've actually heard of, and instead of a gray comb-over, his hair is dyed a not completely natural shade of brown and parted slightly off center, making his face look slimmer.

"Is that what I think it is?" I whisper to Scott, nodding towards the open garage where a sleek and sporty silver convertible

Corvette is parked where Harry's old, staid Lincoln sedan used to sit.

"Yep," says Scott tightly, swinging Daisy up into his arms as the five of us move together towards the porch, for this moment at least united against the onslaught of uncertainty known as Ruth, whom I have secretly nicknamed Ruthless. She is waiting inside and greets us all warmly, exclaiming over how adorable the children are and how nice it is that we have finally agreed to come have lunch. "You all are so important to Harry," she gushes. "I'm so glad you finally agreed to come over." Although I'm tempted to tell her we've got caller ID now so it won't happen again, I bite my tongue and study the woman who has wrecked Scott's family. I am slightly weirded out, but not really surprised to see how much she looks like Candace. Both women are fairly short with the same dark, curly hair and apparently the same weakness for tall, paunchy men who are one taco short of a Mexican lunch special.

Luckily, lunch is almost ready and although my plan was to avoid any personal interaction with either Harry or Ruth by being overly solicitous to the kids, Scott has already stolen my idea and is very industriously entertaining Daisy and Will, so I end up in the kitchen helping Ruth with the last minute lunch preparations. I call Bella in to help and to act as a buffer against any real conversation. I have no desire to get to know this woman who epitomizes the upheaval of one branch of my family. If I weren't thirty-five years old, I'd kick her in the shins, yell, "You're not my kids' grandma" and leave. Unfortunately, I am far too old for that. Bella, on the other hand, isn't, and I eye her speculatively. With just a little prodding.... Nah, I'm pretty sure that falls under the category of bad parenting.

Once Ruth has exhausted all avenues of conversation with Bella, who has responded to all of Ruth's questions with polite one or two word answers, there is an awkward silence. Never one to bear silence very well, I say, "So, how did you meet Harry?"

"We met through an on-line dating service actually," Ruth answers.

"Really? Which one?" I ask curiously as I wash a pint of strawberries. "One of my friends is working on an article about Web of Love."

"That's the one," Ruth says enthusiastically. "It's a great service. After my husband died five years ago, I thought I'd never meet anyone else who shared my interests. And let me tell you, I dated a lot of jerks. Lots of guys with comb-overs and argyle socks with shorts and sandals," she laughs as she glances over her shoulder to where Harry and Scott are talking in the living room. She sighs. "But then I signed up with the Web and met Harry."

I roll my eyes in disgust. I wonder if Meg is right and people consciously lie on dating service questionnaires, or whether they just choose to reinvent themselves. I also wonder why, if they want to reinvent themselves, they can't just do it with the person they're already with.

Ruth, Bella and I carry everything to the table and we all sit down to eat. The meal passes quickly and by some tacit unspoken agreement, we all stick to light, meaningless topics such as the kids and their activities, Ruth's job as a veterinarian's assistant, Harry's hunting lease and Scott's big case.

At least until Will, who has until now been sitting and eating quietly, pipes up. "Grandpa, who's that lady?"

"Why, that's Aunt Ruth," Harry says jovially. "She's very nice and she lives here sometimes."

I choke on the piece of chicken I am eating and cough violently into my napkin. Aunt Ruth? And what kind of idiot tells an already confused four year old about cohabitation? I was kind of thinking we might not broach that subject with Will until he at least had some permanent teeth. Or maybe even some facial hair.

"Where's Grammy?" Will persists.

I have explained to both Will and Bella about Grandpa and how he and Grammy aren't married anymore, but apparently Will didn't get it. Hell, I don't get it. We talked about how people change and sometimes don't have anything in common anymore, but how that happens after forty-five years of marriage is a little outside my comprehension too, especially when Auntie Ruth shows up so soon.

"She lives in Florida now, remember?" Scott says to Will.

"Would you like to see our kittens?" Ruth chimes in. Two points Ruth. The kids jump up from their chairs, clamoring to see the kittens. They follow Ruth into the study.

"Kittens?" Scott looks at his dad quizzically. "You've always said you hated cats. In fact, you've always hated pets, even the hamsters I had as a kid. You used to "accidentally" let them out of their cage and leave the back door open."

"Well, yes. But Ruth fell in love with these little guys and we just had to have them. They're our babies."

Bella and Will come back into the dining room, each holding a small, mewing striped tabby kitten. Daisy trails behind, holding out her arms yelling, "My hold! My hold!"

"What are their names?" Bella asks.

"Well, that one there is Pussy Galore," Harry says, pointing to the one Bella is holding. "And that one (pointing to Will's bundle) is Octopussy because she only has eight lives left. We found them dumped in the woods."

"What's a pussy?" Will asks innocently.

"A grandpa word!" Scott exclaims at the same time that I say, "Another word for kitty."

I look at Ruth who is laughing and staring up at Harry adoringly. Portrait of a crazy woman, I think to myself.

Thirty minutes later, we are back in the car driving home. Daisy is quiet for once, sound asleep in her car seat, and Bella and Will are watching a movie on the DVD player.

"So what do you think of Ruthless?" I ask Scott, ready to put aside my anger for a moment to dish about Harry's girlfriend. "She seems nice enough, but I don't think she has any clue who your dad really is."

"I don't have any clue who my dad really is," Scott says. We don't speak for awhile, and then I say, "He really did meet her through a dating service." When Scott doesn't respond I add, "It's the same one Kate is doing a piece on. Apparently it's one of the only ones that matches you up with someone they think you're compatible with based upon some personality test, instead of you choosing the person you want to date. Kate says they swear they will find you your soul mate in five matches or less."

"Five, huh?" says Scott. "You've just got to wonder if my mom had signed up at the same time if they would have matched him up with her or Ruth."

"Maybe both," I say.

"Yeah, but which one first?" Scott shoots back. After a few minutes, he says, "What do you think would happen if we did it?"

"Did what?" I say, slightly horrified. I briefly wonder if he has found my book and been reading it. Suggestion number four is doing it while driving.

"Signed up," Scott says. "Do you think they'd match us up?"

"Oh," I say with a little laugh. I'm getting paranoid. Scott couldn't possibly know about the book. "I don't know. If we'd done it fifteen years ago, sure. But I don't know about now. Not that we're not happy," I rush to add. "Just that we don't have as much in common now. For example, you work for sane people who can wipe their own butts, and I work for small dictators who can't."

Any further conversation is cut short by Will, who chooses that moment to throw up his lunch. The rest of the afternoon passes in a blur as Scott and I divide our time between completely disinfecting the minivan and taking care of Will, who apparently has some kind of tummy bug. When we finally fall into bed at ten thirty, I am surprised to find myself tossing and turning, unable to fall asleep. Insomnia just isn't in the vocabulary of a mom with three kids. I figure I am about seven years behind on sleep. I used to ask Scott to wake up with the kids one Saturday a month so that I could sleep in, but he'd be so crabby the rest of the weekend, moaning about how tired he was and sleeping on the couch in front of the TV for entire weekend to make up for it, that I decided it wasn't worth it. I figure when Daisy goes off to college, I'm going to turn into Rip Van Winkle. Or, if I don't stop falling into bed before putting on moisturizer, Rip Van Wrinkle. In my current state of sleep deprivation, I can drink a cup of coffee, then immediately fall asleep on the couch. Just ask Scott, as the fact that I can't stay awake through a movie is a major source of contention with him. Tonight however, the tables are turned and I am the one wide awake, listening to him snore peacefully beside me.

I stare at his face, almost as familiar to me as my own, and in his sleep I can see his father in him. I wonder if he is like his father on the inside too, and if in thirty years he will decide to become someone different, someone who won't love me anymore.

After thirty minutes of tossing and turning, I give up and go into the study. I check my e-mail and am delighted to see that Kate has sent me one of those fun "get to know your friends better" e-mails where you answer questions about your favorite things and send it to all your friends, who then fill it out and send it back to you. It sure beats lying in bed thinking about the one hundred things I have to do tomorrow.

Oooh, this looks fun. When I was a teenager, I would spend hours with my friends filling out magazine quizzes such as "What's Your Style?" or "What Color are You?" Once you're a wife and mom, no one really cares what kind of animal you would like to be for a day or whether you'd buy a beach towel with bold stripes or a colorful floral pattern. They're just interested in what's for dinner and whether you went to the drycleaners.

Let's see......

First name: That's easy –Elizabeth/Liz.

Birthplace: Philadelphia

I will not eat: Sushi. Or anything that my toddler has licked first. Unless it's chocolate.

Do you read the ending before you finish a book? No. Picture books don't take that long to read.

Favorite thing to do on the weekend? Sleep. Alone.

Do you prefer small talk or deep conversation? Deep conversation, although I would just settle for adult conversation.

What food or beverage do you get at the movies? Popcorn, plus whatever I can I sneak in my purse; it's not cheap going to the movies with three kids.

Favorite hot beverage: Coffee and anything with Bailey's in it.

I love the smell of: Rain and my kids' hair just after a bath.

Favorite TV character: Anthony, the blue Wiggles (Admit it! He's kind of hot!)

What do you daydream about? Sleeping. Alone.

What did you do last night? Stole my vibrator back from my mom.

Do you believe in UFOs? Yes, I see them every night at dinnertime.

Glass half empty or half full: Half full (But as long as it has alcohol in it, who cares?)

How do you relax? What's that?

What do you do when you're mad? Eat chocolate or shop for shoes.

Clean freak or total slob? Total slob, although I think the word total is a little harsh.

What do you like to do on rainy days? Keep the kids from killing each other.

I would love to try: Sleeping. Alone.

By the time I'm finished I realize I don't have a life. Well, I have a life, but I'm not really sure it's mine. It's pretty apparent that somewhere along the way I have lost control of it. What I like to do and what I want out of life has gotten lost amidst taking care of kids, a husband and a house. I realize I'm not quite sure who Liz is anymore. I think about Scott's and my conversation in the car and wonder if we *would* be matched up if we signed up for a dating service. Having children, and loving those children so much I would do anything for them, has changed who I am. But, I reason, Scott has made this journey with me. Being a father and a husband has changed him too. Surely we are still meant for each other.

Just as I hit send, Daisy starts to wail. I quickly shut down the computer and go upstairs to check on her. It looks like she has the same tummy bug as Will. I change her sheets, give her a quick bath, dress her in fresh pajamas, and then settle down with her in the rocking chair in her room. We sit together, chest to chest, her chubby arms wrapped around me and her head tucked under my chin, my active and independent little girl content for once to sit still in my lap. She breathes a contented sigh, safe and cherished in my arms, and as her eyes close, her breathing becomes slow and rhythmic. I inhale the sweet scent of her freshly shampooed hair, which really is one of my favorite smells in the world. I hold her, snuggled close to my heart all night long, sure of who I am with her asleep and heavy in my arms.

Chapter Seven

Since Halloween falls on a Friday this year and since all of our girls wanted to go trick or treating together anyway, Angie, Kate, Meg and I decided to have a Halloween party at Angie's house, followed by trick or treating in her neighborhood and then Meg's and my neighborhood. The party officially started five minutes ago, so I am impatiently waiting for Scott to get home from work while an equally impatient Darth Vader and Little Red Riding Hood keep looking out the window. My kids obviously have some sort of cape fetish. Daisy, who is dressed up like a cat, is too fascinated with the tail attached to her black leggings to be impatient.

"Yay, Daddy's home!" shouts Isabella as she runs to the window for the sixtieth time. She and Will meet Scott at the door, both talking at once.

"Hurry, Daddy. We're ready to go," admonishes Bella.

"I can't wait to eat candy," Will moans ecstatically. "What are you dressing up as, Daddy?"

"Can I at least put my briefcase down and change out of my suit?" says Scott.

"Sorry," I say. "They're a little excited, and the party has already started."

With a sigh, Scott disappears into the bedroom, returning five minutes later in jeans and a sweatshirt.

"You're not dressed up." Bella says disappointedly.

"I didn't have time, honey," Scott says.

"You could have kept your suit on, put bows all over yourself and gone in your 'birthday suit,'" I suggest.

Scott stares at me blankly. He used to think my jokes were funny, but nowadays he is either too preoccupied with work or he's completely lost his sense of humor.

"What are you dressed as?" Scott asks, as he takes in my neon green athletic pants, green long sleeved t-shirt and neon green windbreaker.

"It's a surprise," I say. "You have to see Angie and Meg to get it."

After we decided to have a party, the three of us got really into planning our costumes. Scott flat out refused to dress up and both Angie and Meg said their husbands would rather watch a chick flick marathon than put on a costume, so we decided to do something together. Kate and Hugh always dress up as something together to go with whatever Chloe is being, so she opted out of the group costume. The three of us got together last Friday afternoon after school and after a couple of margaritas, we decided to dress in our regular clothes and carry signs that said "Nudists on Strike." Apparently it's not a good idea to brainstorm Halloween costumes while drinking margaritas. We had just pulled out some poster board and started making our signs when Isabella and Hannah walked in and read the first sign, carefully sounding out the words.

"What's a nudist?" Hannah asked.

Needless to say, the signs were quickly disposed of and we were back to the drawing board (after we all mentally added money to their future therapy fund). We had agreed it had to be something we could put together with stuff we already had since we'd already spent all of our money on whatever cute costumes our kids had spotted in the plethora of costume magazines that seemed to arrive in the mail daily. Despite the fact that none of us remembered ever wearing an official costume when we were growing up (although we all remembered an entire era of dressing as a gypsy) and we complained about how expensive bought costumes were, it didn't stop any of us from buying our kids the biggest and best costumes we could find. We couldn't agree on anything and finally, three margaritas a piece later, we left without a plan. However, a few days later I had a stroke of brilliance and e-mailed everyone my idea. Angie and Meg quickly e-mailed me back that they could do it. I can't wait until the guys see it. I'd forgotten how fun it is to dress up for Halloween. And I'm totally excited about the party. Despite how good of friends the four of us are, we seldom get together with our whole families, and our husbands, although friendly enough with each other, don't know each other all that well. I think Scott could use a few guy friends that aren't work related.

We all pile into the minivan and drive the short distance to Angie's house. She answers the door wearing an olive green, flowing jersey dress that falls mid calf.

"Come on in," she says throwing open the door. Her house is festively decorated with cotton spider webs strung over the doorways, an assortment of carved jack-o-lanterns and a talking skeleton that scares the crap out of Daisy. Her kitchen table is covered with an orange and black tablecloth and is laden with goodies that are labeled with grotesque names, such as witches fingers (taquitos with an almond sliver at one end), eye of newt (meatballs) and guacamole dip (monster brains). There's even an anatomically shaped ice heart floating in a bowl of green punch. I add our contribution, a graham cracker crumb kitty litter cake complete with tootsie roll poops, to the table. Scott shakes hands with the guys and the kids run around like maniacs, exclaiming over each other's costumes and, in the case of the boys, having light saber fights.   Kate is standing by the punch bowl, dressed as a Hershey's kiss in a sparkly silver metallic dress, silver tights, sparkly silver ballet flats and a cute little silver hat with a piece of foam coming out of the top that says Hershey's .

"You look fantastic!" I say. I glance around the room until I spot Chloe, who is wearing a candy corn dress with white Go Go boots, and Hugh, who is dressed like a tootsie roll. "You guys are adorable."

Although the way they do everything together is a little corny, I feel a pang of envy. There was a time when Scott and I were like that. In fact, somewhere in our attic are matching Lego costumes we wore to a Halloween party a couple of years before Isabella was born. I was a red Lego and Scott was a blue one, and we spent an entire weekend cutting the costumes out of boxes, spray painting them, and attaching three empty, spray painted butter tubs to the front of each box which would fit into the three holes on the back of the other person's box. When we wore them, we could stand front to back and fit together perfectly.

"What ARE you guys?" Kate asks, looking from me, in my lime green track suit, to Angie, in her green dress, to Meg, who is wearing some skin tight, green spandex pants with an equally tight button down green shirt that only Meg could pull off. I suddenly realize this costume might not be my most brilliant idea. While Angie looks elegant and sophisticated in her dress and Meg, who manages to be slim yet still have curves in all the right places, looks like a pin up girl, I look like a giant pickle.

The guys have all meandered over to where we are standing and they too, are looking as us curiously.

"We're wearing green, we're a gang of girls," I hint encouragingly. They all look blankly at us.

"We're Gang Green!" Angie trills.

Scott and John laugh. Hugh says, "That is so wrong." I've never quite been able to figure Hugh out, and I'm not sure if he's joking or not.

"It was Liz's idea," says Angie. "C'mon, let's eat."

We fill the kids' plates and sit them down with juice boxes and admonishments to eat something before they gorge on candy while the men load up their plates, open beers and make their way outside to sit in the driveway. For some reason, once couples have kids they regress back to about age thirteen. The boys cluster together in one group, and the girls get together in another group. And just like thirteen year olds, we all still talk about sex. Tonight the women all end up in Angie's living room, balancing plates of food on our laps.

I am the last to sit down, having had to prepare four plates of food, one of which had to be cut into miniscule pieces for Daisy. It would be nice if Scott would occasionally remember that his children eat three times a day, even at parties, and help fix their plates. Instead, as usual, I am left to take care of it.

"What did I miss?" I say as I sit down and kick off my shoes.

"We're talking about sex," says Angie.

"You know, we only talk about it because we're not doing it," I say.

"Speak for yourself," says Kate.

"Oooooh, Kate. You never kiss and tell. C'mon, spill the beans," Meg teases.

"There's nothing to tell. We just have a very healthy sex life," Kate says demurely.

"How healthy?" I ask. "Once a quarter healthy? Once a month healthy?" I gasp dramatically, and then ask incredulously. "Once a week healthy?"

"Yeah," chimes in Angie. "Exactly what is 'healthy'? Give us a number."

"Well, we usually make love three to four times a week," Kate says.

"What?!" I shriek incredulously.

"You've got to be joking!" exclaims Meg.

"How do you possibly find the time, not to mention the energy, to do it that often?" Leave it to Angie to cut to the chase. "I don't think Richard and I are alone in the same room three times a week."

"Oh, we just squeeze it in whenever we can," Kate says. "Take last night for instance. Chloe was taking a bath and I stepped out of the bathroom to get her pajamas. Hugh was coming down the hall from the opposite direction and, well, one thing led to another and we had a quickie in the hallway."

"Let me get this straight," I say. "You and Hugh were doing it just outside the bathroom while Chloe was five feet away in the bathtub?"

"Yeah," giggles Kate. "And Chloe kept saying, 'Mommy, are you coming?' and I'm like 'Yes, honey, I'm coming. Just a minute, I'm coming, I'm coming.'"

We all burst out laughing. "Now that is wrong!" says Angie.

"What about you?" I say to Angie. "How was the Lickety Split cream?"

"Oh it was good!" Angie says.

"Really? What did Richard think?"

"I don't know. I never tried it on him. It tasted so good I just kept sneaking tastes of it and the next thing I knew, it was gone!"

The guys wander back in to our peals of laughter.

"What's so funny?" Richard asks.

"Never mind honey, you won't get it," Angie says, which sets us off again.

"We'd better get going soon," Scott says, nodding towards the kitchen where the kids, their blood sugar elevated from food, are starting to get wild. We quickly clean up while the guys herd the kids outside, then we all set out to trick or treat.

In true guy fashion, Richard has mapped out our trick or treating route and hands each of us a neighborhood map with our trick or treating trail highlighted in yellow. His well thought out route winds systematically through their neighborhood to ours, with a stop on Meg's street before the trail ends at our house. I wish I had that kind of time.

We follow the kids as they excitedly run from house to house, exclaiming over the most recent addition to their buckets, which are getting fuller and heavier. Scott and I repeatedly offer to take Daisy's bucket, as her little feet are starting to drag and she is getting slower and slower, but she is reluctant to relinquish her booty. "My carry!" she says emphatically. Someone hands her a lollipop (her favorite), and eyeing it speculatively, she suddenly hands me her bucket, keeping the lollipop. "Heavy," she says.

As we reach our neighborhood, we hit more and more houses of people we know and we stop to chat. At two of the houses, the men hand out beers to our husbands.

"Now this is trick or treating!" Hugh says after Meg's next door neighbors give the guys each a Miller Lite.

"I might even dress up for this," Scott agrees. "Who knew you could trick or treat for beer."

As we wander the neighborhood, I am happy to see Scott joking and laughing with my friends' husbands. I watch him as he drains his beer and slips his empty beer bottle into the pocket of his big jacket before turning to laugh at something John says. Despite the tension that has been growing between us lately, I still love him and I'm glad he's enjoying himself.

By the time we reach our street, the kids are ready to sit down and gorge themselves on candy.

"Wait!" I say. "We have to go to my next door neighbor's house," I say.

"I thought it was empty," Angie says.

The house has sat empty for the last six months, ever since our previous neighbors, a sweet older couple, went to jail for embezzling money from their dry cleaning business.

"A new family moved in last weekend," I say. "This is the perfect opportunity to say hello."

I had intended to take cookies or a loaf of homemade bread over to welcome them to the neighborhood, but I haven't had time. I do want to meet them, though, particularly since I saw the movers carrying in a baby bed. Not that I was spying on them or anything. But ever since I saw that I've gotten excited at the prospect of another baby on the street. None of my friends have kids younger than three, and Daisy needs a playmate her own age. I have already begun imagining my new neighbor and me becoming fast friends and popping over to each other's houses to borrow a cup of sugar, or have a cup of coffee or keep each other's kids when one of us has to go to the doctor. I miss that now that all of my friends' kids are older.

It doesn't take much to convince the kids to go to one more house. A woman with long dark hair tied back in a ponytail answers the door with a little girl who looks to be about Daisy's age perched on her hip. An older boy, about Will's age, peeks out from behind his mom, wearing nothing but a pair of white Underoos. Hmmm, maybe they don't celebrate Halloween.

But no, she's handing out little bags of pretzels to the kids. As everyone moves away down the sidewalk, I linger in the doorway and introduce myself to my new neighbor. Her name is Christine and her baby, Scout, is only two months younger than Daisy. We exchange pleasantries and she tells me to drop by anytime. I promise that I will and say goodbye, catching up with everyone as they descend upon my house. Unfortunately, I didn't know everyone was coming to my house and it's not decorated for Halloween, although there are plenty of cobwebs, and with all the toys lying about like we've been robbed it looks pretty spooky.

Excited, all of the kids quickly empty their Halloween buckets in the middle of our living room, comparing their loot and negotiating trades. Scott hands out beer to everyone except Kate, who doesn't like beer, and we all sit together for a few minutes and relax, trying to figure out how to get everyone home since all of our cars are at Angie's house.

The guys finally decide they will walk back to Angie and Richard's, pick up their cars, and then drive back to our house to pick up the women and kids. Angie insists that she and their kids will walk home with the guys as well, as there's no point in Richard going back and forth.

"Besides," she points out. "They've got to come off their sugar high anyway."

Before I know it, everyone has decided to walk back to Angie's house, including Bella and Will, who don't want to be left out of the fun.

"We've got to keep Daddy company," Bella says seriously.

I watch them all leave, a laughing throng of the people I love best. I go back into the living room to check on Daisy. She has fallen asleep on the floor surrounded by her candy, her drawn on whiskers smudged by her fist as she rubbed at her face, trying to stay awake. I carry her upstairs, change her into her pajamas, gently wipe her face and hands and lay her down in her crib. Her eyes don't flutter open once. It's like playing with a rag doll.

I go back downstairs and have just started picking up the kids' candy, pilfering a few Reese's Peanut Butter cups and Snickers along the way, when there's a knock at the door. Irritated, I go to the door, ready to blast a group of trick or treating teenagers for their failure to heed the unwritten Halloween code that you don't go to houses with the lights off. Instead, Hugh is standing on the porch, looking more than a little bit tipsy. Kate doesn't drink much; apparently neither does her husband. I briefly wonder if that could be the secret to their prolific sex life but quickly discard it. If I quit drinking, Scott and I might never have sex!

"Kate left her cell phone," he says.

"Did you drive over here?" I ask, looking past him to the empty driveway.

"Nah," he says. "I ran." I vaguely remember Kate mentioning that Hugh ran in marathons.

I haven't seen Kate's phone, so Hugh comes in and together we ransack the living room, pulling up couch cushions and looking under furniture.

Finally I say, "Why don't you just call it?"

"Call it what?" he says, confused.

"Call her cell phone number," I say slowly. Hugh is either really drunk or really dumb. I think it could go either way.

"Oh, okay," he says. He punches in the number on his cell phone and a few seconds later, my ficus tree starts ringing. I'm guessing Daisy might have had something to do with that.

I hand Hugh the phone and walk him to the door. Just as I'm about to close the door, he lurches forward, grabs my breast and plants a sloppy kiss on me.

"I've always liked you Lizzie," he slurs. "You're so fun."

"And you're so drunk," I say, pushing him out the door. "Just go home and let's pretend this never happened."

I close the door and sigh. You know your life is pretty pathetic when you get felt up by drunken tootsie roll and your first thought, however horrible it might be, is 'at least someone stills find me attractive'.

Chapter Eight

Tuesday, November 4th

Of course my second thought after Hugh hit on me was what do I tell Kate? If this was the first time it had happened, it would be a lot easier to write it off to Hugh simply being drunk. But there was the first time I met him, when he was just a bit too friendly and held my hand a touch too long, the conspiratorial winks here and there, and the subsequent, occasional flirtatious remarks that I brushed off, certain that a man like Hugh could not possibly be interested in me when he had a wife as gorgeous and wonderful as Kate. Four days later, I am still debating whether or not to tell her. So far, I haven't told anyone. I thought about telling Scott, but he seemed to like hanging out with my friends' husbands and I don't want to ruin that by Hugh's moment of drunken stupidity. I actually picked up the phone twice to call Angie, but it felt too much like gossiping if I told Angie but not Kate and Kate doesn't deserve that. So I've decided to keep it to myself, at least until I decide whether to tell Kate or not.

Quite honestly, I've been stewing about it quite a bit since Friday. Not that Hugh hit on me, although that was weird, gross and a little comical all at the same time. I'm just angry for Kate. And I'm angry for all of us. Because if Kate, who is beautiful and well dressed and skinny and smart and keeps her house spotless all the time and has sex four times a week can't find happiness with her husband, then how on earth can the rest of us?

It's Election Day, and although I should probably be thinking more about life and liberty, it is the pursuit of happiness that is dominating my thoughts. In fact, the kids and I are on our way to vote now, just as soon as we drop Bella's friend Olivia off at her house. Olivia's mom is an emergency room nurse and has gotten in the habit lately of asking me at a moment's notice to pick Olivia up from school when her after school care falls through.

Right now the two girls, who are sitting together in the coveted "way back" seat of the van, are debating whose mom is smarter.

"My mom is really smart," Olivia is saying. "She's got a job."

Bella is silent. I decide to chime in and provide a little clarification. Nothing like having to justify yourself to a six year old.

"Your mom is really smart," I say to Olivia. "She helps a lot of people at her job. And she's a good mom and takes care of you, which is an important job too.

"My mom is smarter than you!" she says. Isn't she just precious?

"My mom is smart too," declares Bella suddenly. She has apparently decided that it is a good thing to have a smart mom and she is not about to be outdone by Olivia. Although I have no delusions about her reasons for defending me, I'm grateful nonetheless. I sit back with satisfaction and wait for my daughter's brilliant comeback. "She's…..she's smarter than a cricket."

"Crickets don't have brains!" says Olivia with disdain.

Hmmm. Maybe we need to work on Bella's debating skills.

Luckily we are pulling up to Olivia's house now. We drop Olivia off in front of her house, waiting until she is safely inside before we drive off. It's four thirty and I'm hoping we will beat the post work crowd at the polls. I probably should have voted early, but I really wanted Bella to have the experience of going to vote

73

with me. We find a parking space at City Hall fairly easily, which is encouraging. I get Daisy's stroller out of the back and shiver. It would seem winter has finally arrived, and it has gotten unexpectedly cold. I vow, once again, to try to stay awake for the weather forecast from now on. Luckily the kids all have jackets, but when I got dressed this morning it was still fairly balmy so I am only wearing a thin, three-quarter sleeved t-shirt. Scott's thick blue jean jacket is still in the back from Friday night, so I grab it. I don't have time to put it on since Bella and Will are already heading inside, but I figure I will want it by the time we come back out from voting so I drape it over my arm.

I secure Daisy in the stroller, catch up with Bella and Will, and together we walk into City Hall. Westfield's City Hall is actually called Town Hall since City Hall sounds far too common and mundane for a town as pretentious as Westfield. The political system, however, is still very small town. The whole voting process takes place in the marble-floored vestibule of the building with a dozen or so polling booths set up around the perimeter of the space. Westfield's entire senior citizen population must have signed up to run the election because I don't see a single person working the election under the age of 60. This is precisely why I wanted Bella to come. Civic duty lags in people born after World War II, so I'm doing my part to make sure someone will be there voting for the people who will determine my social security check.

I'm also glad that I brought Bella to help with her siblings because while I am preoccupied with handing my driver's license to the nice little whiskery old man who has eaten more than his share of pumpkin pie at the rest home, Will has let Daisy out of her stroller and she is now toddling off towards the court room. I tell Will to stay with his big sister and I sprint across the room, grabbing Daisy just before she takes a side trip into the men's rest room. I come back with an angry Daisy wriggling and bucking in my arms, trying to get free.

74

"You've sure got your hands full," the man says solemnly. That particular comment is getting a little old.

"Yes!" I say enthusiastically. "Thank goodness for wine!"

I've rendered the poor man speechless. Suppressing a smile, I herd the kids towards an open booth, still holding my squirming toddler who is now complaining more vocally. I look her in the eye and tell her I will put her down only if she stays RIGHT BY MOMMY. She nods and I put her down. I hand her a box of raisins to keep her occupied.

I insert my voting card into the machine and as the screen pops up, I explain to Bella how to vote, showing her how I touch the screen to check the box next to the candidate to cast my vote. It takes all of two minutes, but when I look up Will and Daisy have disappeared. I search the room, finally locating them. Daisy, ever the independent and single minded third child, has apparently taken off again and Will is trying to catch her. Thinking that this is all a great game, particularly since Will is laughing as he chases her, Daisy chortles with delight and runs faster.

"Please go get your sister for me," I say to Isabella.

I turn back to my ballot and cast a few more votes before I'm interrupted by Bella.

"Mom, Daisy dropped her raisins and Will's trying to get them for her. I told them to come back but they aren't listening to me." She has clearly washed her hands of the whole situation. I look over to see both Daisy and Will crawling around on the marble floor. Daisy is busily eating the trail of raisins made by the flung box, while Will is on his tummy trying to reach under a low table, where I presume the raisin box is.

The rest seems to happen in slow motion. I see Will make one last stretch to reach the box, and as he reaches under the table his feet swing around, accidentally kicking the leg of one of the voting tables. The leg must have been a little wobbly to start with because the damn things snaps completely off, sending the voting

75

machine crashing to the floor. An entire women's bridge group rushes over, tsking-tsking over the broken table, the fallen machine, the "poor baby" (who was completely non-plussed by the crash, but took one look at an armada of grandmas rushing towards her and burst into tears), and my parenting skills (or lack thereof) in general.

I rush over with my jacket, Daisy's sippy cup, and Brown Bear, her bedraggled and much loved teddy bear, still clutched in my arms. My voting booth, half filled ballot and the umbrella stroller have been abandoned. Completely flustered, I pick up the still crying Daisy, settle her on my hip, and try to soothe Will, who has now also burst into tears. The grandma armada is still scowling at me, so I apologize profusely and try to help right the table and pick up the fallen voting machine, despite my twenty-five pound accessory. As I bend over, the beer bottle that Scott put in his pocket on Friday night slips out and hits the ground. It resonates loudly as it bounces across the marble floor. The room is quiet enough to hear a pin drop, and let me assure you that a beer bottle on marble sounds a lot louder than a pin! I frantically try to right the jacket, which apparently got turned upside down in the whole table/voting machine crash scenario, but I'm not fast enough. A second bottle goes clattering after the first.

"Don't worry Mommy, I'll get the beer bottles for you," Bella reassures me as she races after the beer bottles.

"I'll help get the beer too Mommy," says Will eagerly, cheered now that it is evident he is no longer the center of attention and disapproval.

"No, no, no!" I say hastily. "Mommy will get them."

Still juggling Daisy, the jacket, the cup, and the dog, I grab the beer bottles and try to shove them out of sight and back into the pockets of the jacket. In my haste, I turn one upside down and the remaining stale dregs of beer left in the bottle trickle down my shirt. Now, in addition to looking like an alcoholic, I smell like one too. I mentally curse myself for my earlier remark about wine. It seems a lot less funny now that I smell like stale beer and my kids have been chasing beer bottles like it's a typical family night activity.

Mortified, I look up at the bevy of disapproving faces and realize I had better leave before one of them calls CPS. I apologize again profusely before quickly herding the kids back to my own voting station. I strap Daisy back into the stroller and finish voting as quickly as possible, randomly punching the screen in my desperation to get out of there as soon as possible. As I finally drive away, furtively checking the rear view mirror to make sure I'm not being followed by a senior citizen on patrol, I wonder who I just voted for. Too bad I will never know, as I have vowed to never set foot in Westfield's Town Hall again.

The next morning, I come home from the grocery store to find my answering machine light blinking. A woman's businesslike voice greets me: "Hello Mrs. Cartwright. This is Penelope Swarthmore, with the City of Westfield."

Oh crap. They've tracked me down. Someone's going to come to my house and interview my kids to see if I'm an unfit mother. Daisy will probably wander in licking the Love Bunny and I'll lose my kids forever.

Wait a minute. What did she say? Something about my driver's license. I rewind the message and listen to it again, then grab my purse and rifle through it. Sure enough, no driver's license, probably because it is still at City Hall, being held hostage by Santa Claus.

Then it hits me; I'm going to have to go back.

Will is at preschool until two, leaving me with just Daisy to wrangle, so as soon as I put all of the groceries away I strap her back into the minivan and head back to the Town Hall to retrieve my license. I am assuming that since the election is over the granny brigade will have gone back to playing bingo at the senior center. I glance in the rear view mirror at Daisy and fervently hope so because the way she's dressed today could easily cement our status as poor white trash. There is a chocolate stain on her shirt from the cookie she had at the grocery store, her shoes are on the wrong feet because she insists "My do it!," and she's wearing her purple sparkly bike helmet which she has refused to take off since she spied it in the garage two hours ago. But if there's anything I've learned as a parent it's to pick your battles, and this one isn't worth it so the bike helmet stays.

According to the message on my machine, my license is in the City Manager's office on the second floor. Daisy and I take the stairs, as she is still mesmerized by going up and down them. A small but nicely decorated waiting area is at the top of the stairs, manned by a very professional looking blond woman who is thankfully young enough to know who the Beatles are.

"May I help you?"

"I'm Elizabeth Cartwright," I say. "I received a call that I left my driver's license here yesterday."

"Hmmm," she says as she opens a drawer in her immaculate desk. She pulls out an envelope and thumbs through it, then thumbs through it again, more slowly this time.

"Do you see it? It's actually Elizabeth Moore Cartwright," I add.

The woman stops thumbing through the contents of the envelope and looks up to study my face.

"Do you need to see some ID?" I joke. Actually, she probably *is* wondering if I'm really who I say I am. The picture on my license was taken about eight years ago, and I know I don't much resemble the slim girl with the heart shaped face in the picture with her tastefully understated makeup, smart top with an elegant scarf knotted around her neck and naturally wavy hair. The clear blue eyes and slightly crooked front teeth are the same, but with my hair in its usual no fuss ponytail (it tends to frizz in Texas) and my one minute makeup routine that consists of applying

78

moisturizer and a swipe of mascara, I realize I may not even qualify as Elizabeth Cartwright anymore.

But no, she is handing me my driver's license and smiling at Daisy, who has discovered the nearby elevator and is busily pressing the buttons. I call Daisy who toddles back over to me. I grab her hand to help her down the stairs when a deep, male voice says, "Liz? Liz Moore? Is that you?"

I look over to see a nice looking man in a well cut suit studying me intently. He's sitting in the waiting area with a briefcase open in his lap and has obviously overheard my entire conversation. I peer at him curiously. Could I possibly know this gorgeous male specimen? Surely I would remember having met him at one of Scott's boring office parties. He is impossibly good looking, with slightly tousled brown hair, warm brown eyes with just enough lines at the corners to assure you that he is a man who smiles often, gorgeous cheekbones and a sexy five o'clock shadow that gives him a rugged look. A long time ago, before I met Scott, I dated a guy who looked a little bit like him, but without the facial hair and cute eye crinkles. Oh no! It couldn't be! Not here in Westfield, not when I'm twenty pounds overweight and wearing faded black yoga pants and an old t-shirt.

"Charlie?" I say incredulously.

In one fluid movement, his lap top is on the chair next to him and he is standing next to me, close enough for me to smell him--a heady but somehow still familiar blend of aftershave and something intangible but so uniquely Charlie that I would have known it was him anywhere. And just like that, I tumble back twenty years to long lazy weekends at the beach, his strong arms encircling my waist, my head cushioned against his smooth, muscled chest as we watched the flames from a dying bonfire flicker against a starry sky, when we lived and breathed each other and believed true love lasted forever.

Of course, proof otherwise is standing next to me wearing a purple bike helmet. I reach for Daisy's hand to anchor me to the life that is now mine. My hand grasps thin air. Alarmed, I look around. There she is by the elevator again, entranced by the buttons that light up. Oh no. The elevator door opens and Daisy walks into it, immediately turning to the enticing button panel inside. This is not good. I sprint towards the elevator, jumping in just before the door closes on my past.

As we ride down to the first floor, Daisy babbles excitedly, oblivious to my inner turmoil. I debate going back upstairs and laughing off the whole thing, saying, "So hey there Charlie, sorry about that. You know how kids are." But maybe he doesn't. Maybe he doesn't have kids. Maybe he's not even married. Oh crap. What if he's not married? What if he is?

In the months following our breakup (and to be honest, on and off over the years), I've had the occasional fantasy about running into Charlie again. I mean, everyone fantasizes about running into their ex don't they? Of course, in my fantasies I'm usually dressed to kill, have an awesome job and have just come back from some exotic locale looking rested and tanned.

"Charlie darling, is it really you?" I coo, all blasé and nonchalant. Of course, I've never called anyone darling in my life and I doubt I've ever cooed either, but you get the point. In my fantasies I don't look like someone's cleaning lady with a street urchin in tow! Maybe he'll think he was mistaken and I wasn't really who he thought I was. No, me saying his name and practically swooning probably eliminate that particular scenario. But going back upstairs is inconceivable. I can't go back. So I load Daisy into my minivan and drive home to the life that I have chosen.

Chapter Nine

Thursday, November 6th

I am not a woman who dreams. In fact, from the moment my head hits the pillow until either my alarm goes off or I hear Daisy over the monitor by my bed, I enter what Scott only half-jokingly refers to as a coma-like state. A light sleeper himself (unless of course a baby's crying or a child appears beside the bed after having a nightmare – then he sleeps like the dead), he has witnessed our cat Bandit kneading me all over with his big, soft paws for thirty minutes at a time trying to wake me up until he gives up and jumps down, disgusted. For all I know, Scott has done the same.

However last night, after watching the election results, I fell into a fitful sleep fraught with dreams. In one of them a young Charlie was running for president, but he was vacuuming in every speech he gave. In another, I was running a marathon, and as I approached the finish line my kids appeared on the sidelines, except instead of cheering me on they were saying, "Mommy, can you make me pancakes?," "Mommy, I want a drink," "Mommy, I need my pink shirt washed."

Now, sitting at the breakfast table, I realize that at least my kids were calling me mommy in my dreams.

"Can someone pour me orange juice?" Will asks. I look around. Scott has already left for work and Bella hasn't come downstairs yet, so unless he thinks Daisy can do it he must mean me.

I pour three glasses plus one sippy cup of orange juice. Two minutes later Bella bounds down the stairs, her reading log in hand. "Can someone sign my reading log?" she asks. Although it's true that Will has just mastered writing the four letters that comprise his name, each letter tends to be about three inches tall and meanders off the page, so I'm pretty sure she also means me. Somewhere along the way I have become the invisible entity—"Someone"—that does stuff for them.

"Sure, let your brother do it," I grumble irritably.

"Cool!" shouts Will.

"Mo-om," chides Bella with a roll of her eyes and enough sarcasm to make a teenager proud. And so begins another day.

I put a movie on for Will and Daisy and spend the morning cleaning the house and obsessing about yesterday and my chance encounter with Charlie. My thoughts flip flop between reliving the past and rewriting the debacle of yesterday into a better version where I run into him again, this time looking fantastic. Disgusted with myself, I finally throw in the towel (literally) and go to the grocery store.

When we get back home, the garage door won't open so I park in the driveway and begin unloading the groceries with Will's dubious help. Will helping consists of him showing me how strong he is by insisting on carrying the heaviest bags, and then howling for help halfway to the kitchen. Once we're inside, I discover what I had already suspected when the garage door wouldn't open. Our power is out again. I sigh. For some reason we've been having an unusual amount of power surges lately. Usually it's back on within an hour, but I have no idea how long it's already been down.

"Woo hoo!" shouts Will. "We can play pioneer!"

The first time the power went out it was dark, a favorite episode of Dora was interrupted, and the kids were scared, so I made the whole thing into a great adventure, pretending we were pioneers. Basically we just ate fruit snacks, played games, and I told them stories by candlelight, but they had so much fun they were disappointed when the lights came back on. Now, even when the power goes out in broad daylight, they beg me to light candles and play pioneer.

"Let's be pioneers unloading groceries from the general store," I suggest.

"Okay," says Will. He prances back out the door and grabs a twelve pack of Coke. "I've got beer for the saloon," he announces. He has a rather disturbing preoccupation with beer right now. I can't imagine why.

Then I notice my new neighbor Christine standing in the driveway.

I smile at her apologetically. Hopefully she is also the type of mom whose kids pretend that Coke is beer. Otherwise there's not much hope for our budding friendship.

"I'm so sorry to bother you," she says in her quiet, melodic voice. "But I have to take Scout for her eighteen month check up and the power is out and I have no idea how to open the garage door. Is your husband possibly at home?" she adds hopefully.

"No, he's at work, but I can do it for you," I say. "Just let me put the drinks inside."

I chase after two cans of Coke which are rolling down the driveway and grab the broken cardboard Coke box which Will just dropped. I plop the drinks inside the door, extract Daisy from the pantry where she has been busily helping herself to every snack she can open, and the three of us walk next door with Christine.

I am always amazed at the helplessness of many married women. Were they honestly this helpless when they were single, or does marriage simply make women stop relying on themselves? Is there some secret incantation in the wedding vows that causes flower arranging men to start wearing tool belts and lawn mowing women to don aprons? I have always prided myself on my independence. I remember my dad spending whole afternoons walking me through how to change a flat tire when I was sixteen. No way was I going to be at the mercy of a man to take care of me. Of course I would be lying if I said I still do everything myself. It is nice to have someone to lean on, the proverbial big strong man to take care of the unpalatable stuff. But I *can* still do it myself if I have to, which is a good thing because with the hours that Scott works, I do end up having to do a lot of "guy stuff" myself. Smoke alarms chirping annoyingly every thirty seconds? I've got a ladder, a screwdriver from my pink "do- it-herself" tool kit and a nine volt battery and I'm not afraid to use them.

Granted there are a few things that I leave for Scott, such as fixing the toilet and of course, having sex. Although thanks to Angie, I guess I have a little blue "do-it-herself" kit and a nine volt battery for that too, but I *am* afraid to use them. Too bad my mom and Daisy have no such qualms.

Christine is obviously not a do it yourself woman. We traipse through her house and out to her garage where I impress her by pulling the red emergency disconnect cord hanging from her garage door and effortlessly lifting the door, liberating her car.

We stand in her driveway chatting for a few minutes and I quickly realize that she is also not exactly the same type of stay at home mom as me either. She's more the "let's all sleep in one bed," La Leche bumper sticker sporting, soy milk drinking, free form, Mother Earth kind of mom. However she seems really nice, so I'm hoping that she doesn't hold my son's sometimes inappropriate imagination against me.

I tell her goodbye, conscious of the fact that she has a doctor's appointment to get to.

"You should bring your kids over to play sometime," she urges. "They can play on the swing set in the backyard."

I must admit I've noticed her play set. It's very unique - kind of plastic looking, but not really. Definitely nothing like the generic wood one in our backyard with its requisite sling swings, fort and a slide.

"Sure," I say, turning to go. "It looks like fun."

"It's made of completely recycled material," she says proudly as she gets into her hybrid car. "Mostly recycled diapers and tampons."

Chapter Ten

"Seriously?" Angie asks incredulously for the fifth time.

"That's what she said," I say.

It is three hours later and Angie and I are surreptitiously checking out the playground equipment next door. Of course, in order to see over the tall wood fence that separates the yards we have to climb into the fort attached to the swing set in my backyard, much to the delight of Will and Tyler, who are thrilled that their mommies have climbed up here to play with them. Not wanting to admit to our kids that we are nosy snoops, we are alternating between acting like pirates, shouting out the occasional "Arggh, me hardies" or "Walk the plank" to the boys and trying to figure out how you recycle a tampon and why anyone would want to.

Uh oh. We're busted. Christine and her kids have come outside. She sees us in the fort and waves. I wave back.

"Thank you so much for helping me this morning," she calls over the fence. "I made you some cookies to say thanks."

"You didn't need to do that," I call back. "It was really no problem."

Her son, wearing only a pair of white skivvies again, is watching Will and Tyler longingly so I say, "Come on over. The kids can play."

She bends down to talk to him, and then straightens up. "Great!" she says enthusiastically. "We'll be over in a minute."

Angie and I extract ourselves from the play fort and go inside. Two minutes later, the doorbell rings. I answer it, surprised to see Christine's little boy, who looks to be about Will's age or a little older, still wearing only his underwear.

"Rebel likes to pretend he is Mowgli from the Jungle Book," Christine explains. "He wears his underwear everywhere."

As is typical of weather in Texas, the temperature has climbed from a chilly forty degrees yesterday to a balmy sixty eight and sunny today, and it is too gorgeous outside to hold any little boy inside for long. Rebel races out into the backyard and is immediately recruited for the pirate crew, blinding white underwear and all. I just hope the pirates never decide to surrender or poor Rebel may find himself going commando. Inside, Scout and Daisy are eying each other warily over their sippy cups.

Christine hands me a plate of cookies still warm from the oven.

"Mmm, these smell so good," I say. Although I contemplate setting them aside for later, Angie is eyeing them greedily so I figure I had better share. Christine only has one, but Angie and I devour three a piece because they taste as good as they smell.

"Anyone want a cup of tea?"

Angie lifts an eyebrow at me archly. "I was thinking it's just about time to fill mommy's little sippy cup, if you know what I mean."

Laughing, I grab an open bottle of merlot and three glasses.

"Oh, none for me," Christine says quickly. "I'm still breastfeeding."

"Wow," says Angie. "That's great. Once mine got teeth, I was out."

87

"We've had a few mishaps, but they are both pretty good about it now," Christine says.

"I'm sorry," Angie says with a laugh. "I thought you said both."

I'm glad Angie said something because I swear that's what I thought she said too. But surely not. After all, Rebel is at least four. Then I remember the La Leche bumper sticker on her car.

"Oh yes," Christine is saying. "I still breastfeed both of them, although Rebel only has a little nip here and there."

Angie and I both cringe. Bad choice of words. Simultaneously, we both jump up.

"I'm just going to check on the boys," Angie says.

At the same time I say, "Let me just go check on the girls. Who knows what they're doing upstairs."

"If you don't mind, where is your restroom?" Christine asks, nonplussed. I point her to the powder room and beat a hasty retreat.

When I come back downstairs, Christine is standing in the long hallway that leads to the powder room, looking at the photographs on the wall. I love to take pictures, and when I stopped traveling to exotic locales with McMillan Hotels I turned my lens on my newest passion, my kids. Consequently, I have literally thousands of photographs of them. I have framed my favorites in a series of collage frames that line the hallway.

"These are fantastic!" Christine exclaims. "Who took these?"

"Oh, I did," I say, slightly embarrassed.

She points to a collage that bears the title "A Day in the Life" and says enthusiastically, "I love this! These are just the kinds of things you want to remember when they're all grown up, not them posing in a fancy dress against some cheesy backdrop that isn't even in your own house."

Wow, that's exactly how I feel, and why I take the pictures I do. It's nice to have someone get it. That collection is one of my favorites too. It includes black and white candid photos of my kids going about the business of childhood – Bella lying on her tummy, bare feet in the air and long hair half shielding her face as she reads a book; Will on a swing in the backyard, head tilted back and eyes closed, utter bliss captured in the grin on his face; Daisy at six months, lips pursed, frowning in concentration as she studies her hands.

"Would you do this for me?" Christine says.

"What do you mean?"

"Come over and take photos like this of my kids. Please. I'll pay you whatever you typically charge."

As if I typically charge anything other than my MasterCard! I'm flabbergasted. Someone wants to pay me to take pictures. Cool.

"You don't have to pay me," I say. "I don't do it professionally. But I'd be happy to come over and take some pictures for you."

Christine thanks me profusely, and then rounds up Rebel and Scout to go home. Angie and I walk them to the door, thanking her again for the cookies.

"Those are the best chocolate chip cookies I have ever had," Angie says.

"I'm glad you liked them," says Christine. "I made them with breast milk."

As the door closes, Angie and I both start gagging. Angie is rubbing her tongue with her hand as if to scrub away the evidence, and I run to the bathroom and rinse my mouth four times, coming back to the kitchen with a bottle of Listerine that we pass back and forth, taking healthy swigs like alcoholics on a bender.

"Ugh!" Angie wails. "I will never, ever be able to eat chocolate chip cookies again!"

"Me either," I agree. "I guess that's one way to lose weight."

We conclude that the only way to get over the trauma of having eaten cookies made with another woman's breast milk is to have another glass of wine. As we sip our Merlot, I tell her about running into Charlie.

"Wow," she says. "That sucks. You should always look hot when you run into an ex. Never give them the upper hand!"

"Exactly," I say, grateful that she so completely understands. "I wish I could somehow run into him again but be prepared this time so he doesn't think that's what I normally look like."

"I've got it!" Angie says triumphantly, jumping up so quickly she sloshes her wine. "Come here."

She drags me over to my little desk in the kitchen where I pay the bills and collect every piece of artwork my kids have ever created and types something in on my computer.

"Voila!"

"Facebook?" I say, puzzled.

"Yes, Facebook," she says. "I can't believe you're not already on it. If you join, we can chat."

"We already chat," I point out.

"We're doing this so Charlie can find you, dummy. We'll post a picture of you looking really hot and gorgeous and include some fabulous tidbits about your life. I guarantee you he'll be looking you up after running into you again."

"You think?" I say dubiously. "I don't think there are any fabulous tidbits about my life. And you didn't see what I looked like yesterday."

"Honey, I know! You were his first love. You could look like a vagrant and I bet he'd still want to know what you're doing now. But we better get it set up now because he's probably already trying to find you."

One hour and an entire box of Popsicle bribes later, I am officially on Facebook. We had to peruse quite a few photographs to find the right one, but I'm happy with the one I've posted. It was taken when we were on vacation in Colorado five years ago, and I look cute in a bright blue sweater, my cheeks flushed from the cold, my eyes sparkling, and looking pretty good if I do say so myself. My profile is fairly vague (after all, I don't want any weirdoes trying to friend me), but it does include my maiden name and where I live so Charlie can find me without looking too hard if he wants to. Angie promises me that when she gets home she'll invite me to be her friend.

"Oh goody," I say sarcastically, "Can we hang out in the quad and eat lunch together?"

After Angie leaves, I set out some hamburger patties to thaw and bathe the kids. Scott arrives home from work early for him (it's 6:30) and offers to cook the burgers as soon as he changes out of his work clothes. I sit outside on the patio while the kids run around the backyard in their pajamas, not wanting to waste a single second of what will mostly likely be the last nice day for awhile.

Scott, now comfortably dressed in old shorts and a Duke sweatshirt, sticks his head outside the back door.

"Could someone light the grill?" he says. I sigh. Him too?

Later, after the kids are tucked in and Scott is blissfully snoring in front of the TV, I close myself in the bathroom and take a good look at myself. Should I just resign myself to a life of anonymity or is there someone in there? Not just someone who pours the juice and checks the homework and lights the grill, but SOMEONE, someone special and interesting and exciting, someone with a life of her own? Is it the someone I used to be or someone completely different that I need to get to know? I like my life with Scott most of the time, and I adore my kids and being home with them, but some part of me longs for more. I long to be someone again.

Chapter Eleven

It has been a week and a half, and although I keep in touch with Angie and Kate almost daily on Facebook, as far as I know Charlie Bennett has not tried to find me. Several other people from my past have, such as weird Brenda Watkins (who now also lives in Dallas and has invited me to a Gay Pride Rally) and Kevin Malone, the president of my senior class, who from the number of friends he has on Facebook is still trying to compensate for his small penis size by how many friends he has. I mean, who really has twelve hundred friends for crying out loud? Facebook is kind of cool though. Kind of like going to your high school reunion without having to lose twenty pounds and buy a new outfit.

It's scary how addictive Facebook is. It's also interesting to see what people end up doing with their lives; how dorky John Graham is now ripped and living in Hawaii, how wild Susan Walker, who did it with every guy on the football team is now a gray-haired Earth mother who raises Alpacas and spins yarn on a farm in California, and how gorgeous, smart cheerleader Vanessa Campbell is now a stay at home mom devoted to the local PTA. I can't help but wonder what my old friends think of me and what I've done with my life. I wonder if they read my profile, shake their heads, and say, "Wow, she had so much potential. I can't believe she's doing nothing now." Or maybe that's just my own fears and insecurities talking.

In between checking Facebook to see if Charlie has tried to friend me I surf the internet, which is how I found some woman named Nina's "Fabulous Lingerie You Can't Live Without" list on Amazon's list mania. I was actually browsing for workout DVDs and had just added the Dirty Dancing Official Dance Workout DVD to my cart when I saw the Nice and Naughty gift suggestion links. But did I click "nice?" No, of course not! One click led to another, and before I knew it I had spent a small fortune on a fishnet open bust three piece garter set, a pair of festive red marabou slippers and a crotchless thong. I had to order that one out of morbid curiosity. When you take away the back *and* the crotch of a pair of panties what can possibly be left? I might as well just tie a string around my waist. Although I haven't been able to find the book since I shoved it in the dark abyss that is my night table drawer last month, I'm pretty sure naughty lingerie has got to figure somewhere in *52 weeks of Spice*.

I am actually going to test one of my new purchases out tonight since the package arrived yesterday and Scott and I have a sitter for tonight. He has been working a lot of late nights and I am looking forward to having a real conversation with him. I haven't even had a chance to tell him about the pictures I took for Christine, which turned out way better than I expected, especially given little Rebel's underwear fetish. The kids looked adorable and I followed them around as they made cookies and had a bath and read bedtime stories. I even made a DVD slideshow of all the pictures I took and set it to music. Christine was thrilled and I have to admit I was too. It was nice to be good at something besides thinking up new ways to get a four year old to eat green vegetables.

Out of habit, before I log off the computer to go take a shower I check Facebook and there it is—a friend request from Charlie Bennett. How about that! Angie was right. I accept his request and within seconds he writes on my wall.

"Was that you I saw at Westfield Town Hall a few weeks ago?"

"No," I reply. *"That was my evil twin who is known for bad hair days and an abhorrent lack of clean laundry."* As an afterthought I add, *"She also stole my usually clean and color coordinated child and turned her into a vagrant."* What can I say? I'm used to the preschool mom crowd who often judge you by how well your child is dressed.

"Ha, ha," he writes back. *"I thought you looked great. Do you live in Westfield? Would love to meet for coffee or lunch and catch up."* He has included his phone number and e-mail address.

I may have been married for ten years but I haven't forgotten the art of playing hard to get, even if the guy in question is just an old friend. Okay, so he's an incredibly hot old friend who once knew every inch of my body, my dreams, and my soul. But that was ages ago. I'm happily married and Charlie can't possibly mean anything to me now. It's not like I'm even going to ever see him again but Angie is right. You've got to keep the upper hand when it comes to exes, and right now I've got it. Without responding, I log off and skip to the shower, humming Bon Jovi's "Never Say Goodbye."

Lindsey, a very responsible sixteen year old straight A student who lives four houses down from us, is babysitting and I have already told her that we will be late tonight and I will pay her handsomely for it. Given that I planned our last ill-fated date at the tennis courts, I have told Scott we can do whatever he wants tonight. I am anticipating dinner at his favorite steak restaurant followed by a typical guy shoot 'em up movie. Although I'd much rather curl up with a good book, going to the movies is one of Scott's favorite pastimes that we rarely get to indulge so I'm happy to let him pick the movie. The part of our date *I'm* looking forward to is an intimate dinner and some actual conversation with my husband since I have felt so disconnected from him lately. It's not like we've been fighting or disagreeing over anything, just more like we've been leading separate lives. He comes home from work late, burnt out and disinterested in conversation, so we sit on the couch together while he eats dinner and watches TV and I read a book, and then we both go to bed with a perfunctory good night kiss. I feel more like I have a roommate than a spouse. I'm sure that a night out alone together is just what we need. In honor of the occasion I am wearing my new crotchless thong (which really is just a piece of string up my ass), my favorite broken in pair of Levi's that hug every curve, and a black turtleneck sweater. I have even added some festive silver jewelry.

My hopes are slightly dashed when we pull out of the driveway and Scott suggests we go to Antonio's Pizza. Sure they have great pizza, but that's somewhere we can go with the kids. I say as much to Scott.

"I know," he says. "But the movie starts at 7:00, and Antonio's will be quick."

Quick? I see my hopes for intimacy and conversation vanishing. But wait a minute. If the movie's at seven, it should be over about nine, giving us plenty of time alone.

"Okay," I say. "Maybe after the movie, we can go have a drink or a coffee."

"Exactly," he says, as giddy as Will on his way to a birthday party.

"There's that new wine bar," I suggest, thinking about how dark and cozy it looks from the outside.

"Actually," Scott says, "I told Joe that we'd meet him and Jules at Station 29 for drinks."

In my head I hear the faint kaswoosh of a toilet flushing as I see my plans for the evening vanish. I like Joe, Scott's best friend from work, well enough, although we typically don't have much to say to each beyond polite inquiries about kids (mine) and work (his). But Jules, his hottest and latest in a long line of hot and sophisticated girlfriends, completely terrified me the one time I met her at a work function. She is tall, thin (although kind of anorexically so, if you ask me), immensely fashionable, and

96

urbane—in short, everything I'm not. Furthermore, from what I know of Station 29, it is just like Jules--a hip place to see and be seen near downtown Dallas, and the kind of place I was happy I would never have to set foot in again after I said "I do."

Oh well, at least we have Antonio's, which has somehow gone from being the worst part of the evening three minutes ago to now being the best.

"Hello, I'm Liz," I say, grabbing Scott's hand as we sit at a table waiting for our pizza. "I feel like I haven't really talked to you in ages. What's going on in your world?"

Scott launches into a story about his latest case involving the corporate merger of some start up telecom company and one of his biggest clients. My eyes are starting to glaze over when our pizza arrives. I seize the moment.

"I have some exciting news. Remember me telling you Christine wanted me to take some pictures for her?"

Scott looks at me blankly. "Who's Christine?"

"Our new next door neighbor," I say impatiently. "I told you about her. Anyway, she wanted me to take some pictures of her kids, kind of like the ones in our hallway, and so I did and she loved them! One of the women in her La Leche group wants me to take some pictures of her baby when it's born, and another one of her friends has already called to see if I'll do her Christmas card family photo. "

"That's great," Scott says. Because he seems only mildly enthusiastic, I add, "And they want to pay me. I have a jobette."

"How much?" he asks, slightly more interested now that money is involved.

"Well, not much," I admit. "Christine insisted on giving me $200. But that's pretty good for the amount of time I spent. Plus you have to take into account that I can do it on my own time so I don't have to pay for day care."

Scott laughs. "Liz, that's great and I'm glad you've found a hobby. But I don't think you need to start talking about day care. It's not like it's a real job."

I feel like a little kid who has been patted on the head and told to run off and play and leave the grownups alone. There is obviously no point in telling Scott that when I took those photos I felt important, like I had something real to contribute for the first time in a long while.

Changing the subject I say, "Remember me telling you I signed up for Facebook?"

Another look of puzzlement.

"Honestly Scott, do you listen to anything I say? Anyway, you wouldn't believe some of the people who have come out of the woodwork and contacted me."

"Anyone I know?" he asks.

"Mostly people from high school, and of course Angie and Kate and some other mom friends. And I get to talk to Heather more (Scott knows Heather since she and I were roommates when he and I started dating). Oh, remember Michelle? She was in our biology lab at Duke. She's a pediatric heart surgeon in Boston now."

"Oh yeah?" Scott says. Guys could care less about this kind of stuff. He'd probably be more interested if I told him she'd become a waitress at Hooters.

"And my old boyfriend Charlie looked me up too," I add nonchalantly.

"That's cool," Scott says, reaching for his wallet. "We'd better go or we'll miss the previews."

Two and a half hours later, our minds numb from watching thirty eight people get shot, thrown off of a building, or blown up in a car crash (I admit I kept a body count—I had to do something to entertain myself), we are headed downtown to meet Joe and Jules. Although Scott does not seem too interested in what is going on in my life, I figure he might like to know what's been going on with his kids. Besides, I can usually make him laugh with my only slightly embellished stories of their antics.

"You know, Will pulled his penis out at Bella's soccer practice on Monday," I say. Hey, the truth can make for a better story than fiction. I know Scott will get a kick out of this one. "Right there in front of everyone and he starts waving it around. I'm trying to be all nonchalant so I say very casually, like it's a matchbox car, 'Will, put your penis away.' That's something I never thought I'd say!" I add with a laugh.

"Liz, could we not talk about the kids tonight?" Scott says with a sigh. "I'd just like to enjoy some time with you."

If that's the case, then I'd like to know why we are driving across town to spend the rest of our rare evening out with other people. When we walk into Station 29, my senses are bombarded. The bar scene is just as I remembered it. There is enough smoke to make me slightly jones for a cigarette (I smoked for two years in college), the music is throbbing, and there are scores of beautiful people drinking martinis, tossing their gorgeous manes of hair and flashing impossibly white teeth as they talk and laugh. You can practically feel the energy of the place. Scott spots Joe and Jules at a table for four near the band and grabs my hand, pulling me through the throng of people to their table. Joe stands up and slaps Scott on the back, then gives me a hug. Jules remains seated, although she nods at us and purrs hello. Her aloof gaze takes in my jeans and sweater, as out of place here as if I were wearing flippers and a wetsuit in the Sahara.

"I'm not quite dressed for this place," I say breezily, as if it doesn't bother me at all. "I thought we were just going to the movies." Truthfully, I'd be perfectly happy if the floor opened and swallowed me up. What looked casually hip and even sexy in my bathroom mirror seems hopelessly provincial here. And Jules' look lets me know that even if she were just going to the movies, she wouldn't be caught dead in what I'm wearing. I want to announce that at least I'm wearing a thong, but I wisely keep that information to myself.

The guys are deep in conversation, leaving Jules and me to try to find some common ground.

"Do you come here often?" I say. Great, I sound like I'm trying to pick her up. "I mean, I've never been here before."

"Really?" Even Jules' voice is impeccably cultured. "Do you drink in the suburbs then?" I can't tell if she's making fun of me or just trying to make conversation.

"Usually," I agree. It's not a lie. Angie's kitchen table and Kate's patio are both, technically, in the suburbs.

"What an interesting necklace," she says. I touch the silver cross that Bella painstakingly made for me last Mother's Day out of jewelry wire and a paper clip.

"Thank you. My six year old daughter made it for me," I say proudly.

"How quaint," Jules says.

We are saved from further conversation by the waitress, who approaches to take our drink order. Although I usually stick to red wine or margaritas, this evening is definitely going to require something harder. I peruse the drink menu and order something called a gumdrop martini. That sounds yummy.

As the evening wears on, it becomes painfully apparent that I am the odd man out. I have nothing to add to Scott's, Joe's and Jules' discussions about work, the Dallas night life scene or their mutual interest in French movies so I just keep ordering drinks and slugging them back. I'm feeling a bit fuzzy headed and have mostly tuned out their conversation when I hear Jules say, "All women wear thongs."

Thongs. Now there's something I can talk about since one has recently disappeared up my butt. Seriously. The last time I went to the ladies room I couldn't find it all. Luckily it's crotchless so it didn't really matter. Before I can get my mouth to work Scott

100

says, "Not true! Not every woman wears thongs. Liz doesn't."

I'm sure he means well but he is so not helping me here. I'm sure Jules already thinks I'm a hopeless frump anyway.

"What do you wear then, granny panties?" Jules says incredulously.

"I wouldn't say they're granny panties," I say indignantly. "They're just, you know, briefs. Like a bikini bottom."

"Some women like Liz are just more reserved," Scott adds.

Reserved? I'm not reserved! Okay, maybe I'm a little reserved but I'm wearing a crotchless thong for crying out loud. Of course I don't wear one every day because half the time when I use the restroom I have an audience of three very curious little people who have been know to randomly share stories of my personal hygiene with perfect strangers. That and I don't have time to constantly dig underwear out of my crack. There's something to be said for comfort.

"You're just not sexy if you don't wear a thong," Jules says dismissively.

That does it. It is my moral obligation to stand up for all the real underwear wearing women out there. I'll show Scott reserved. I stand up. I'm a little wobbly so I wait a minute to regain my balance. Then I march over to the where the band is getting ready to start another set.

"Shcuse me," I say to singer. "I need to borrow your microphone for just a wee little second." I wave my thumb and forefinger, with a miniscule amount of space between the two, in his face to show him just how little I'm asking for.

"Is this thing on?" I say into the microphone. Apparently it is because my voice is reverberating through the bar and suddenly everyone is looking over at the stage.

"This place is full of gorgeous women," I announce. A few of the women cheer and a guy in the back whistles. I nod and say, "Iss true. I've never seen so many gorgeous women in one place.

101

And my friend here thinks that all of you gorgeous women are wearing thongs." I nod towards Jules, who is staring at me open mouthed. I must say it is not a particularly attractive look for her.

A few men make wolf calls. Encouraged by their enthusiasm I continue, "I say that's not true. I say most women, even most sexy women, don't wear butt floss on a daily basis. Help me out here. Who doesn't wear a thong?"

I scan the crowd.

"Aha!" I say triumphantly, waving my hand vaguely at the smattering of raised hands in the audience. "And I'll bet that a bunch of you women who *are* wearing a thong tonight (and let me tell you guys, it's all for you) won't be wearing one tomorrow when they're at the gym or grocery shopping or watching Desperate Housewives. But that doesn't mean they're not still sexy! Am I right ladies?" I see more smiles and nods and one woman yells, "You tell them sista!" She actually looks a little scary but I appreciate the vote of solidarity.

"We are sexy women!" I yell. "And we are here to tell you that we can be sexy without a thong!" I raise my fist in a rallying gesture. Unfortunately I drop the microphone in the process. I turn around and bend down to pick it up and when I turn back around the crowd is going wild and cheering me on. Except for Scott, who is making some weird gestures at me.

"And jeans are sexy too!" I yell, caught up in the moment.

"They sure are, baby" some guy calls.

The next thing I know Scott is pulling me off the stage. "I think it's time for us to go," he says, grabbing his jacket off the back of the chair.

"I'm not finished yet," I say indignantly. "Look, they love me."

"Sure they do honey," he says with a smile. "'Cause when you bent over to pick up the microphone your jeans split, and I'm not sure what happened to your underwear but let's just say you look like a hypocrite."

I reach back and my hand touches flesh. There is a rip at least two inches gaping across my left cheek.

"Oh," I say. Then, "Oh!" I pull my sweater down as far as it will go as Scott turns to say goodbye to Joe and Jules. Jules is smiling at me, a real smile, not the fake, polite, condescending smile she bestowed on me earlier.

"Wow!" she says admiringly. "You're a lot more fun than I thought. I must come and drink in the suburbs sometime." She slips me a business card. "Call me. We'll do lunch."

When we get home, Scott pays the babysitter while I go upstairs and check on the kids, tucking blankets around warm little pajama clad bodies and kissing soft, smooth cheeks. When I get back downstairs, Scott is already in bed.

"Wow, you were something tonight," he says. "I'm not sure you're going to feel so great tomorrow though."

"I was something, wasn't I?" I say proudly. "And you haven't seen anything yet." I waggle my eyebrows at him suggestively. "I'll show you just how reserved I am! Don't move! I'll be right back. I'm just going to go change into something a little less comfortable."

I disappear into the bathroom and close the door. Sadly, I peel off my jeans and throw them in the trashcan. Dang, they were my favorites. My crotchless thong is gone. All that I can see is a thin band of lace resting on my stomach, which bears those faint silver scars of childbirth otherwise known as stretch marks. Definitely not the sexy look I was going for. I remove the thong and dig around in the closet for one of my other new purchases, the fishnet open bust three piece garter set. Man, this thing is REALLY confusing to try to put on when you're drunk. I end up with the stockings on backwards and one breast poking out of the neck hole. After four attempts I finally get it right, and then spend another five minutes attaching the stockings to the garter. Scott had better appreciate this.

I emerge from the bathroom with a grand flourish. There lies my husband, sound asleep with a pillow over his head, softly snoring. It's the last straw. I walk over to Scott's side of the bed and roughly nudge him awake. Sleepy and disoriented, he squints at me through sleep blurred eyes.

"What's the matter?" he mutters grumpily.

"What's the matter?" I yell. "That you even have to ask is what the matter is. I haven't talked to you in weeks, much less shared a romantic second alone with you, and on our one night alone together you take me to a cheap pizza place, to a stupid guy movie and then to some horrible singles bar with *your* friends. And I may as well have been talking to myself for the last week since you don't remember anything I've told you. You don't care about anything that's important to me and to top it all off, you have the nerve to fall asleep while I'm putting on some stupid sexy lingerie that I bought for you."

Awake now, he lifts up on one elbow and takes in my outfit, his eyes widening appreciatively. "You can still seduce me," he says hopefully.

"Forget it," I say huffily. "For some reason, I'm just not in the mood anymore!" I turn and stalk out of the bedroom with as much righteous indignation as I can muster wearing an open busted garter. I almost slam the door, but I remember the kids sleeping upstairs so at the last minute I click it closed with quiet resolve instead. I wrap a blanket from the powder room linen closet around me and go into the study. I sit down at the computer and log on to Facebook. I click on Charlie's name to send him a private message. *"How about Starbucks next Monday around 9?"* I type and hit send.

Chapter Twelve

Tuesday, November 18th

It's amazing how one glimpse into your past, no matter how brief, can propel you back in time. Charlie responded to my message the day after I sent it and agreed to meet me for coffee next Monday. Since then, I have done nothing but think about him. It's as if the past fifteen years have become foggy like the bathroom mirror after you take a hot shower and the only thing that is sharp and clear are the three years that Charlie and I were together. In the vast spaces of mindlessness that is motherhood- change diapers, cook meals, build with blocks, fold laundry, clean up, repeat- there is plenty of time for your mind to wander, and I find myself constantly thinking about Charlie, the memories playing in my head like a movie. Our first date, when he tried to impress me by making lobster for dinner and we ended up feeling so sorry for the lobsters that we let them go in the creek behind his house and went to Burger King. The taste of his lips, warm and wet on mine as we sat in his hot tub, the feeling of my stomach dropping to my toes the first time his hand slipped behind me to gently untie my bikini top. The way he looked when he picked me up for prom, incredibly handsome and uncharacteristically shy in a tuxedo vest. Stolen visits to his apartment at Penn State, playing at being grown ups, and the inevitable heartbreak six months after I went to Duke and he told me he couldn't do a long distance relationship.

I have been so preoccupied with my memories that even Scott's blatant attempts to get out of the dog house have barely registered. My tirade Friday night must have gotten through to him because he has definitely been trying hard this week. I realized how bad he felt on Saturday when he made the ultimate guy gesture of love-he washed my car. He has been coming home before the kids go to bed, he actually put Daisy to bed one night, he has made sure to ask me about my day and then listened attentively as I recounted the monotonous details of going to the grocery store or my parent teacher conference with Isabella's teacher, and he brought me flowers on Monday. But while I have appreciated his gestures and outwardly praised his thoughtfulness, all I can think about is Charlie. Thankfully the memories seem to have finally played themselves out today, only to be replaced by guilt. Is it a mistake to see him again? Sometimes I'm certain that it is, that I should message him back and tell him something has come up and I can't make it, but have a nice life. But then I think, what's the harm in seeing an old friend? I'm happily married, he's probably happily married; it would be nice to catch up and revisit my life before kids. Seeing Charlie again is more than just seeing my first love; it is the chance to see myself through the eyes of someone who knew me before I was someone's mother, when I belonged only to myself. He is part of who I used to be; it might be just what I need. And of course I will sleep better for the rest of my life knowing that the last time he saw me I didn't look like hell. That's all I really want. To see him one more time when I'm looking great and acting cool and composed, to let him know how fabulous my life turned out without him. But I still feel guilty. Maybe it's because Scott is trying so hard to be nice.

Thank God Bella has soccer practice tonight so I can run it by Angie, Meg and Kate. Although Angie, who got me in this mess to begin with, will probably show up to help me get ready like some suburban Madame, I'm pretty certain Meg and Kate will tell me if

106

meeting Charlie for coffee is a really stupid idea. At least I'm hoping they will.

We arrive at the park where the girls practice a few minutes late, thanks to Daisy pooping in her diaper right as we were walking out the door. There must be some Pavlovian response in babies to poop when the front door opens. Isabella races onto the field to join her friends and Angie waves me over to where she and Meg are sitting in their folding chairs under a tree near the playground. Will immediately begs to join the other boys on the playground and Daisy occupies herself moving wood chips from one square of sidewalk to another, leaving me free to chat with my friends. My mother once commented that when my brothers and I were young, children didn't get to do the thousand and one activities kids today are constantly signed up for. I didn't have the heart to tell her it's not really for the kids. Seriously, what three year old (or even six year old) is interested in organized anything, for crying out loud? It's purely selfish. We parents are too isolated locked away in our big suburban homes behind privacy fences, or busy working nine to five (or more likely eight to six), to make friends with other neighborhood moms and meet over coffee each week. So we manufacture circumstances in which we see the same group of moms on a regular basis in order to replace that ability to connect with other women. In the new millennium of motherhood, soccer practice and ballet and tae kwon do are our means to connect with each other. Whether our kids actually get anything out of soccer or ballet or karate at this age is irrelevant.

"Where's Kate?" I ask, unfolding the chair I have schlepped from the car along with Daisy's diaper bag, two juice boxes, Bella's water bottle and an odd assortment of sand toys.

"Her dad's in the hospital again," Meg says. "I brought Chloe."

I frown in sympathy. Yet another thing that sucks about getting older—not only do you have to take care of your kids and your husband, but you now have to take care of your parents too.

Sometimes all I want is someone to take care of me.

"Cookie?" I offer them, holding out the bag of chocolate chip cookies I brought.

Angie shudders. "You've got to be joking," she says.

I laugh and turn to Meg. She is hunched over a bundle wrapped in a blanket and at first I think she must be holding someone's baby. On closer inspection I see that it's Buttons, the kitten they found abandoned in a grocery store parking lot about six months ago and decided to keep. Frankly, I can't believe the cat has survived Meg's boys. On second thought, Buttons isn't looking so hot. She's kind of stretched out in Meg's lap looking all dopey.

"What's wrong with Buttons?" I ask.

"Oh, we got her fixed today," Meg says. She strokes the cat's head gently. "My poor baby," she croons.

"Don't worry," I say. "Bandit was the same when he got snipped. But he was back to his old self in a day or two. Of course, the fact that Scott shared sausage biscuits with him every day for a month out of guilt over taking his manhood probably helped."

"A little sausage in exchange for his sausage, eh?" Angie laughs. I make a face at her.

"They can still have sex even though they're fixed can't they?" Meg asks.

"No!" Angie says, laughing. "Cats just have sex to procreate, so if they're fixed, what's the point? Then they just like to cuddle. Hmm, maybe I should have agreed to get my tubes tied after all. Then I would have an excuse for just wanting to cuddle."

"Yeah, but then John would expect you to purr and rub against him," I point out.

Meg waves her hand at Angie dismissively. "You don't have cats," she says. She turns to me. "That's not true is it Liz?"

"Angie's probably right," I say. "Although Bandit did get out one night before he became a eunuch, so I like to think he had one night of bliss to remember in his old age."

"Poor Buttons!" Meg exclaims in horror. "I had no idea she was going to be a virgin for the rest of her life. I'm so sorry, sweetie," she croons to the cat.

Ten seconds later, in typical Meg fashion, the cat and her lamentable virginity are both forgotten as Meg leaps to her feet, almost dumping poor, dopey Buttons on the ground. "Oh my gosh, I almost forgot to tell you guys! You know Jorge, who does my hair?" Angie and I nod. Despite Meg's somewhat strapped financial situation, she somehow manages to scrape together $60 every three months to get her hair cut by Jorge, a gay Hispanic man whose colorful lifestyle and antics are a constant source of entertainment for all of us.

"Your hair looks great," Angie offers.

"Thanks! So I was at Jorge's on Saturday, and he was telling me about this place you can go and get real designer handbags. We're talking Coach, Louis, Dolce and Prada, for almost nothing. You have to know someone to get in, and they don't really have a permanent location so you have to know where they are, but Jorge is going to e-mail me the info so I can go after Thanksgiving. I'm going to do all of my Christmas shopping. You guys want to come?"

"It sounds too good to be true," I say dubiously. "Are you sure it's legit?"

"Absolutely," Meg says. "Jorge has been going for years. I think they are slightly flawed so they can sell them for much less. And they have shoes too."

"Oh, well then," I say. Obviously, if they have shoes I must go.

"I'm out," Angie says, holding her hands out. "You guys can go fund the Mafia without me. Besides, I know this is

109

Westfield and all, but I'm going to wait until Hannah's at least eight before I buy her a Prada."

We sit in silence for a few minutes, watching our exuberant girls run across the field after the soccer ball, graceful and strong and free and confident in the way that girls are before they hit puberty, before little clouds of self-consciousness begin to follow us everywhere, sprinkling us with the suspicion that we're not smart enough, or pretty enough, or perfect enough.

"So, remember how I ran into my ex-boyfriend Charlie at Town Hall? He friended me on Facebook. He wants to meet for coffee and catch up." I say it all nonchalantly, as if the whole thing hasn't been completely monopolizing my thoughts every waking second.

"Get out!" exclaims Meg.

Angie whacks me with the magazine that it is her lap. "What?!! When? You rat! Why didn't you call me immediately? What did he say? Is he married?"

"Hold on, hold on," I say with a laugh. "I haven't even decided if I'm going or not."

"Of course you are!" exclaims Angie at the same time that Meg says, "Of course you're not!"

They stop and frown at each other. "She shouldn't go!" Meg says firmly. "Seeing an old boyfriend is asking for trouble."

"She's not asking for trouble," Angie retorts. "She's getting revenge. The last time she saw him she looked like shit. Does she want the guy who broke her heart thinking she's turned into a frumpy housewife?"

"Thanks Ang," I interject sarcastically, even though she's got a point.

They both ignore me. "What if she realizes he's her true love and it completely ruins her life, wanting what she can't have? " Meg counters.

It's like watching my id and ego battle it out in front of me. I should have known Angie would be the figurative devil on my shoulder.

"It's not like she wants to hook up with him," Angie says. "She's happily married." They both turn to look at me. "Aren't you?"

I squirm a bit. "Sure," I say. "I mean, definitely. Scott and I are definitely happy." It even sounds to me like I'm trying to convince myself. "After ten years of marriage and three kids, of course it's not the same as when we met. We have responsibilities now. We have more to think about than the next place we're going to have sex."

Angie nods. "That's why I gave you the vibrator," she says. "The bunny is there for you!"

I shoot daggers at her. "Don't even go there," I say. "We're happy. It's just that sometimes I feel like I've lost myself somewhere along the way. Remember that 'Get to Know your Friend' quiz Kate sent? I put Anthony the blue Wiggle as my favorite actor because I can't remember the last time I watched an adult show. River Monsters doesn't count. I've even imagined what he looks like naked," I confess.

"Don't worry. We all fantasize about the Wiggles," Angie says. "When you watch talking cartoon animals all day, four real men are pretty irresistible, even if they are dressed like dorks. Although I always fancied Greg myself. He's so tall, and he has a nice smile."

"I think Captain Feathersword is cute." Meg says. "I have a thing for pirates." Angie and I look at her quizzically.

"The point is that you haven't lost yourself any more than any other mom has," Angie says. "It's harder when you stay home I think. There's nothing to keep you grounded in the adult world. But you're still you."

111

"Honey, maybe you should meet your ex," Meg says. "Maybe it's the reality check you need to realize how happy you really are in your all-grown-up life. And you'll probably realize you're not so different than you used to be."

"Damn straight," says Angie. "Look great, knock him dead, and then call and tell us everything."

11:08 p.m.

I used to love the rain. The steady sound of it has always comforted me, and some of my happiest memories are being lulled to sleep by the rhythmic patter of rain on the roof. In the early days of our marriage, Scott and I would make slow, languid love to the sound of a light spring rain, and have primal, intense sex to the clamor of a torrential storm.

Now we lie side by side in bed, wide awake but not touching, wondering which of our three children will wake up first. It's Daisy, whose fearful cry comes across the monitor mere seconds after the first big boom of thunder. I'm out of bed and up the stairs in less than a minute, gathering her up in my arms and comforting her with whispered reassurances.

"My sleep in Mommy's bed," she demands, trying to climb me like a monkey jonesing for a bunch of bananas.

Another crack of lightning and the subsequent crash of thunder shake the house, making me jump. "Sure baby," I whisper. I am fumbling for a diaper (no point in sleeping in a wet spot when you don't even get an orgasm out of the deal) when Will appears, his blond hair sticking up every which way.

"Listen Mommy," he says, grabbing my hand and pressing it to his small chest. "My heart is beating so fast I think it's gonna run to China'

"You scared of the thunder buddy?" I ask. He nods emphatically.

"Let's get your sleeping bag. You can sleep in Mommy and Daddy's room too."

He races back into his room to get his stuffed duck, Quackers, and reappears in seconds, relief clear on his face. I peek in Bella's room and find her sitting up in bed, the covers pulled up to her chin, trying to be brave.

"You want to come sleep in Mommy and Daddy's room until the storm passes?" I ask. She nods, grabs her blanket and follows us down the stairs.

I return to the bedroom with my entourage, dump Daisy on the bed with Scott, and then help Will and Bella set up their sleeping bags on either side of our bed, tucking them in for the second time tonight. I climb back into my bed, Daisy safely hemmed in on the big king-sized bed with Scott and me on either side of her.

Another crash of thunder reverberates and Daisy wraps her little arms as tight as she can around me, pressing her face into my neck.

"Mommy?" A tentative little voice says from the other side of the bed.

"It's okay," I say reassuringly. "Mommy and Daddy are right here. You're safe."

"I know," Will says sleepily. "I was just checking to make sure *you* were okay."

As the storm slowly moves away, taking its reluctant thunder with it like a truculent child, I hear Will's soft snores along with Scott's louder ones. I check on Isabella, my quietest child even in sleep. She is also fast asleep. Too bad her little sister isn't. Daisy tosses and turns in bed, a firecracker with no where to boom. I sing softly to her, smoothing the fine, dandelion hair off her forehead with my fingers until finally, her eyes get heavy.

"I love you," I whisper, more to myself than to her.

113

Her blue eyes open and she says sleepily, "Thank you," then drifts back to sleep.

Four hours later I wake up to find that my three foot tall child has somehow stretched herself horizontally in the bed like Stretch Armstrong, taking up so much space that Scott and I are now huddled on the edge of either side of the mattress. Bella is sprawled out on the floor on my side of the bed, making getting up to go to the bathroom akin to walking through a mine field. I have no doubt that Will, sleeping on the floor on Scott's side of the bed, looks the same.

This is what kids do to marriage. They take up all of the space between you until you find yourself clinging to the edge on opposite sides, the kids between you. But they are so small, and our love for them is so big, so we tell each other to move over and we let them in.

Chapter Thirteen

Three days later, as I maneuver my minivan into a miniscule space at the mall thanks to the huge SUV that parked over the line in the space to my left, I'm still wondering if I'm doing the right thing. Unless I chicken out, I am meeting Charlie for coffee on Monday. As luck (or fate?) would have it, Scott's mom Candace is arriving on Sunday to spend Thanksgiving with us and has offered to keep the kids for me on Monday so I can run some last minute errands. This is going to work out quite nicely since one of those errands will include picking up some coffee at Starbucks at about 9:00 on Monday morning.

This morning however, I am determined to buy myself something to wear on Monday that doesn't scream "mom." Or at least that doesn't scream "mom who has totally let herself go." For the last week, I have taken every opportunity to lock myself in the bathroom and peruse the stacks of Redbook and Parents magazines that I pile up in there in the event I ever have time to read them, trying to figure out what a fashionable mom might wear. I have been staying in there for so long that Scott often knocks on the door to make sure I'm okay.

So I am at the mall, armed with my MasterCard and a purse full of snacks and toys to keep Daisy occupied, while I shop for clothes at "real" stores that I haven't frequented in years. When I was in college and even in my early married years, shopping was a fun hobby and social event, and I would spend entire days browsing stores and trying on clothes with Heather or another girl friend, stopping only long enough to grab an overpriced frou frou salad or sandwich at some trendy lunch spot. Now I just grab the bare necessities, shop online, or on the rare occasion I am alone, try to cram a year's worth of shopping into three hours, manically trying on clothes and purchasing everything that looks remotely decent. I'm sure Angie, Meg and Kate go shopping, but I honestly have no idea where because we never go together.

My excitement over shopping at the mall quickly wanes as Daisy proves to be in a crabby mood. She doesn't want a snack, she keeps dropping or throwing the toys I give her onto the floor, and she keeps arching her back in the stroller yelling, "My want out!" She seems content as long as we are trucking through the mall at a pace that would leave a long distance runner in the dust, which sadly doesn't allow for much window shopping. I pause to catch my breath just outside of Saks Fifth Avenue and she looks inside, mesmerized and amazingly still quiet despite the fact the stroller has stopped. Hmmm, maybe she's just a high end shopper. I tentatively step inside the store. Still quiet. Although it's probably way out of my price range, I figure I'll look around since Daisy seems willing. I browse in the misses' sportswear section along with two other women, who despite being thirty years apart in age look like well heeled carbon copies of each other who have just stepped out of the pages of Vogue. As an equally well-manicured sales lady approaches, Daisy yells, "Mommy, you tooted!"

She chortles with laughter, just as her brother and sister did when she repeated the word they taught her last weekend. I ignore her and calmly peruse a rack of cardigan sweaters that cost more than a year's worth of birth control.

"Mommy, you tooted!" she says more loudly.

"You silly girl," I say, deliberately misunderstanding. "Mommy didn't hoot. Owls hoot, don't they? They say, 'hoo, hoo.'"

"No, Mommy. You tooted!" Daisy has very good language skills for a not quite two year old and is very single minded when she wants to be, which is apparently now. "You tooted. Mommy tooted," she says again.

"I did not!" I whisper loudly to her.

"You tooted!" she says with delight.

I catch myself before I get into an argument with a toddler over whether or not I tooted and hastily leave the hushed aisles of Saks, breathing a sigh of relief when we reach the cacophony of sounds and fluorescent lights of the main mall. Undoubtedly, one of the reasons God gives us children is to keep us humble and help us realize our place in the world. Message received; I do not belong at Saks Fifth Avenue. I also did not belong at the gym. When I took advantage of a trial membership when Isabella was little and I was pregnant with Will and unable to wear my wedding ring, Bella would point to ripped, African American men and exclaim, "Daddy!" It was a toss-up who was more horrified, them or me.

We end up at Macy's, and in sheer desperation I let Daisy out of her stroller. She seems content to crawl in and out of the rounders of clothes while I look at clothes. I am holding a cute, flirty red floral blouse up to a pair of black silk trousers when I hear a man say with censure, "My goodness. Where's your Mommy?"

Oh crap. Where's Daisy? I look inside the rounder where she was just swatting at tags but she's not there.

"Daisy?" I call loudly.

I rush across the aisle to the dressing rooms where an elderly man is sitting, obviously waiting for his wife who must be in the fitting rooms. And there, in front of the three-way mirror is Daisy, undressing herself with the practiced moves of an

117

experienced stripper.   Mortified, I scoop her up along with her discarded clothes and disappear into the fitting rooms where I try on the pants and blouse I was holding and play pat a cake with her until I am sure the elderly couple have left the store and I can slink out undetected.

Monday, November 24th

Despite my catastrophic trip to the mall, after which I renewed my vow to only shop online until Daisy is in kindergarten (probably at a magnet arts school for exotic dancers), I did manage to purchase a new outfit which I am wearing this morning. The red blouse and black pants, paired with a pair of black boots I splurged on last year, make me feel dressed up, but not so much so that I won't fit in at the carpool line. I feel pulled together and confident. I woke up extra early this morning so I would have time to wash, dry, and straighten my hair, and it looks great all sleek and straight and shiny, falling just past my shoulders. After studying pictures of movie stars in a People magazine I bought at Wal-Mart yesterday, I decided that accessories is what makes the look so I am wearing a chunky black necklace, gold hoop earrings, and my DKNY watch with the black crocodile band, along with a big, fashionable black leather tote. I fancy I look a bit like Katie Holmes about to go to the Farmer's Market with Suri, or perhaps Julia Roberts grabbing a cup of coffee before picking the twins up from a play date.

I am meeting Charlie at the Starbucks at Westfield Commons, a brand new, red bricked outdoor shopping and dining Mecca that has been meticulously created to look old. It is beautiful though, with lots of tree lined walkways, and the Starbucks has an outdoor patio that overlooks the small, man-made lake. I pull into a parking place and walk the short distance to the coffee shop with a combination of nervous excitement tinged with trepidation. What if he just wanted to see if I really was the train wreck I appeared to be so he could congratulate himself on dodging that bullet? Or what if he's gay? Crap, why didn't I think

118

of this earlier; what if he brings his wife? I shake off the "what ifs" and open the door to the coffee shop. There he is, definitely alone and undeniably gorgeous. He is watching the door and his eyes light up when he sees me. He gets up from the table where he is sitting and meets me halfway, where we both awkwardly stop, uncertain whether we should shake hands, hug or do nothing. I opt for nothing, opening my black tote to deposit my sunglasses.

"Liz! It's great to see you," he says warmly. He grabs both of my hands and takes a step back, looking at me intently. For some reason, I feel like it is the first time a man has really looked at me in quite some time. "You look fabulous!"

"You too," I say. "I can't believe we ran into each other in Westfield of all places." After all, back when we knew each other we both lived half a continent away from here. Talk about fate. To him I say incredulously, "Do you live here?"

"No," he says. "I'm just here on business. Let's grab some coffee and I'll tell you about it."

We both order coffee (a latte for him, a skinny mocha for me), awkwardly making small talk about the weather and the shopping area while we wait for the baristas to make our drinks. Once they are in hand, we return to his table by the window.

"So," I begin, taking a tentative sip. The hot beverage singes my throat. "What are you doing here?" Back in my life.

As Charlie talks, I learn that he is an architect that designs upscale town home communities and he has been in Westfield several times over the last month on business because his company is trying to build a complex on the extremely tony north side of town. In addition to having to come into town for periodic on-site inspections and meetings, a group of homeowners have been lobbying to stall the project and he has been elected to liaison with the community leaders, which is why he was at Town Hall the day I went to pick up my driver's license.

"So what about you?" he says. "Obviously you live here. But what were you doing at Town Hall? In trouble with the law as usual?" I look into his eyes, which are dancing merrily.

"That is so unfair!" I say in mock indignation. "The one and only time I have ever been in trouble with the law is when you convinced me to try to buy a six pack for you at the shore over Spring Break."

"Hey," he says with a laugh, holding up his hands. "You can't blame me. No one could ever look into those big blue eyes of yours and say no. It was a fail proof plan."

"Sure," I say dryly. "If a police officer hadn't been buying a cup of coffee and a donut one aisle over."

"C'mon," he says. "I took care of you didn't I?" He had, in fact, pulled the police officer over to the side as I stood quaking in my flip flops at the prospect of having committed the misdemeanor offence of trying to purchase alcohol as a minor and told him a very convincing story about how my entire family, all fifteen of them, were depending on my scholarship to Yale law school to reverse the poverty that had ensued after my father was injured saving a small child and her dear old granny from a burning building, and how any blemish on my record would ruin everything. The police officer, accustomed to turning a blind eye to the hijinks of the hordes of high school and college students that swarmed the New Jersey shore during that one week every March, had agreed to overlook it provided I pay a fine of $50, which Charlie had promptly handed over.

"Yes," I agree, dryly. "You definitely saved me from a life of crime. Not to mention the poverty me and my twelve siblings would have endured."

And just like that, the awkward distance of fifteen years evaporates and we are once again at ease together as only two people who have known each other when they were young and shared a lifetime can be.

Charlie asks about me so I tell him about finishing my degree at Duke, my career at McMillan Hotels, meeting Scott and my subsequent move to Dallas.

"Do you still work in PR?" he asks.

"No, I stay home with my kids right now. I have three," I say.

"Oh yeah?" his eyes light up. "Tell me about them."

"Seriously?" I look at him, dubious.

"Definitely" he says. "I love kids."

"Well, Isabella is six going on about thirty. She's way too smart for own good, but she's so sweet and charming. Will is four and he is all boy, a constant chatterbox who is cuddly and sweet one minute, and then trying to lasso the cat the next. Daisy—her real name is Margaret, after my mom, but we've always called her Daisy—is the one you saw at the Town Hall. She'll be two in March and she gets away with murder because she's so cute and funny." I pull out my phone and show him pictures. He runs his thumb across the image of Bella and smiles.

"She looks just like you," he says.

"You think?" I ask, pleased. My kids are all blond like Scott, so most people don't think they resemble me at all. When people ask where they get their blond hair, I usually say the mailman. Or the pool boy. Of course blow up pools don't require that much maintenance, but they don't need to know that.

"Do you have kids?" I ask. I don't see a wedding band on his hand (yes, I looked!) but that doesn't necessarily mean anything.

"One. His name is Logan. He's thirteen." My, my. Someone certainly got busy after we broke up. So much for my fantasies of him pining away for me.

"He lives with his mom in Virginia. I see him once every couple of months and he usually comes out to spend some of the summer with me." He looks sad and out of some long-forgotten

121

but deep-seated habit, I put my hand over his. It is warm, smooth, and utterly familiar. The electricity that flows from his hand to mine is just as familiar, and I pull my hand away quickly.

"Are you honestly old enough to have a thirteen year old?" I ask, feigning shock.

He laughs, and the spell of the moment is broken. "Might I remind you that we're the same age?"

"Yeah, but you're four months older, which is like two years if you're a dog."

"Are you calling me a dog?" His eyes are dancing with laughter again.

I feel years younger and freer just talking to Charlie. Can two years, the age difference between Scott and me, make such a difference? Or is it because Charlie and I have not grown older together, have not crossed all of those milestones into adulthood side by side, that we are able to be who we were when we left off. Charlie's and my firsts together are so different from Scott's and my firsts. Charlie was my first love, the first boy I gave everything to first, the one who rode the teenage roller coaster of intoxicating highs and devastating lows with me—high school football games and stolen kisses under the bleachers, parties and SAT tests, graduation and a future still waiting to be discovered. Scott is my grown up love, the one I have financed a mortgage with, the one I have created new life with; surely that should mean more.

"So you're divorced?" I finally ask.

Charlie tells me briefly about his ex wife Jennifer, whom he met, dated and married in the space of one year while doing his architecture internship right after college graduation. We talk about Philadelphia, where Charlie still lives, and his parents and mine. Our conversation moves to hobbies and he asks me if I still like to take pictures. I look at him, stunned.

"I liked to take pictures when we were together?" I ask. Why don't I remember that?

"Sure. Don't you remember? You were always toting your camera around and making people pose for you, or taking pictures of weird stuff like the carousel on the boardwalk that would always come out looking cool and artsy."

How could I have forgotten this?

I tell him about the pictures I have been taking recently and he listens with such interest that I find myself telling him my dreams of being a photographer, dreams long buried that I hadn't quite realized myself until now.

"I'd like to see them," he says. "Will you e-mail me a few, or just post them on Facebook?"

"Why?" I ask suspiciously.

"Because they're important to you. Because you were always a great photographer and I want to see them. Because I want to say I was one of the first to recognize your talent before you become wildly famous. Because I need some ideas to steal for my Christmas cards. Do you need more reasons?"

"Okay, okay" I say with a laugh, but I am secretly pleased. His interest in me as a person, as a woman, is intoxicating. Our coffee cups have been empty for a while now and I glance down at my watch absently. What? How on earth could two and a half hours have possibly passed? I still have a hundred things to do and even Candace will find it odd if I don't come home with a turkey after spending the entire morning out. Perhaps especially Candace.

"I've got to go," I say with regret. "But I am so glad you contacted me. It has been amazingly nice to see you. Well," I add. "I know I technically saw you before, but I was chasing a toddler into an elevator so that doesn't count."

Charlie smiles his crooked smile at me.

"Let's keep in touch?"

"Okay," I say. "I'd like that." I scribble my cell phone number on a napkin and hand it to him.

We stand up to leave and this time we embrace, a warm hug that is as natural as it is spontaneous. His strong arms encircle me in an almost bone crushing bear hug, and I can't help but notice how different from Scott he feels to hug; he is slightly shorter and not as broad as Scott, but wiry and defined. I reluctantly pull away.

"See you later, Charlie Bennett," I say with a smile.

I turn to go and look back over my shoulder. He is still standing at our table, watching me leave.

"Goodbye, Lizzie Moore, more, more," he says softly, using the nickname he gave me long ago because he said he always wanted more, more, more of me.

I smile until I remember that Lizzie Moore is no more.

Chapter Fourteen

Saturday, November 29th

You would think that having three rowdy kids home from school on Thanksgiving break, a repentant (i.e. brown nosing) husband, a visiting mother-in-law and a very complicated recipe for cranberry chutney would be enough to keep my mind off of Charlie, but a mole on an albino hasn't been examined as closely as I have analyzed our coffee date last Monday. I have replayed every look, every flirtatious remark, and every casual touch that sent electricity coursing through my veins. A great deal of introspection over the last week has finally given me the perspective I need. I have concluded that while I still find Charlie intoxicatingly handsome and having coffee with him made me feel like a roasted marshmallow – all warm on the outside and gooey on the inside- I have simply been suffering from Dr. Jacobson syndrome.

Dr. Jacobson is my gynecologist. Although he is an incredibly warm and compassionate doctor, he's not much to look at. Tall and gangly with too much body hair and too little head hair, he won't be gracing any "Doctors of the ER" pin-up calendars. Of course, that's probably why he went into obstetrics and gynecology in the first place. What woman wants some good looking guy peering at her dainty bits between the stirrups in the cold sterility of a doctor's office? Good looking guys are meant to ogle you when you're wearing something more romantic than a paper gown. But when I went to see Dr. Jacobson for my six week check up after Isabella was born, he held my hand kindly, looked me in the eye and said those three magic words, "How *are* you?" Suddenly, he looked tall and lean instead of gangly, and I noticed how warm his brown eyes were and how cute his smile was.

It was the first time in six weeks that someone had actually asked about me and cared about how I felt. Sure, everyone made a half-hearted attempt to ask how I was, but they had usually started cooing over the baby before I had chance to mention my sore nipples, my hemorrhoids, the fact that I hadn't slept for more than three hours in a row or the third degree tear that necessitated me wearing an ice pack in my underwear (if you could call the giant, mesh hospital issued undergarments underwear). Not that I could blame them. From the moment Isabella was laid on my chest, all red and wrinkly, peering at me intently with big, beautiful blue eyes, her mouth a perfect little "o," my heart had left my body and taken up permanent residence in her tiny one, recognizing it's rightful owner. I had never loved another being so much. Still, I had just suffered every indignity imaginable, not to mention excruciating pain, in order to bring her into the world. Was it so much to ask for someone to care about how I was? And then Dr. Jacobson did, and he really meant it. It took Bella finally sleeping through the night and a few post baby romantic encounters with Scott (aided by a glass or two of Chianti) for me to get over my sudden infatuation, which was luckily a distant memory by the time I went in for my three month post-natal check-up, saving me certain embarrassment.

Obviously, the same thing has been happening with Charlie. He is simply the first male in a long while who has really looked at me and cared about who I am and how I feel. It doesn't hurt that he's pretty gorgeous. And that I know what those long, slender fingers are capable of. But never mind, I'm finished thinking about him and our coffee date last Monday. He's just another Dr. Jacobson, only hotter.

Of course, that hasn't stopped me from checking out his Facebook page on a regular basis. And now that we're Facebook friends it seems totally natural to read what he's doing and send a funny comment here and there, which he reciprocates. In a way, we are rediscovering our friendship. And we did have a friendship, a pretty good one that began before we started dating and somehow remained intact throughout the roller coaster ride that is first love. Even when teenaged insecurity and passion threatened to tear us apart, our friendship was the strong thread that bound us together.

In high school I had a lot of guy friends. They were easier to be with; I didn't have to deal with gossip and pettiness and the constant, ever changing drama of who liked whom. It wasn't until I became an adult and needed someone to actually understand me (along with the concept that chocolate and shopping are basic human needs) that I began to truly appreciate having women friends. Now my female friends far outnumber my guy friends. In fact, the only guy not related to me that I really talk to on a regular basis these days is the Starbucks guy. I wouldn't trade Angie, Meg and Kate for the world, but reconnecting with Charlie has reminded me how fun a guy friend can be, something I had forgotten since by some unspoken rule guy friends become off limits once you (or they) are married. As if you can't be trusted not to tear your clothes off if you spend five minutes alone with someone of the opposite sex whom you're not married to.

When his status update read *"Charlie is struggling with eighth grade English. What the heck is an appositive?"* I responded with a glib, *"Looking on the bright side?"*

"You always were a smart ass," he quickly responded with a smiley face.

After a moment, I took pity on him and sent another post. *"It's a noun that defines a noun next to it. Here's an example: 'Charlie, **the brightest boy in my English class**, seems to need some after school tutoring.'"*

His flirtatious response, *"I seem to recall you were pretty good at that…"* had me smiling, blushing and immediately logging off.

When I posted a note detailing my non-cooking sister-in-law's attempt at a Thanksgiving turkey, from forgetting to remove the neck and gizzards to tying the turkey's legs together with mint-flavored dental floss, he sent me a note saying, *"Damn, I've missed you. Haven't laughed that hard in ages."* And when I posted an all out plea for a good last minute appetizer recipe to take to a party, Charlie sent me his recipe for Sausage Cheese Balls with a mustard dip, which brought back long forgotten memories of him making the same dish when he came to my house for Christmas our first year of college, prompting my parents, who adored him anyway, to declare him "a keeper."

"I'd forgotten about your sausage!" I posted back. The minute it popped up on his wall, I read it in horror and didn't log on to Facebook for three days.

At their request, I have begun posting some of the photos I have taken for the handful of families who have hired me to take pictures of their kids and families, and I know that Charlie checks my photos page because he is always leaving comments like *"loved the angle in that one"* or *"the goldfish in the background was brilliant"* or *"how on earth did you make her eyes so blue? You're amazing!"* I bask in the glow of his praise, which is all the more meaningful to me since Scott can't be bothered to even look at my pictures, much less share my enthusiasm over them. When I was in line at the grocery store, it was for solely for Charlie's benefit that I surreptitiously snapped and then posted a photo of the plump woman in front of me who was wearing revealing short shorts with the word 'Juicy" emblazoned across the bottom. *"Too good to pass up,"* I tagged it, and within an hour Charlie had responded, *"Now there's truth in advertising."*

I might possibly convince myself that our rediscovered friendship is completely innocent had I not seen Charlie's "Back in the Day" post from over a year ago featuring a veritable scrapbook of photos, most of which I am prominently featured in and looking happier than I remember ever looking, tagged as *"the one that got away."* And of course, if I didn't have that secret pull in my stomach every time I thought of him.

Chapter Fifteen

Saturday, December 6th

Meg is picking me up to go on our little purse shopping expedition in fifteen minutes and I am trying very hard to be ready on time, particularly since my friends like to joke that there is real time, and then there is Liz time. It's true that I'm a little punctually challenged; I was even late for my own wedding (well, not exactly late, but let's just say I wasn't the first, or the second, or even the third one to arrive at the church).

"Scott," I call out in frustration. "Can you come get Daisy?" She is serenading me with an endless loop of Twinkle, Twinkle, Little Star. Each time she finishes, she demands, "Say' beautiful,' Mommy!" I am a well-trained Mommy so I say, "That was beautiful," and she says, very graciously, "Thank you!"

I give up on Scott coming to get her and carry her into the kitchen where he is making the kids lunch.

"Meg will be here soon. Can you take Daisy?"

He looks at me like I have grown three heads. "I'm making lunch," he says. "How am I supposed to do two things at once?"

I am saved from responding by Meg, who is tooting her SUV's horn in my driveway.

"Got to go," I say breezily, giving Scott a quick peck on the cheek and thrusting Daisy in his arms, leaving him to figure out how to handle what I deal with every day. "See you later."

When I climb into Meg's Tahoe, I find Angie already there, putting on lipstick with the aid of the tiny mirror in the flip down visor.

"I didn't think you were coming," I say. "Something about illegal activity and your latent Catholic school girl hang ups."

"I haven't been able to get the scoop on your little coffee date with our man Charlie," she says. "You've been way too cagey when I've tried to worm the information out of you on the phone. So Meg and I are going to dangle expensive shoes in front of you and not let you try them on until you spill the beans."

I laugh. "I can take you both. Actually, there's not that much to tell. He's gorgeous, successful, divorced (I look pointedly at Angie, giving her the real information she is looking for), has a thirteen year old son and still lives in Pennsylvania. We enjoyed a little harmless flirtation and....that's it. Back to life as we know it."

"What kind of harmless flirtation?" Sister Meg asks primly. "You could make the argument that scx in a motel room is harmless as long as he used a condom."

"Meg!" I say, outraged. "You did not just say that! Harmless as in I looked hot and made him salivate a little, we talked about old times, and I got the satisfaction of knowing I've still got it and he lost out on it. We keep in touch a little on Facebook. Oh, and he did refer to me at "the one that got away" in an old picture he posted, but I swear it's strictly platonic. And Meg, you were right. Talking to him made me remember I used to love photography."

"See," Meg says. "I knew you'd see that you haven't changed."

Only I'm not so sure she's right. If I haven't changed, then why do I feel so unfulfilled? How did I ever forget what I used to be so passionate about and what was important to me? And why, oh why do I never feel more alive than when I get an e-mail from Charlie?

"So tell us everything," Angie persists. "What happened? What did he say? What did he look like?"

"Gorgeous," I say, falling dramatically back against the seat. "He still has gorgeous thick curly dark hair, but with a little touch of gray at the temples, just enough to make him look distinguished. Some laugh lines around his eyes. Incredible abs. I swear, it was kind of like stepping back in time he looks so much the same, just in a more, I don't know, grown up and masculine way. I kept looking at the little hairs on the back of his hands and trying to reconcile those strong man hands to the boy I used to know. But then he would smile at me, and he still has the same crooked little eye tooth and that same way of smiling with a quick little wink that makes you feel like you are the only woman in the room and it was like no time had passed at all."

"Did you kiss him?" Meg asks.

"No," I assure her. "Just a very platonic hug."

"So what are you going to do about him?" Angie asks. "Are you going to do him?"

"No," I say with a sigh. "I'm going to forget about him. Just like I did fifteen years ago."

As we pull into a dingy looking strip shopping center, Angie says, "Then give me his number. I'll do him."

We all laugh as we get out of the car. I look around for a handbag store, but all I see is an insurance agency, a Fiesta grocery store and a few mom and pop type restaurants.

"Are you sure this is it?" Angie asks dubiously.

"Right this way," Meg says confidently.

The store has no sign of any kind outside, but once we step inside it looks like any other handbag store. That is if the purses were made by blind monkeys sewing with their feet.

"This stuff is crap," I say to Meg. "Look at this." I hold up what is apparently meant to be a crocodile Hermes bag, but in a misguided attempt to come as close as possible to the genuine article, the inside embossed tag reads Herpes-Paris instead of Hermes-Paris. I guess it's also possible the seamstress was trying to make a personal statement.

"We're not supposed to shop out here," Meg says. "These are the replica handbags. Just a minute."

Angie and I follow her as she approaches an ageless Asian woman.

"We'd like to see the real handbags," she says.

"The handbags are right here, ma'am," the woman says.

"No, no," Meg says imperiously. "The real ones, you know, in the back." Instantly, a big guy who looks like he just ate a beach ball is next to us. His hair is greased back and he's got beady eyes like a snake.

"Ladies," he says smoothly, as if the grease from his hair has seeped down into his vocal cords. "I am afraid you have come to the wrong store. If you do not see something you like, perhaps you should try Macy's."

Meg leans close to Mr. Greasy and says in a stage whisper, "Jorge sent me."

"Jorge sent you?" The man is suddenly quite cordial. "And did Jorge recommend anything in particular?" He is looking at Meg expectantly.

"Well we sure don't want Herpes," I say dryly under my breath. Meg elbows me.

"Yes," Meg says. "He said I should really look at the limited edition purple Louis Vuitton bags."

I'm not an expert, but I really doubt good old Louis makes a purple bag.

I'm expecting the secret handshake next, but instead Mr. Greasy is hustling us down a corridor. "The restrooms are right this way ladies," he says.

Restrooms? I don't recall any of us saying we needed to use the restroom. I look at Angie, who shrugs.

Mr. Greasy apparently thinks one of us is about to have an accident because we are practically running down the hall. At the end of the corridor, he stops and speaks into a walkie-talkie, and then presses a code into a number pad located on the wall.

"Beam me up Scotty," I mutter. Meg gives me a dark look of reproof. A buzzer sounds, then the door opens and we are shoved inside. I look around and realize that I have died and gone to shopping heaven. Who knew that Saint Peter would be disguised as a greasy Italian who opened the pearly gates with a walkie-talkie? There are designer handbags and shoes everywhere. I squeal with delight.

"Look at this," I say, reverently lifting up a Jimmy Choo sling back pump in lime green. "They're $45! I can't believe it!" I practically swoon as I start gathering up shoe boxes.

"Check this out," Angie says. She's holding up a brown Louis Vuitton tote bag with the trademark gold letters and emblems. "I don't see anything flawed on it at all!"

"How much is it?" I ask.

"$129," she says.

"Get out!" I say. Meg is frozen in place, taking it all in with a look of rapture on her face.

Our shopping frenzy is interrupted by Mr. Greasy, who has come back with a big, burly black guy in tow. He's got a gold earring in one ear, and his white t-shirt is stretched tightly across his muscular chest with a very scary tattoo just visible under the sleeve.

"This is Rodrigo. He'll be happy to help you."

I'm pretty sure Rodrigo was not hired for his fashion knowledge. My suspicions are confirmed as he follows us throughout the back room, making sure I don't slip on a pair of shiny black stilettos and try to pass them off as what I put on this morning with my black yoga pants and Duke sweatshirt.

Unperturbed, Meg is becoming quite chummy with Rodrigo. She keeps saying stuff to him like 'are we tight Rod?' and 'these kicks are off the hinges!' I think all of this discount shopping has sent *her* off her hinges.

An hour later, loaded down with purses and shoes and the occasional pair of sunglasses, we decide we'd better leave before we spend all of our Christmas money on ourselves. Although we all said we were Christmas shopping, most of the shoes I'm buying are in my size, although I did pick up a nice purse for my sister-in-law. It has been so long since I have bought stuff for myself that I'm downright giddy.

Angie and I have already checked out and are waiting for Meg to finish her transaction when all hell breaks loose. There's a flurry of walkie-talkie activity, and then several police officers bust through the loading dock doors at the back of the room. A man who was comparing the merits of Fendi versus Kate Spade with Angie has somehow procured a pair of handcuffs and a firearm and is handcuffing Mr. Greasy. Just when you think you know someone! Out of the corner of my eye I glimpse Rodrigo making a run for it before being tackled by one of the uniformed officers.

Meg, Angie and I are unceremoniously herded into an adjacent empty retail space by a woman police officer along with two other women who were also shopping in the back room, and the police woman begins sternly asking each of us whether we knew the merchandise we were purchasing was fake. The first woman bursts into tears, protesting that she wasn't really going to buy anything and babbling on about how she just happened to see the store while she was grocery shopping. Right!

Meg is muttering, "They better not have run my credit card since I didn't get my stuff. Hey, can I have that Dolce bag you bought? You guys wouldn't have even known about this place if it wasn't for me."

I shush her as the police officer turns her attention to me. Since evidence to the contrary is piled up around me, I don't think

I can claim I wasn't really going to buy anything. I pull out my cell phone. "I need to call my attorney," I say haughtily, and then I call home.

Scott arrives an hour later, all business in a suit, tie and wing tipped shoes, his unshaven Saturday face miraculously shaved and still smelling faintly of aftershave. To his credit, he didn't even ask any questions when I called; he just told me to hang tight and he would get here as soon as he could. I don't see the kids trailing behind him, thank goodness, so he must have foisted them off on someone. I hope it was someone we know. He nods to me, gives me a barely perceptible wink, and then turns to the police officer. He introduces himself and the two of them move into the corner where much earnest conversation and gesturing occur.

"Sorry to say it Liz, but your husband has never looked hotter to me," Angie says.

I have to agree. He's looking pretty hot to me too. After about twenty minutes, Scott comes back over to where we are sitting and says, "Ladies, you are free to go."

We all jump up to hug him, and I give him a big kiss on the mouth, smiling at what the police officer and two other shoppers must be thinking. They already know I'm amoral and unscrupulous- I just got busted for buying illegal shoes. Let them wonder how I pay my attorney's fees!

"How did you do it?" I ask.

"It's technically not illegal to purchase knock off designer products, just to sell them," he says. "Although I'm not sure what you girls were thinking. Didn't it occur to you that something might not be legitimate when you were taken into a secret back room?"

"We thought they were seconds, you know, the real thing but with a few imperceptible flaws so they couldn't sell them for full price. Obviously they couldn't let everyone know about it or they'd be mobbed," I say. As I'm explaining our actions to Scott,

I'm starting to see how dumb they sound. "That's what Meg's hairdresser told her," I finish lamely.

"How come they weren't shut down earlier?" Angie asks. "Anyone could come shop in the front part."

"You're allowed to sell merchandise that looks like or is 'inspired by' designer products as long as you don't represent that they are the real thing. So the front of the store is legit. Just not the stuff in the back that you guys bought, which, by the way, you will have to turn over to the police."

Angie and I hug our purchases protectively. Meg moans, "It is not fair to have a $40 Dolce bag slip through my fingers not once, but twice!"

"I'll make sure you get your money back," he says gently.

We reluctantly turn our bags over to the police, sign some paperwork, and head to the parking lot where I say goodbye to Angie and Meg. I get into the car with Scott and sigh.

"Thank you," I say simply. "Although it's going to take me awhile to get over losing those gorgeous green sling back pumps."

"You're welcome," my husband says with a smile. "And Liz? When something seems too good to be true, it probably is."

Chapter Sixteen

Christmas Eve

It's Christmas Eve, and although I want to be filled with peace and Christmas spirit, all I feel is tired. For the past three weeks I have run myself ragged trying to find everything on the kids' Christmas lists, putting things together, wrapping presents and hiding them strategically around the house. After a few scares when I couldn't remember where I'd hidden two presents, I spent an entire evening making a chart that would make an OCD cartographer proud that showed where everything was hidden-- silver locket for Isabella in back of top drawer in china cabinet; Power Rangers for Will under sweaters in cedar trunk; baby doll for Daisy behind stack of size 6 jeans that I haven't been able to fit into for eight years. It is one of my greatest fears in life that something will happen to me before Christmas and no one will be able to find all the presents.

I think Scott must still believe in Santa Claus because when he wakes up on Christmas morning, an abundance of gifts have magically appeared under the Christmas tree. He is completely uninvolved in shopping for Christmas gifts; he claims he is too busy. Not only does he not shop for anything (other than gifts for me, which he either has his secretary order online or picks up in a panicked rush on the 23rd), he doesn't even help wrap anything so he has no idea what anyone is getting, or what I go through to get to Christmas day. When Will changed his mind three days ago and sent Santa an updated letter saying what he really wanted was a bike instead of a Playmobile Pirate Ship (which I had gone to five stores to find), it was me who ran out to get it. When I gently told Bella that perhaps a CD player and an American Girl doll were too much to ask for and she said, "Don't worry Mommy, I'll just ask Santa for one and you and daddy for one," it was me who pored over our budget and newspaper ads trying to find an additional $50 and a sale on CD players. I have shopped for the equivalent population of a small African village searching for just the right thing for the kids, Scott, my family, Scott's family, my friends, Bella's friends, the kids' teachers, Bella's soccer coach, and the mailman. Just when I had crossed the last name off my list and heaved a sigh of relief, I read the school newsletter reminding everyone to remember the behind the scenes people who worked so hard for our children, so I had to run to Starbucks for more gift cards for the crossing guards, the school nurse and the nice cafeteria worker who intercepted the wine box I put in Bella's lunch.

When the barista asked cheerfully, "Another one, Mrs. Cartwright? How do I get on your Christmas list?" my first thought was 'holy crap, was I supposed to get the Starbucks guy something.'

However, tonight is Christmas Eve and everything is finally finished. The last present is wrapped, the last cookie baked, the last Christmas card mailed. Now there is nothing left to do but let the spirit of the season sweep over me, washing away the stress and tension and the endless pursuit of stuff that has dominated the month. As soon as Scott gets home, we will all go to the Christmas Eve service at our church. Afterwards, we will come home and the kids will each open one present (matching red fleece pajamas with cute little reindeer on them), then we will all pile on the couch in front of a nice blazing fire and sip hot chocolate sprinkled with cinnamon and little marshmallows while I read "The Night Before Christmas" and the story of Jesus' birth. We'll sprinkle reindeer food in the yard (oats mixed with glitter) so the reindeer can find our house, set out cookies and milk for Santa, and then I will tuck everyone into bed with admonishments to go to sleep quickly so that Santa can come.

This storybook scene will come to a grinding halt as soon as the last child falls asleep, at which point I will consult my flow chart and retrieve boxes containing American Doll furniture, a bike, a kitchen and a vehicle for action figures from the attic and manically put them together, cursing profusely when I end up with extra screws or realize I've put stickers in the wrong place. I will undoubtedly need Scott's help, so we'll fall into bed at 1:00 a.m. for about four or five hours of sleep before the kids wake us up, eager to see what Santa brought.

My fantasy evening lasts until we get home from church. We arrive home feeling that same sense of belonging and timelessness that we feel every Christmas Eve. There is something magical about singing "Silent Night" by candlelight in the courtyard of the church we attend, the cool, crisp night lit with stars so bright you just can't help believe in the magic of Christmas. Bella and Will have just scampered upstairs to change into their new pjs, Scott is chasing a naked Daisy around trying to put her pajamas on, and I am heating milk for the hot chocolate when the doorbell rings.

"Who on earth could be at the door on Christmas Eve?" I wonder aloud.

"Probably carolers," Scott says.

"That's perfect!" I exclaim, still happily ensconced in my Christmas fantasy world where everything is sleigh bells and sugar plums. "Get the kids. They'll love this!"

Scott rounds up the older kids, I turn off the stove and wrestle Daisy into her pajamas while the carolers keep incessantly ringing the doorbell. When we are all assembled in the front hall, I throw open the door expectantly. Harry and Ruthless are standing on the doorstep.

"What took you so long to answer the door?" Harry says as he pushes past me, his arms filled with several large brown bags. Ruth follows him carrying a laundry basket overflowing with wrapped packages.

"What is he doing here?" I demand under my breath to Scott. He shrugs and says, "I'll go find out."

Harry is in the kitchen busily unloading his bags, which contain two large bottles of vodka, two bottles of cranberry juice, a liter of Sprite, a mesh bag of lemons and a blender.

"Let's get this party started," he says jovially. I look meaningfully at Scott. He clears his throat.

"Ummm, Dad?" he says. "We thought you guys were coming over tomorrow afternoon with everyone else for Christmas dinner."

"I know, I know," Harry says. "But since we didn't get to see you kids at Thanksgiving, we wanted to spend as much of Christmas with you as possible. Besides, Ruth misses her grandchildren so we thought it'd be fun to see the kids open their presents tomorrow morning." I'm sure Candace misses her grandchildren too. Let Ruthless go hang out with her own grandchildren.

Scott must know I am about to explode because he says firmly, "Dad, you can't stay. We have our own family traditions to keep and the kids have to get to bed early."

His father interrupts him. "Don't worry. You all just go ahead and do your thing and Ruth and I'll stay in the kitchen. You won't even know we're here!"

There is no way I can send my father-in-law home at 7:00 on Christmas Eve, especially not with my kids clamoring around him like a bunch of puppies that have just discovered table scraps. "Grandpa Harry, what did you ask Santa to bring you?" "Grandpa Harry, Grandpa Harry, what happens if the reindeer poop when

141

they're flying?" "Grandpa Harry, mommy says you'll probly get coal in your stocking. If you do, can I have it?"

After hugs all around, I usher the kids back into the family room while Harry and Ruth stay in the kitchen, where they are going to whip up a pitcher of Ruth's allegedly famous Christmas cocktails. We are halfway through *The Night Before Christmas,* me raising my voice to be heard over the whirring of the blender and Harry and Ruth's loud laughter coming from the kitchen, when there is a loud commotion outside.

"It's Santa, it's Santa," Bella yells.

Will bursts into tears. "Oh no, oh no! We're not in bed. He won't come. Come on Bells. We have to hurry!" He is running around in circles in distress. Scott assures him that it cannot possibly be Santa yet while I spring from the couch to see what is the matter. I peer out the dining room window and see my parents' fifth wheel parked out front. My mom is helping my grandma down the steps and my dad is ambling towards my front door. I sigh. According to the minute by minute itinerary my dad e-mailed me last week (Tuesday, 12: 25: see World Trade Center made of rusted debris in Oakridge), they weren't supposed to arrive until 11:21 tomorrow morning. So much for my peaceful Christmas Eve.

I open the door and feign delighted surprise that they have arrived early. It's not that I'm unhappy my family is here for Christmas. It's just that I was just looking forward to a quiet evening to enjoy Christmas with my husband and kids before I have to cook for everyone and find tissues or spoons or turn the heat down or clean up after everyone (my family can use drinking glasses at a rate per person that is ridiculous) and worry about whether Grandma is washing her underwear in the toilet. Ever since her stroke a few years ago, Grandma hasn't been quite the same.

142

"We just decided to skip Graceland and come straight to you guys," Mom says enthusiastically. "It's Christmas! We should all be together."

"We've already seen it anyway. Your mom just wanted to get Daisy some Elvis head booties. We'll hit it on the way home so we can attend his birthday bash. You got anything to eat?" my dad asks as we go inside. "Your mom just couldn't wait to get here, so we didn't even stop for dinner."

"There's some leftover lasagna in the refrigerator. We were just about to read the Christmas story and put the kids to bed," I hint.

"Sure, sure," my dad says with a wave of his hand. "Don't worry about us. We can take care of ourselves. You and Scott just go ahead with what you were doing. I told your mother we shouldn't have just barged in on you on Christmas Eve." He stops short when he spies Harry and Ruth sitting at the bar in the kitchen. "Oh, hello," he says stiffly. Even when Harry and Candace were married, my parents have never gotten on with Harry. Harry "putting the old cow out to pasture," as my mother likes to refer to him divorcing Candace, has certainly not helped. Nor has she warmed to Ruth, whom she calls the imposter grandma.

The men shake hands and Harry pours a glass of Ruth's punch for everyone. Scott brings his into the living room where I once again assemble the kids to read *The Night Before Christmas*. We make it to the part where jolly old St. Nick is calling his reindeer when the doorbell rings again.

"For crying out loud!" I sputter, slamming the book shut and getting up to answer the door.

My brother Tom, my sister-in-law Michelle and my 15 year old niece Nicole are standing on the front porch. The same brother Tom who lives on base at the Lackland Air Force base in

143

San Antonio and was not supposed to arrive until tomorrow! My other brother, John, isn't coming.

"We were evacuated due to flooding," Tom says by way of explanation. "Hope it's okay if we crash here tonight."

"Sorry," Michelle adds, trailing in behind him. Nicole is too busy texting on her cell phone, which I can't help but notice is way nicer than mine, to say anything.

Everyone congregates in the kitchen where Ruth is now whipping up her third batch of whatever cocktail she makes, and Harry is showing everyone his new tattoo, a kind of creepy looking mermaid that he is boasting that Ruth designed. My brother gratefully takes a glass of Ruth's concoction and drains it in one long swallow. I grab one and do the same.

"Slow down," Harry warns. "These things are so strong they'll rust your weinee."

There's a visual I could do without. Looking on the bright side, my brother gets along with everyone and will provide a nice buffer between our parents and Harry and Ruth. I pull him aside.

"Look," I say to him. "We're going to read a few Christmas stories and then put the kids to bed. Think you can use your fancy military negotiator training to keep the body count down in here?"

"Sure," he says, busily pouring himself a second drink. "No problem. You kids go have fun."

As we go back into the living room Scott says, "Why don't we just go read upstairs?"

"No," I say firmly. "The nice roaring fire is in here, the Christmas tree is here, everything is here! How am I supposed to have Christmas spirit upstairs? This is my house and I want to read the f-ing Christmas story downstairs!" I am practically screaming.

The kids are staring at me wide-eyed with shock.

"Honey," Scott says mildly. "I think you might be missing the whole meaning of Christmas."

I know he's right, but I had wanted this night to be perfect. Not a day goes by that I don't thank God for my three beautiful children, and because I know they are mine by grace alone I work hard to deserve them. I want them to leave childhood with an arsenal of happy memories, so that no matter where they go or what life throws at them, they will know they are loved. But I guess acting like a screaming banshee isn't quite the right tactic.

"You're right," I say taking a deep breath. "Let's just skip to the real Christmas story, get the kids to bed and then we'll deal with everyone in there."

I open the family Bible to the chapter of Luke. Harry comes wandering through the living room.

"Sorry," he says in a loud stage whisper. "Just have to use the restroom."

I ignore him and begin reading. "In the sixth month the angel Gabriel was sent from God unto a city of Galilee, named Nazareth to a virgin espoused to a man whose name was Joseph, of the house of David; and the virgin's name was Mary." I stop reading at the sound of snickering. If Scott is laughing so help me.....but it's not Scott. It's his dad, who has paused in the doorway on the way to the restroom and is standing there giggling like a school boy over the word "virgin."

Ignoring him and Ruth, who has come in looking for him, I continue reading. "And the angel came in unto her, and said, Hail, thou that art highly favoured, the Lord is with thee: blessed art thou among women." I read about how the angel tells Mary that she will conceive and give birth to a son who will be called Jesus. We get to my favorite part, where after the angel goes on about how great this son of Mary's will be, how he will be called the Son of the Highest and will reign over everyone and his kingdom will never end, all Mary can say is how the heck that can happen since she's never had sex. Just like a woman to cut straight to the chase.

"Then said Mary unto the angel, 'How shall this be, seeing I know not a man?'" I read.

"That's what she said," Harry says with a guffaw. "That's her story and she's sticking with it, eh?"

"Dad, please! The kids," Scott admonishes.

Grandma and Nicole have come in to see what's going on. "I love this story," Grandma says, sitting down. "It's what Christmas is all about."

At least someone gets it, I think, slightly mollified. I continue reading.

> And it came to pass in those days, that there went out a decree from Caesar Augustus that all the world should be taxed. And this taxing was first made when Cyrenius was governor of Syria.) And all went to be taxed, every one into his own city. And Joseph also went up from Galilee, out of the city of Nazarth, into Judaea, unto the city of David, which is called Bethlehem; (because he was of the house and lineage of David) To be taxed with Mary his espoused wife, being great with child. And so it was, that, while they were there, the days were accomplished that she should be delivered. And she brought forth her firstborn son, and wrapped him in swaddling clothes, and laid him in a manger; because there was no room for them in the inn. And there were in the same country shepherds abiding in the field, keeping watch over their flock by night.
>
> And, lo, the angel of the Lord came upon them, and the glory of the Lord shone round about them: and they were sore afraid. And the angel said unto them, Fear not: for, behold, I bring you good tidings of great joy, which shall be to all people.

For unto you is born this day in the city of David a Saviour, which is Christ the Lord. And this shall be a sign unto you; Ye shall find the babe wrapped in swaddling clothes, lying in a manger. And suddenly there was with the angel a multitude of the heavenly host praising God, and saying, Glory to God in the highest, and on earth peace, good will toward men. And it came to pass…

Pppppwwarrrrpppppp. "Grandma!" exclaims Nicole. Everyone busts out laughing. Everyone except me and Grandma, who has no idea what everyone is laughing at. My Christmas Eve is ruined. I quickly read the reminder of the story and slam the Bible shut.

"Time for bed," I announce, and go upstairs to put the kids to bed.

It takes a while to get them all settled, as riled up as they are from the constant influx of grandparents, aunts and uncles and the imminent arrival of Santa. When I get back downstairs, everyone has congregated in the living room in front of the fire, talking and laughing and drinking Ruth's cocktails. It's the perfect Christmas tableau, the one I imagined; only I'm not in it! I was too busy doing all the work. And call me Scrooge but I have no intention of letting everyone sit around drinking and having fun while I put all the toys together myself.

"Alright, everyone," I say grumpily. "We have a ton to do. Since you're all here, you might as well help. Who wants to put together the kitchen for Daisy?"

Grandma and my parents, who are tired from driving straight through from Tennessee, decide to go out to their camper and go to bed. Nicole goes with them, feigning fatigue and excitement over sleeping in the RV. In reality, I'm sure she just wants to text her friends and boyfriend at home without her mom bugging her. Tom and Michelle have agreed to put together the kitchen, Scott is assembling the doll bed for Bella, and Harry and Ruth are going to put Will's bike together while I go into the bedroom to stuff the kids' stockings. Forty-five minutes later, I check on everyone's progress. Daisy's kitchen has been put together (not surprisingly) with military precision, the stickers meticulously applied and the tiny condiment bottles lined up like little soldiers. Will is sleeping in Bella's room to make room for Tom and Michelle, so when their work is done they say goodnight and tiptoe upstairs. The American Girl doll Bella asked for is reclining in a four poster doll bed decked out with miniature orange and pink throw pillows. The only thing missing is the bike.

I find Scott and Harry in the garage, the bike still in pieces around them. "You guys need some help?" I ask, although I'm not quite sure who might help them. I certainly don't know how to put a bike together. I look around.

"Where's Ruth?" I ask.

"Went to bed," Harry slurs. "Too many cocktails. But not us eh?" He punches Scott lightly in the arm.

"Scott, please tell me you're not drunk on Christmas Eve," I implore.

Scott makes an exaggerated attempt to look sober. "'Course not," he says with a hiccup. "We're almost finished." He looks around the garage. "We just gotta figure out where these four wheels go." They both burst out laughing. The bike is a two wheeler, Will's first.

Disgusted, I go inside and climb into bed, my cell phone in my hand. Although I know she's probably sound asleep and won't read my text until tomorrow, it still makes me feel better to vent to my best friend.

"The family has descended and the elves are all drunk," I text.

Angie responds almost immediately. *"Perhaps Mrs. Claus needs a hot toddy?"*

I smile. *"Why are you still up?"* I text back.

"I've got a hot teddy instead of a hot toddy and I'm just waiting for Santa to come…."

I laugh out loud at the double entendre.

"Enjoy yourself! I'm going to put myself out of my misery and jump out my bedroom window. Merry Christmas!"

"I'm not worried. Your bedroom is on the first floor. I'll call you tomorrow. Merry Christmas sweetie."

I smile as I lay my phone down on my night table, grateful that I have a friend like Angie who will talk me off the ledge, even one a foot off the ground, in the middle of the night on Christmas Eve when she's having sex.

Chapter Seventeen

Christmas Day

Thanks to Ruth's cocktails, everyone was too hung over to get up early so Scott and I got to open gifts with the kids by ourselves after all. When we first walked into the living room to see what Santa had brought, I almost sat on Harry, who had passed out on the couch. I debated whether I should wake him up or not, but I decided I didn't want to deal with him, so I just covered him up with a fleece throw and pretended he wasn't there. He didn't wake up the entire time we were opening gifts, although he did snore loudly from time to time, making the kids giggle. Needless to say, Scott is hung over as well, but he is doing a fair job of pretending he's not. Somehow he and his dad managed to get the bike together last night, and Will was ecstatic to see it parked under the Christmas tree this morning. Other than a bottle of ketchup, it was what he most wanted for Christmas. However I'm still going to get Tom to check out the bike before Will actually tries to ride it.

Eventually everyone else stumbles out of bed and wanders in looking for coffee, and once we're all assembled we start all over again with the present opening. An hour later, the kids look like Bandit the year he drug the Thanksgiving turkey carcass out of the trashcan and fell asleep next to it after he had eaten his fill-fat, happy and satiated with more toys than they can possibly play with in one day. In addition to the gifts from Scott and I, which always seem to be reasonable in number when scattered about the house but obscenely excessive on Christmas morning, our families seem to be in some sort of gift giving competition when it comes to the kids. By the look of it, the categories are "largest quantity of gifts" (my parents have that one wrapped up), "most obnoxious" (Mike and Elise, who have obviously never had children or they wouldn't have given Daisy the excessively loud and slightly creepy Elmo that randomly sings and demands to be tickled) and "most expensive" (easily Harry's win since he surprised them with a Wii game system). Even Ruthless got in on the action, giving each of the kids their own Wii games. She gave me dust mop slippers.

Unfortunately, I have to waste the one day that I am guaranteed endless free time while the kids are occupied with their new toys cooking for, and then cleaning up after, fifteen people. Although most of the women have said that they will help out (Scott said he'll "watch the kids"), so far I have been in the kitchen by myself while they all create Mii characters that look like themselves on the Wii. As I toss the salad, I wonder what Charlie is doing today. I have had to physically restrain myself from sneaking off to the computer to log on to Facebook and see if he's posted anything. Does he have his son with him? Does he go to his ex-wife's house to celebrate Christmas? Is he alone, standing in his kitchen wondering what I am doing?

The ham and the green bean casserole are in the oven, the potatoes are boiled and mashed, the gravy is warming on the stove, and I am starting to make the squash casserole when my mom comes in.

"Sorry dear," she says. "That was just so fun. Can I help with anything?"

"Sure," I say, handing her a colander filled with sliced squash. "Could you squeeze the water out of the squash for me?"

She looks at the squash as if it has personally offended her.

"Squeeze it? That's not how I make squash casserole," she says.

151

I take a deep breath. "Really? How do you make yours mom?"

"I just steam the squash and then add some butter. You'd know that if you'd ever shown an interest in cooking. I tried to teach you but you always had more important things to do." She sniffs at the thought.

"Mom!" I say with exasperation. "I was fourteen. When you're fourteen you have no idea that one day you'll ever eat squash casserole, much less want to make it."

Just then, Michelle and Nicole walk in. "Your Mii character is wearing too much makeup," Michelle is saying.

"Um, Michelle, it's a video game," I remind her.

Nicole flashes me a grateful look and then says, "Need any help Aunt Liz?"

Mom turns around and waves her wooden spoon at me. "See?" she says accusingly. "Nikki's a good girl. Grandchildren are God's reward for enduring our children."

"Oh, for crying out loud," I mutter. I put Nicole to work crushing Ritz crackers to go on top of the casserole. "Don't worry," I whisper to her. "I'll make you a hot Mii guy and you can run off to the Mii plaza together."

I am mixing all of the ingredients for the casserole together when Ruth comes in, conveniently showing up after all of the work has been done. She dips her little finger into the squash, scoops out a bit and licks it. Ewww.

"What does this have in it?" she asks.

"Squash, polenta, Parmesan cheese," I say, ticking off the main ingredients.

"Hmmm. That's not how I make my squash casserole."

"Me neither," my mom says vehemently. "I make mine with plain old cheddar cheese and sour cream and it's perfect.

"Me too," Ruth agrees, and I can see my mom softening just a bit towards the imposter grandma.

"Great!" I say brightly. "Next year one of you can make it."

Thirty minutes later, the guys are outside, Michelle and Scott's sister Elise are setting the table, my mom is filling water glasses and Nicole is playing Littlest Pet Shop Monopoly with Isabella, leaving Ruthless with no one to talk to except Grandma. As I slice the ham, I can't help but overhear their conversation.

"Now how did you meet Harry?" Grandma asks.

"We met through a mutual friend," Ruth says neutrally. "I can't recall where Elizabeth said you live."

"Oh, I live in New Jersey," says Grandma. "A nice little retirement community where there's always someone around to play bingo with. And what about you? Do you live alone?"

"I live with Harry," Ruth says.

"Oh my," says Grandma prudishly. "How long have you known him?"

"We met in June."

"Well you're moving right along dearie, aren't you?" Grandma says, and then shuffles off to wash her hands for dinner. I suppress a giggle. Being able to say whatever you damn well please almost makes getting wrinkly and senile worth it. I'm already getting wrinkly and senile, so maybe I should start practicing speaking my mind.

Once we are all seated at the table and have said grace, Harry taps his glass.

"I'd like to make a toast," he booms. We all dutifully raise our wine glasses. He looks around the table and sees that Michelle doesn't have one. "What? You don't have a drink? Let's get you one! Scott, where's that bottle of Merlot?"

There is an awkward silence, and then Michelle says, "My father was an alcoholic. I don't drink."

"Oh," Harry says without missing a beat. "Then we'll just get you white instead." He grabs a bottle of Chardonnay and Michelle, aware that any protest she might make will fall on deaf ears, politely allows Harry to fill her glass before he continues.

"I know you all don't know Ruth that well, so I wanted to say thank you for including her, and us, this Christmas." As if we had a choice. I dig into the green bean casserole.

He clears his throat. Oh. Apparently he's not finished. I reluctantly put my fork down. He continues, "As you all know, I have never been happier than when Ruth came into my life." I wonder how he knows it's Ruth that's made him happy since she arrived at approximately the same time as the Corvette, the home gym and the bottle of brown hair rinse.

"Although we haven't formally announced it, Ruth's been more or less living at the house for the last four months. And since I'm a man of honor...." He stops to look at me, as I have choked on a green bean and am having a coughing attack into my napkin. "Are you alright Elizabeth?"

I try to nod. My brother whacks me on the back. "She's fine," he says.

"Anyway," Harry continues, slightly muddled now. "Well, call us old-fashioned, but Ruth and I have decided to get married."

The whole table erupts. There is a chorus of "When?" and "Where?" and the occasional "Congratulations."

I wish I were sitting next to Scott, but he is at the opposite end of the table, looking shell shocked.

"Well, we're thinking something small with just family and friends," Ruth is saying. "We've set the date for April 18th."

Tom leans over to me and whispers, "That's probably enough time to hire a mercenary if you want to knock her off."

"Are you going to the Justice of the Peace?" I ask innocently.

"No," says Ruth, confused.

"Las Vegas?" I ask hopefully.

"Actually, we're getting married at St. Luke's and then having the reception at the Sheraton. We'd love for Isabella and Daisy to be flower girls, and Will could be the ring bearer," Ruth is saying.

I nod numbly, distantly aware that Bella is squealing with delight. It is her greatest disappointment in life that she has reached the ripe old age of almost seven and has never been a flower girl. I'm sure it will eventually hit her that the wedding is between two people in their sixties so it may not be all it's cracked up to be, but for now I may as well let her enjoy the moment. Someone should be happy about it.

"Does Mom know?" Scott asks quietly.

"Oh well, yes," his dad stammers. "I e-mailed her this morning."

"You e-mailed her?" Scott is incredulous.

Nicole sidles up to me. "Aunt Liz, I hate to miss all the fun but my boyfriend is in between Christmas dinners and I told him I'd call him as soon as we finished eating. Is there anywhere I can go in this house where it's quiet?"

"If you find it, let me know," I say to her. Unexpectedly, memories of being Nicole's age and enduring what seemed to be endlessly long holiday meals with my family when all I really longed for was to talk to Charlie surface, so I lean over to her and whisper, "Go into my bathroom. Lock the door and if anyone knocks, just say "whooeee" really loud and flush the toilet and they'll leave you alone. Believe me, it works."

"Thanks Aunt Liz. You're the best," she says with a quick hug before disappearing down the hall.

The next thirty minutes are dominated by talk about Harry and Ruth's upcoming wedding. I'm trying to figure out how to escape when Nicole's screams pierce the air. We all jump up from the table and rush down the hall. I'm the first to get to her, since I'm the only one who actually knows where she is. Nicole is huddled in the corner of the bathroom, her cell phone still clutched in her hand, a look of horror on her face.

"Aunt Liz, your bathroom is haunted," she says breathlessly.

"What?" I say incredulously. "Calm down. What happened?"

Her courage bolstered by the appearance of the fourteen of us standing in the bathroom doorway, she agilely runs over to join us, casting sidelong glances at the vanity as she passes it. "I was just standing here and this, this scary noise started coming from the vanity," she says.

"What kind of noise?" Michelle asks, her arm protectively wrapped around Nicole, believing as all mothers do that we can protect our children from harm if we just hold them in our arms and put ourselves between them and the world.

"It was a whirring noise, like some sort of crazed machine. Like...like Texas Chain Saw Massacre or something," she says hysterically.

"Is your cell phone on vibrate? Maybe you laid it on the counter."

Nicole looks guiltily at her mom. "No, I had it in my hand."

"It was probably just something outside," my dad says.

"Or the heat coming on," my mom adds.

"Whatever it was, there's no noise now," I say reassuringly. "Let's just go back to the kitchen and..."

I am interrupted by a loud buzzing sound coming from the bank of drawers between Scott's and my sinks. I jump, Nicole and

156

Michelle scream, and Elise pulls the kids away from the doorway. My brother, trained for crises such as this, strides forward purposefully.

"Everyone stand back," he says authoritatively.

"Daddy!" Nicole squeals.

Tom cautiously opens the top drawer. We all push a little closer to peer cautiously inside at the jumble of hair elastics, makeup brushes, hair brushes, and lip gloss tubes. Nothing out of the ordinary in there, although it does look as if it could use a little organization. Tom slowly closes the top drawer, takes a deep breath and then yanks open the middle drawer. There is a collective gasp as the noise gets louder. Afraid of what might be in there-a rabid mouse, some kind of insect that might hurtle out of the drawer into my face, a miniature Leatherface wielding a tiny chainsaw-I quickly peek into the drawer.

There's my vibrator, happily bumping around the drawer, knocking into my glasses case, a stack of CD cases and a bottle of hairspray.

"Oh my gosh!" I say, horrified.

"Oh my gosh!" Scott says, thrilled.

"Oh my gosh!" Michelle says with a giggle.

"Oh my gosh!" my mom says with excitement. "There's your nifty little egg beater, Liz." She plucks it from the drawer and waves it triumphantly in front of her. "Anyone want meringue on their pumpkin pie?"

According to the blue numbers on my alarm clock, it's midnight. The surprises of Christmas—the gifts, the wedding announcement, my inopportune malfunctioning vibrator—are over, yet I lie awake, unable to sleep. The combination of too many Christmas Eve cocktails, waking up too early this morning, and going to bed too late last night has taken its toll on Scott, and he is out cold. Not me. Since I have been tossing and turning for over half an hour I get up, put on my soft pink fluffy robe, and go out to the living room where the fire has died down to glowing embers. No one remembered to unplug the Christmas tree and hundreds of white fairy lights twinkle in the dark. For the moment I ignore the fact that our house could have burned down and look around at the room illuminated by the light of the tree. The house, decorated for Christmas, is a pretty good reflection of my life. The nativity scene, lovingly set up by Bella each year in its place of honor on a table in the foyer, is surrounded by an assortment of action figures. Although the Red Ranger is holding the three wise men at gunpoint, an assortment of Will's action figures-Batman, the Joker, Spiderman, Mr. Incredible, Luke Skywalker, Darth Vader and an army of battle droids- have all come together to worship the baby Jesus. There's our Christmas tree, which we picked out and cut down the weekend after Thanksgiving at a nearby Christmas tree farm, now held upright by the liberal use of fishing line looped around the curtain rod ever since we came home from school and discovered it leaning precariously to the left, the trunk weakened and rotted by a rainy fall growing season. An assortment of handmade gifts, most featuring my children's handprints made into everything from reindeer to angel's wings, is liberally sprinkled throughout the house.

I close my eyes and allow myself to think about Charlie. I replay the texts we have exchanged since I saw him a month ago, the ones I showed Angie and Meg, and the more recent ones I didn't, the ones that were alternately flirty, asking if we could get together again when he was in town last week, then pouty when I told him I couldn't. I don't trust myself to see Charlie again yet. But texts are different, safer. With texts, the flirtation is heady, but not quite real. Texts I can read and reread on the days I am feeling frazzled and unattractive without having to act on them.

I sit back in Scott's recliner and stare at the tree. After a few minutes, I take off my glasses and look at the tree again. This is the hidden blessing, the silver lining of being half blind and enduring Coke bottle glasses as a child until you are old enough to put your foot down and demand contact lenses. When you look at lights with imperfect vision, uncorrected by glasses or contacts, they look different. Out of focus, the outline blurs into tiny halos of light, and instead of seeing a plastic light with a filament inside, you are looking at something magical. It makes me almost feel sorry for people with perfect vision.

When I was little, my parents would sometimes pile my brothers and me in the car and drive up to Valley Forge where we would stop at the top of the ridge and gaze down at the lights of King of Prussia below. I always loved looking down on those lights, imagining the magical creatures that lived there among the fairy lights. Then when I was twelve, my mom took me to an optometrist, who discovered that my eyesight was pitifully bad. The day we picked up my new glasses I rode home in shock, pointing out stores and landmarks and signs that had always been there, but that I had never been able to see before. It was amazing, this brand new world I could see. Then one evening we drove to the top of Valley Forge. With my new glasses on, there were no fairy lights or gnome village after all, just a regular town sharply lit by plain fluorescent street lights.

I never forgot that disappointment. I have worn contacts for so long now that I have forgotten what it is like to not see clearly. But every once in a while, I still like to take them off so that I can see the magic.

NEW YEAR'S RESOLUTIONS

Lose 20 pounds

Have sex 40 times

Get at least ~~eight~~ six hours of sleep per night

Don't forget resolution number 2 in trying to achieve resolution number 3

Exercise for 30 minutes every day

Psych self up for wedding

Ask Meg about happy pills

Potty train Daisy or buy stock in Pampers

Advertise photography business (come up with company name?)

Buy perfect birthday cards for Angie, Meg and Kate in January. Remember where I put them.

Limit Facebook time

Delete messages from Charlie

Forget Charlie

Chapter Eighteen

Wednesday, January 7th

"Come on guys," I yell up the stairs to Bella and Will. "Hurry up or I'm going to be late."

I have a photography job today which I am really wishing I hadn't taken since the kids are still out of school for the holidays, while Scott, who barely stopped checking his phone long enough to open presents, is back to his typical ten hour workday, leaving me to scrambling to find something to do with the kids. Kate has invited Bella over to play with Chloe for the afternoon, but I can hardly ask her to take Will and Daisy. I'm sure she would take them if I asked, but I'm not sure I could afford to replace the damage done to her *House Beautiful* home by my *World Wrestling Entertainment* kids. So Christine is taking Daisy to play with Josie and Will is going to Meg's. It's taken me over an hour just to get the kids ready, making sure everyone has the right sippy cup, diapers, change of clothes, lovey, and so on, leaving me with five minutes to slap some makeup on and grab my camera bag, hoping that everything in it is ready to go. I don't know how working moms do it. Well, all moms are working moms; those who work outside the home just have two full time jobs instead of one.

Forty-five minutes later, having dropped all of my children at their respective play dates (returning home once to pick up Brown Bear whom we somehow forgot) and having effusively thanked all of my friends who are bailing me out with promises to return the favor, I arrive at Emily Davis' house. I feel like this is my first real photography job since she really has no personal incentive to use me, but saw my photos and sought me out on her own. We have spoken on the phone to discuss the scope of the photo shoot, but we have never met.

I ring the doorbell and am greeted by a beautiful slim woman about five years younger than me with gorgeous long wavy golden blond hair and brilliant blue eyes. She is flanked on either side by two petite blonde little girls who appear to be about three and four and are dressed identically in designer denim overalls trimmed in pink and black with big black velvet bows in their hair. I introduce myself and we go inside, sitting across from each other in the tastefully decorated living room which is somehow completely devoid of the disarray of Barbie clothes, discarded socks, action figures and miscellaneous toys that constantly litter the floor of my living room. A gorgeous hunk of a guy appears in the doorway, introduces himself as Emily's husband, and then takes the two little girls to another room in the back to watch television while Emily and I talk. I fight back a touch of jealousy at the perfection of this woman's world. For a moment, I wistfully imagine what it would be like to be in her shoes, younger, slimmer, richer, organized, with immaculately dressed children who are quiet and well-behaved and a husband who could be a model.

She begins to tell me what she has in mind for the photo shoot, basically a "day in the life" type approach where I follow her around as she makes cookies with the girls, gives them a bath, reads them stories, and goes about the business of being a mom. I nod, making notes.

"I just found out I have breast cancer," she says. "Hopefully they'll get it all, but I know there are no guarantees. So I want some pictures of my life with the girls, just in case, so they can remember me. And so I can remember me." She speaks matter of factly, with an acceptance that I think can only have been achieved by hours and hours of anger and tears and soul searching

162

until finally reaching resignation. I'm not sure I would ever get past the anger and tears.

As she speaks I look up, flabbergasted. Suddenly, I am ashamed of my jealously, my vanity and superficiality in my misguided belief that this woman must be happier than me because the accoutrements of her life look perfect. I imagine what it would feel like to be her, not knowing if I would be around to kiss my children goodnight each night, to watch them grow up and teach them how to ride a bike without training wheels and walk them to kindergarten on the first day of school and help them get ready for their first date. I want to cry for her, this woman who has had to face my deepest, darkest fear. But right now she doesn't need my tears or my sympathy. She needs my talent, so I spend the next five hours giving her the best that I have to give.

I open all of the blinds in her immaculate home, letting in the natural sunlight and ensuring that when she or her children look back at these photos they'll remember how blue her eyes were. I follow her around, fading into the background as I snap hundreds of photos of Emily, her husband Steve, and their daughters, Grace and Sarah, going about the everyday tasks of life that she will never take for granted again. Standing around the butcher block island of their kitchen, Emily's hand over Sarah's, guiding hers as she stirs the cookie batter. All four of them laughing as they decorate each other's noses with flour, Little Grace licking the spoon, a half eaten cookie left on the counter like a life interrupted. The girls in the bath, Emily hugging a damp and sweet smelling Sarah wrapped in a pink hooded towel. Emily flying Grace on her feet as Grace squeals with laughter. The whole family piled onto the sumptuous white, king-sized bed, engrossed in reading Owl Babies. The four of them outside, the two little girls holding hands as they skip ahead, Steve with his arm protectively wrapped around Emily, walking a few steps behind. A reflection in the mirror of Emily brushing Sarah's hair into a ponytail, a stolen snapshot of Steve watching, a look of pure love on his face.

When I leave Emily's house I am exhausted, but I have the bone deep satisfaction and sense of accomplishment of knowing I have done something brilliant and life changing today. I refuse to let her pay me, insisting that her only payment be living a long life so that she can recommend me to everyone she knows.

I pick up Bella, Will and Daisy, and I am a kinder, gentler mom that night as I make dinner, give them a bath, read them stories, and tuck them into bed. I linger in their bedrooms a little longer than usual, appreciating the sweet curve of Daisy's cheek, Will's gap toothed smile and the softness of Bella's hair. I hold them a little closer, a little tighter, and a little longer when I hug them goodnight, grateful that I am alive and here and their mother—a job that is more rewarding than any success I may find as a photographer. I hope I won't take it for granted, although I know that I inevitably will anyway.

After the kids are all asleep, Scott calls to tell me he is going to be home really late, if at all. "Sorry, hon," he says. "I've got trial on Monday and I'm on a roll."

I want to tell him about Emily. I want to tell him about the photos I took, photos which I realized as I uploaded them onto the computer are really, really good. I want to tell him how glad I am to be alive, and to have him and our beautiful children to share my life with. But he isn't here, and I say nothing. I know Scott, and when he is preparing for trial he is preoccupied. Lonely, I log onto Facebook, posting a selection of the photos I took earlier today. I type, "*Liz is appreciating her life and the amazing mystery of grace.*" It's a bit heavy, I know, but I'm feeling subdued and reflective. More than anything, I wish I had someone to talk to about it. I wish I could call Angie, but she's skiing with her family in Colorado.

"*Feeling pensive are we?*" Charlie messages me almost immediately.

"*I just spent the day photographing a woman who just found out she has breast cancer,*" I type back.

His response is short, but speaks volumes. *"Want to talk?"*

I do. I dig out his cell number and dial his number on my cell phone. He answers on the first ring.

"Hey there," his voice, although a little different on the phone from how I remember it, is warm and friendly.

We talk for almost an hour. I tell him all about the photo shoot and how heartbreaking, yet strangely powerful, it was to chronicle an afternoon in this amazing woman's life. He tells me how poignant and beautiful the photos are and reassures me that regardless of what happens, I have given this woman and her family a priceless gift. It is exactly what I need to hear and as we talk, the lump that has been in my throat all evening finally starts to dissipate. Charlie tells me a story about when he went camping with our high school friend Nate, and how he ate jalapenos out of the jar and then went to take a whiz in the backyard and started screaming with pain when he pulled his business out, that makes me laugh so hard my side aches.

"Thanks, Charlie," I say before we hang up. "I really needed this...you."

"No problem," he says lightly. "That's what friends are for."

Scott still hasn't come home by the time I go to bed, and as I lie in bed I imagine him in his office, sitting on the floor, shirttails untucked, surrounded by legal files. I imagine Charlie lying awake in bed like me, the yin to my yang, and wonder if he is thinking about me as much as I am thinking about him. I remember how in high school we used to talk on the phone every night, me sneaking the phone into my bedroom so my parents wouldn't know, and he would talk me to sleep, the deep timbre of his voice the last thing I would hear as I drifted off. My soul aches for that connection again and I think about calling him back.

I'm reaching for my phone, but before I can call him back it starts to rain, huge buckets pouring out of the skies, and before long the kids end up in bed with me. They instantly fall back asleep, tucked into the warm cocoon of Scott's and my king sized sleigh bed, but I lie awake, listening to the storm rage outside. As the lightening cracks and the thunder roars, I think of Emily, and how behind her cool façade this is how she must really feel—angry and violent. The wind is strong and the rain lashes furiously against the house and I wonder if Emily's husband is lying awake too, listening to a storm that mirrors his soul. I realize that I am angry too—angry at a world where beautiful young mothers with small children get cancer, and angry that Scott is at work when he should be home with me. The rain falls in rhythm with my tears until it slows to a drizzle, and I fall asleep.

Chapter Nineteen

Tuesday, January 13th

    Christmas break (or rather "winter holiday" as it is now referred to at our elementary school so as not to offend the Jewish, Hindu, Atheist and other cultures that don't celebrate Christmas; not that any of my Jewish or Hindu friends have ever actually been offended by this) is over, which means that both Bella and Will are back in school. Daisy is taking a nap, exhausted from two weeks of non-stop entertainment and attention from her older siblings, so I have decided that today is the day to start my diet and workout regime guaranteed to help me achieve my first New Year's resolution to lose 20 pounds. In exchange for giving them a comfy place to turn flips, practice their drop kicks and grow big enough to live in the outside world, each of my children has given me ten extra pounds by which to remember their occupancy in my body. Technically I probably need to lose 30 pounds, but I've decided to settle for 20. I was probably too skinny before (whatever; yes I'm lying), and what 35 year old woman weighs what she did in high school anyway? Well, I can think of a few, but I call them bad names behind their backs so I've decided to keep my ten pounds just to ensure my friends' goodwill.

    In order to get started, I have purchased a nice journal in which to record my daily caloric intake, a case of Slim Fast chocolate shakes, and Wii Fit, an exercise program I can do from the comfort of my own home. Thank goodness for technology. If you're playing a videogame, it probably doesn't even feel like exercise. It's got to be better than the treadmill, which I couldn't use anyway since we use it to hang Scott's work shirts on. Over the holidays, after everyone left I finally got a chance to create my own Mii character. The Wii Liz looks just like me only slimmer, with a red outfit, blue eyes, and dark hair (no hint of gray in sight) pulled in a ponytail. After one particularly harrowing day when Scott was out of town and the kids had done nothing but whine and fight all day, I created an alter ego Mii with bloodshot eyes and wild, unkempt hair. I named her Mom.

Now, having duly recorded what I ate for breakfast (oatmeal, coffee with skim milk and a banana for a respectable caloric intake of 200 calories) and lunch (a Slimfast shake for another 200 calories; I feel like I'm on a game show), I turn on the Wii and get ready to videogame myself into shape. Despite the fact that my Mii character turns significantly dumpier looking once I enter my weight, the computerized balance board says, "Ow!" when I step onto it, I'm passed during the first minute of a virtual run by a pigtailed cartoon version of my youngest child who can barely walk without falling down in real life, and I fall off the balance board trying to achieve the Tree yoga pose, the time passes quickly. When I look at the clock, I realize it's been almost an hour since I started. Crap. I've got to pick Will up from preschool in twenty minutes. I'm starving, so I grab two sticks of celery and go upstairs to wake Daisy up. Ten minutes later I am pulling out of the driveway when my cell phone rings. I don't recognize the number. It's probably the guy I called last week to come look at the electrical wiring in our kitchen and see why the recessed lights keep burning out.

"Hello," I say curtly, my annoyance at how long it has taken him to return my call resurfacing. The connection is so bad I can barely hear him, which adds to my irritation.

"Hey there, gorgeous," a male voice drawls seductively.

The nerve of male contractors, particularly Texan ones! No matter how long I live here, I will never get used to this excessive familiarity of strangers. I rip into him.

"Don't hey there me," I say hotly. "I called you over a week ago and you're just now returning my call?"

"You did?" I hear a hint of amusement and maybe even satisfaction in his voice.

"Yes, I did and you damn well know it."

"Okay. Well I didn't get the message. Besides, I'm calling you back now aren't I?"

This from the guy who was originally scheduled to come out on a Monday, called to say he couldn't make it until Tuesday, and then called at 11:00 on Tuesday to say that since it was almost lunch time and the day would be half over, there was no point in him coming until the next day. I'd find another electrician, but I've already paid him $300 to figure out what's wrong.

"A week may be nothing to you, but I've been cooking in the dark! Do you know what happens when you can't see and put Creole seasoning into cookies instead of ginger? It's not pretty!"

"Liz?" the voice on the other end of the line now just sounds confused. "Is that you? This is Charlie."

Oh, right. Not the electrician. Charlie. I knew there was something vaguely familiar about that voice. Crap.

"Charlie, I'm sorry," I say, raking my fingers through my hair in exasperation. "I thought you were my electrician. You caught me at a bad time. I'm late to pick up my son from preschool, I had a fight with my toddler over shoes, all I've had to eat all day is a lousy bowl of oatmeal, a banana, a chocolate shake and two sticks of celery and I'm starving!"

Charlie laughs that sexy throaty rumble of his. I can practically see his eyes dancing. So much for Resolution number 12.

"You want me to call you back later?"

"No! I mean, yes. Um, I can talk for a second."

"Although I'd love to help with your, err....cooking problem, I was actually calling about something else."

"Okay," I say cautiously.

"A few days ago our in house advertising guy was talking about doing an artsy brochure and slideshow for our new development. We started talking about potential photographers for the job, and I immediately thought about you. Your work is fantastic, especially those recent ones you posted. You'd be perfect for the job. So I showed your photos around and everyone agreed your style is just what we need for the project. You interested?"

Oh my gosh! Is this really happening? I'm driving a minivan with a toddler strapped in the back, but somehow I feel like I'm fifteen and the cutest guy in school just asked me to the school dance. I can't decide if I'm more elated about talking to Charlie again or the photography project. Act cool, I remind myself. Be professional.

"Sounds interesting," I say noncommittally. "What exactly does the project entail and what's the time frame?"

"The development is a beachside community near Santa Barbara. We're having a pre-opening the first weekend of March. We were thinking of flying you out for a long weekend so you could get to know the development and have plenty of opportunity to photograph everything. I'll be there too, so I can show you around. Our budget for your end of the project is $5000."

I almost plow into the subcompact in front of me. Five thousand dollars? The opportunity of a lifetime to jumpstart a new career? The chance to spend an entire weekend with Charlie?

Charlie mistakes my silence for indecision.

"I'll e-mail you the details and you can think about it. Take your time. The project's yours if you want it, so just call me when you've had a chance to look it over. And go get a pizza!"

170

"Okay," I say numbly. I say goodbye and end the call just as I'm pulling up to the front of the carpool line. Will climbs in the car and begins giving me a blow by blow account of his day, but I don't hear a word. In my mind, I'm in California taking photographs of million dollar homes and walking along the beach with Charlie.

Chapter Twenty

True to his word, Charlie has sent an e-mail that is waiting for me when I return home from picking Will, and then Bella, up from school. The pictures he's sent of the development, called Harbor Falls, are stunning, making we wonder why they want to pay me $5000 to take more.

"Don't underestimate yourself," Angie says to me when I call to tell her about the job offer. "You're really good."

"But I'm just a mom," I bemoan, self doubt setting in. "I take pictures of kids! What do I know about taking pictures of fancy real estate developments?"

"First of all, you've got to stop thinking of yourself as 'just a mom,'" Angie says sternly. "You are a nurse, a psychologist, a sleep expert, a chef, a chauffer, a tutor, a conflict negotiator, a professional organizer, an accountant, secretary, professional shopper, laundress, handyman, computer data entry person, facilities manager and domestic technician. Plus, you've got a damned good eye and are a talented photographer. If you can take fabulous pictures of kids who whine and cry and spit up and dribble chocolate on themselves, how hard can a building be? They don't even move!"

"You're right," I sigh. "Why am I so worried about this? It's the opportunity of a lifetime."

"That's why you're so worried about," Angie says gently. "And then there's the whole Charlie factor."

"Yeah," I sigh. "What am I going to tell Scott?"

"Tell him the truth."

Five hours later, the kids are all tucked into bed and Scott has taken up his nightly residence on his side of the sofa, the dinner I just warmed up for him in front of him, TV remote in hand and *River Monsters: Killer Fish* on.

"Can we talk?" I say.

"Sure," he says, eyes still glued to the giant catfish some man has just hooked on his fishing line.

"Uh, you think you could turn that off for a second? I have something I want to talk to you about."

Scott sighs. It's barely perceptible, but I can hear it. He mutes the television and turns to me.

"Okay. What?"

Now that I have his undivided attention, however reluctantly given, I don't know how to start.

"Remember how I ran into Charlie Bennett, my old friend from high school a few months ago?"

Scott is looking at me blankly.

"We had coffee?" Nothing. I sigh. This might be easier than I thought. "Anyway, I had told him about my new photography business and…"

"You have a photography business?" Scott looks surprised. "I thought you were just taking some pictures of your friends' kids for fun."

"Well, I was," I say. "But I'm really good at it, and it makes me feel like I'm somebody again to actually do something with my life."

"You are somebody, Liz, whether you take pictures or not" Scott says. "And you are doing something with your life. You're a great mom, the best in fact, and I couldn't even begin to be as

173

successful as I am at work if you weren't taking care of everything at home."

"You just don't get it!" I say in exasperation. "I'm sure it's great for you and the kids, but it's not enough for me. Maybe it used to be, but it's not anymore. I want more! I want to do more than arrange play dates and fold laundry and make your dental appointments and come up with a hundred different ways to cook chicken."

"I thought you loved being at home with the kids," Scott says, perplexed.

"I do love being at home with the kids! I love them more than anything in the world, and I love being here everyday with them. I love Daisy's sticky hugs, and the way Will smells like a wet dog after he's been playing outside, and watching Bella get her first goal at soccer practice. But I love me too, even though I'm not quite sure who that is anymore."

"So what do you want Liz? Do you want to get a job?"

"I have a job! That's what I'm trying to tell you. I'm a photographer, and Charlie's company wants to pay me to fly out to California and do the photography for their newest residential development. They're willing to pay me $5000. I want to do it."

Scott whistles softly. "Wow. Okay. When is it?"

"March 5th. There's a pre-opening that weekend, so I'd have to leave Thursday morning, and I wouldn't get back until Sunday night. It would mean you'd have to take a couple of days off work to watch the kids."

Scott's gaze inadvertently drifts back to the TV where three men stand knee deep in a muddy river, holding a fish that's at least six feet long. "I'm sure I can take a few days off or at least work from home those days. If you're sure this is what you want."

"I'm sure," I say, and for the first time in a long while, I am.

174

Chapter Twenty-One

Friday, February 27th

It's been six weeks since Charlie's phone call, and while I feel like my entire life is on the cusp of change, in reality it has just kept chugging along, business as usual. I have religiously eaten Cheerios, salads, and Slim Fast shakes, and despite devouring half a package of Oreo cookies in a moment of weakness, I have lost five pounds. I've gone shopping with Ruth for beautiful white dresses for the girls to wear in her wedding to my father-in-law, had the carpets cleaned, and constructed a Valentine box the night before it was due out of a shoebox, paper doilies and glitter without teaching my kids any new curse words. I've logged on to Facebook daily, casually keeping in touch with Charlie. I've had two more photo assignments, one of a sweet, newborn baby boy and one of a couple expecting their first baby, and I marked the fifth birthday of my own little boy by making a dinosaur cake and hosting a party for ten five year olds at an indoor bounce house facility aptly named Wild Thing. After the party, as I lay next to him in his bed while we said prayers and sang his favorite bedtime song, I realized that this was the last birthday he would have as a preschooler, since he starts kindergarten in the fall. Noticing my silence, he said, "What's wrong Mommy?" I looked at him, his face as familiar to me as my own hand, and could see a glimmer of the strong and sturdy bones of the man he would become beneath the sweet, boyish, freckled face.

"I was just thinking that before long you'll be too big to want to cuddle with your mom," I said lightly.

Taking my face between his hands like he used to do when he was a toddler, he said with the certainty of a five year old, "Even when I'm 25, I'll still want to cuddle with you."

Like his son, Scott has wanted to cuddle more lately too, but who could blame him? He's gotten sex a dozen times in the last month and a half, which is a bit behind the pace I set for myself with my New Year's resolution but way more than our usual average. Last Saturday, after having made love the night before, Scott said flirtatiously, "You know, I was thinking we could try something new."

Thinking he was going to suggest covering me in whipped cream or doing it on the kitchen table, I said cautiously, "Okay…what?"

"I was thinking we could do it two nights in a row. It's been awhile since we've done that.'

"No it hasn't," I protest. "We've definitely done it two nights in a row in the last couple of months."

"No, we haven't," he says. "I know these things. I keep a log."

"You do not!" I say incredulously. I'm pretty sure he's joking, but you never know.

"I do. It's in the guy handbook. I keep track of these things."

"Really? Let me see your log!" The second the words are out of my mouth I realize I have been set up. Scott winks at me, confirming what I have guessed.

"Why, I thought you'd never ask," he drawls.

More often than not, our lovemaking is just like everything else between two married people, comfortable and routine, and if I occasionally feel a weird detachment afterwards I don't dwell on it because he's obviously never been happier. He's also gotten noticeably nicer, talking to me while he eats dinner instead of turning on the TV, and holding my hand when we walk together somewhere.

Angie swears that all you have to do to get a man to fall in love and stay in love is to have sex with him on a regular basis. My theory is that to keep a man interested, even when you've been married to him for ten years, you have to be a little independent and hard to get some of the time. I suppose it's no wonder that Scott is acting love struck-he's having regular sex with an emotionally detached woman! Isn't that the ultimate male fantasy? Well, maybe after two women at once. The truth is I'm not really trying to play hard to get; it's just that for the first time in the fourteen years we have been together, Scott's not the only man on my mind.

Tonight I don't have to think about anything but having fun because it's Girl's Night Out, and Angie, Kate and I are taking Meg out to celebrate her birthday. She is the first one of us to turn forty so in the spirit of paying tribute to her lost youth, we're going to a Duran Duran concert in downtown Dallas. I am the designated driver for the evening, so I hop in the minivan and head over to pick up Angie. From her house, we drive to pick up Kate, who hops in the car looking like the poster child for trendy thirty-something women everywhere. She's wearing leggings, a hot pink tunic, and fuzzy boots. Her outfit is accentuated with a funky pendant and a boho beaded headband around her dark hair that is smartly cropped into a cute little pixie cut, accentuating her killer cheekbones. Damn. I really thought I had it this time, with skinny jeans, a hoodie and my favorite go anywhere black boots.

"How do you do it?" I ask incredulously. "I don't think I've ever seen you wear the same thing twice, and you always look so…so, perfect."

"Oh, please," Kate protests as she buckles her seatbelt. "I finally got so sick of never having anything to wear that over the holidays I took everything out of my closet and put it all back in again organized into outfits, complete with accessories."

"You what?" Angie says.

"Seriously?" I echo.

"Seriously. So on each hanger I have the pants or skirt, the top, the jewelry and the shoes. You'd be amazed at how many outfits you actually have when you do that."

"Will you come do mine?" I beg. Kate has that deer in the headlights look so I clarify. "I mean, for my trip to California. Just like eight or ten outfits."

Kate looks visibly relieved. I'm slightly offended; my wardrobe's not that bad. Well, maybe compared to Kate's it is.

"Sure. When are you going to California?" I forgot Kate hasn't kept up with the whole story. With soccer season over and Chloe in private school, I haven't seen Kate on a daily basis right, so she hasn't been privy to the details of the Charlie sage. She knows I met with my "old beau" as she calls him, but that's the extent of her knowledge. "Are you driving? Route 66 to California is just wonderful." I look back at her and sure enough, she's got that dreamy-eyed Kate look. "I remember when Hugh and I drove from Dallas to L.A. We stopped at the Grand Canyon and it was so fun just driving and talking and singing along with Barry Manilow and Neil Diamond.

"Really? Really?" Angie demands, bemused. She and I exchange a smile. This is what we love about Kate. She may be perfect on the outside, but she's a dork on the inside just like the rest of us.

"I'm going in two weeks," I say. "It's a photography assignment."

"That's wonderful," she enthuses. "Who's the assignment for?"

"Her hot ex-boyfriend," Angie sings.

Further conversation is mercifully cut short as we stop to pick up Meg, who has dressed for the occasion in her usual funky style that only Meg can pull off. She practically bounces into the car, a piece of poster board tucked under her arm.

"What's with the poster board?" Angie says.

Meg holds it up and waves it at us.

"'John, you're my freebie?'" Angie reads off the glittery sign.

"Yes, John Taylor is so hot!" Meg says. "He's definitely at the top of my list as far as freebies go."

"What's a freebie?" Kate asks.

"The one guy you'd have sex with besides your husband if there were no repercussions. Oooh, I hope John sees this!"

We all laugh and my trip to California is forgotten. At the concert, we dance and scream and sing along with hundreds of other thirty and forty something women for whom the song "Rio" was a Spring Break anthem. Meg flashes her poster from time to time, but much to her disappointment John does not pull her up on stage and make out with her.

When the concert's over, we pile into the minivan, still laughing and talking about the concert, the guys in the band, and the memories each song evoked. Angie puts a Duran Duran CD into the CD player and we crank up the volume, singing along at the top of our lungs. Because I'm singing along to "Hungry Like the Wolf," I somehow miss my turn onto I-75 and instead we find ourselves driving down lower Greenville, a strip of restaurants and bars that definitely draws a weekend party crowd, most of whom are a good bit younger than us.

By now we have traded out Duran Duran for Madonna, and Meg, who is sitting in the front seat and has had more drinks than I could keep track of at the concert, rolls down everyone's windows.

"C'mon," she says to us. "Sing it like you mean it!"

I slow down to a crawl and we belt out "Like a Virgin" at the top of our lungs to the young, beautiful people on lower Greenville.

"Like a virgin, touched for the very first time." Meg's really getting into it, running her hands down her chest as she sings out the window. She leans out the window and holds up her sign. "Where are you John?"

"Do something," I say urgently to Angie and Kate. Angie unbuckles her seat belt and reaches up to the front seat, grabbing Meg and pulling her back into the car.

"I can be John," a drunk, twenty-something frat boy type calls back. "But who's Will? Should I be jealous?"

Will? What's he talking about? Oh shit, Will. My Will, whose name is plastered on the back of my minivan on a decal of a soccer ball, right next to the one with Bella's name and her soccer team, The Groovy Girls.

"Roll up the windows!" I hiss

"What?" Angie shouts over the music.

"Roll up the windows," I say, louder this time. "Think about it. We're driving down lower Greenville in a white minivan with kids' soccer decals on the back."

"Hmmm, I see your point," Angie says. She rolls the windows up as we quietly drive off. "Let's go back to my place. We can hit the hot tub."

We stop at a local Mexican restaurant en route to Angie's because we are all starving. Two hours later, we're happily ensconced up to our necks in marvelously warm bubbles, a nearby table littered with empty wine bottles and half full glasses of Merlot.

"Sadly ladies, we have been relegated to the suburbs now that we are forty," Meg says with false dejection.

"Speak for yourself," I shout. "I've still got a few more years."

"Goodbye, party days," she laments. "We're married women with families now."

"Sorry it didn't work out with John," Kate says with mock sympathy.

"Yes, well, maybe next time," Meg says dismissively with a wave of her hand. "So, who's yours?"

"My what?" Kate says, confused.

"Your freebie."

"Ooooh, my freebie. Hmmm. I don't know. Let me think. Definitely George Clooney. And Keith Urban. He's cute."

"Don't forget Neil Diamond," Angie says with a laugh.

"Okay, okay, laugh all you want," Kate says good-naturedly. "Who's yours?"

"Brad Pitt, Jon Bon Jovi and David Beckham, preferably all at the same time. Not that I've given it any thought or anything," Angie says. We all laugh.

"What about you?" Angie says to me. "Who's your freebie?"

"I've never really thought about it," I say. "Unlike others who shall remain nameless. I wouldn't turn Brad Pitt down, after you were finished with him of course. And definitely Matthew McConaughey. Mmmmm, he is sexy!"

"What about Charlie?" Angie says wickedly.

"Ah yes," I say with wistfully. "I can't forget about Charlie!"

Chapter Twenty-Two

Monday, March 2nd

"Wow, you have a lot of clothes." Kate is standing in the walk in closet I share with Scott, although share may be too generous a term for it since my clothes take up more than two thirds of the space.

"Well," I say defensively. "It's not like I wear them all. These," I say, pointing to a section, "are the clothes I can almost wear if I lost about five more pounds, and these are the clothes for when I get a personal trainer and get my college, pre-kid body back. And these over here are my fat clothes left over from when I was pregnant with Daisy, which I occasionally wear right before I get my period."

"So where are the clothes you actually wear?" Kate asks bewilderedly.

"Oh, right here," I say, pointing to the smallest section of my closet.

Kate begins pulling things off hangers and throwing them on the bed. Before I know it, there are five cute outfits I would never have thought of putting together laying on the floor, complete with shoes, handbags and accessories, looking like chalk outlines at a crime scene. She's like my own personal Pinterest board.

"Are you going to need a swimsuit?" she asks.

Oh damn. I didn't see that one coming. What could be worse than having to wear a swimsuit around your hot ex, who's also kind of your boss, in the middle of winter? "Probably," I say miserably. "There's a pool."

"Show me what you've got!" Kate demands.

I start to take my clothes off. "Your swimsuit, dummy," she says, laughing.

I dig out the suit I bought last season, and she frowns as she surveys the floral swim skirt and tankini top.

"What?" I say defensively. "I've gotten lots of compliments on this suit."

"Yeah? From anyone under the age of sixty? Never mind. Anything else?"

"Well, there's this," I say, digging into the back of the drawer and pulling out a fairly modest black two piece I haven't worn in a while.

"Perfect," she says, snatching it up. She thrusts it at me. "Go put it on."

When I come out of the bathroom, I sneak a peak in the mirror. Hmmm, not as bad as I expected. It's amazing what a difference five pounds can make. I subject myself to Kate for her approval. She nods and says, "That's it!"

"There's no way I'm walking around in a two piece!" I protest. "I've got stretch marks."

"You can barely see them," Kate assures me. "And you've got great boobs. One of the few pluses of pregnancy. Besides getting the baby of course. But okay." She looks at me thoughtfully for a moment and goes back into the closet, rummaging around for a minute before emerging with a big leopard print scarf and a pair of strappy, black sandals. She ties the scarf around my waist, and I slip my feet into the sandals while she pulls my hair to one side and secures it with a red silk flower.

"Wow!" I say, looking at myself in the mirror. I recognize the girl in the mirror, but it's been a long time since I've seen her.

"Will you need something dressy?" she asks. I nod, and within minutes, my little black dress has joined the stack, kicked up a notch with a brightly colored scarf (to be tied around my neck), killer high heels and an armful of clunky bracelets.

"How about lingerie?" she says.

"Kate," I say, laying my hand on her arm. "He may be hot and I may love to imagine what it would be like to be with him again, but it's not going to happen. I'm married. I'll be sleeping alone."

She nods. "Then any old beekeeper outfit will do," she says. We laugh, but suddenly the weight of the secret I have been carrying since October seems unbearable.

"Hugh made a pass at me at the Halloween party," I blurt out. "He was drunk, and I'm sure it didn't mean a thing, he probably doesn't even remember it, but I just thought you should know."

"It's okay," Kate says hugging me, although I'm pretty sure I should be the one hugging her. "I'm glad you told me, but it's not a huge surprise. It's happened before. He's even had a couple of affairs."

"Oh, Kate," I say, and now I *am* hugging her. "I'm sorry. I had no idea. You two seem so happy."

"We are happy," Kate says. "That's just it. I don't know why he does it, but he's always sorry, and he always comes back to me and Chloe."

"So why do you put up with it?" I ask, angry on her behalf.

"What am I going to do, leave him? I love him," Kate says simply. "Plus I have Chloe to think about. Hugh and I have been together since high school, and I can't imagine being with anyone else. You may think I'm crazy, but I just can't throw it all away."

184

I don't know what to say, so we just sit there with our arms around each other, Kate and I, and stare into my closet filled with clothes that I can't throw out any more than Kate can throw out Hugh, in hopes that one day they will fit again.

Chapter Twenty-Three

Tuesday, March 3rd

At Angie's insistence, I have dropped Daisy off at her house and am sitting in the waiting area of the Butterfly Salon awaiting the waxing appointment she has made for me with her technician, Jennifer.

"Friends do not let friends go to an important weekend getaway at a posh resort without a hedge trim," she said when I protested. I'm not sure if she thinks I need the "hedge trim" for laying out at the pool or for Charlie, and I don't really want to know, so I let her make the appointment and take Daisy for me. What can it hurt? Actually, having the hairs unceremoniously ripped off my tender bikini area can probably hurt a lot, but I'm willing to give it a try. After all, Angie does it.

"Miss Cartwright?" A slight Chinese woman is looking expectantly at me. Since I'm the only one in the waiting room, I'm fairly sure she's talking to me.

"I'm Elizabeth," I say. "But my appointment is with Jennifer."

"I Jennifer," she says brightly. "Right this way."

She leads me to a small room in the back that has just enough room in it for a small table covered with paper and a little Bunsen burner with a small pot on it, which I brilliantly deduce must contain the hot wax.

"Your friend Angela say you want Brazilian, yes?"

"Uh, okay. What is a Brazilian?"

"I remove all hair. Front, back and everyting in between. You want landing strip or Hollywood?"

Landing strip??? I don't think I want that. "What's a Hollywood?" I ask, slightly panic-stricken.

"Bare like the baby's bottom," she says.

I blanch. "Landing strip," I say weakly. I am so going to kill Angie for this.

Jennifer turns to a pot of wax and stirs it with what looks like a Popsicle stick. "You go ahead and take everyting off and we get started," she says nonchalantly.

I wait for her to leave, but she just keeps stirring the wax, which I can now see has steam coming off of it. Am I supposed to just undress in front of her? Apparently so. At least the gynecologist has the decency to leave the room while you undress. There is barely enough room to turn about, but I somehow manage it, slipping my jeans off with my back to Jennifer. I turn back around, glad that I'm wearing a nice pair of underwear. Good thing I did laundry yesterday, or this could have been even more embarrassing than it already is.

"So does it hurt very much?" I ask apprehensively.

"So so," she says, wobbling her hand from side to side. "You take some Motrin beforehand?"

"No, I didn't think to," I say. "Should I have?"

She shakes her head at me. "You want someting for pain?" She digs through her purse and then turns to me, two strange looking orange pills in her opened hand. "Since you friend of Angie's, these for you," she says. "Just don't tell anyone where you get them. And if you get hot flash or really angry, you no worry unless it last longer than two days."

"Umm, no thanks," I say nervously. "I have a really high pain tolerance. So, do you wax your, uh, area?" I say, stalling for time.

"No, no, no," she says with a laugh. "That for crazy Americans. Now you take rest of clothes off and we start."

The rest???

"Shouldn't you buy me dinner first?" I joke. Jennifer looks at me blankly. I suddenly realize I can't do this. I'm not as brave or sexy as Angie is, and quite frankly, I'm okay with that. Besides, no one but Scott and I will ever know if there are a few bushes outside the cave or not.

"Uhh, look Jennifer. I'm sorry, but I can't do this. Can I just get an eyebrow wax?"

Jennifer eyes my white cotton underwear speculatively. "You sure? Your man think Brazilian very sexy."

"I'm sure," I say firmly, desperate to just leave. "I'll still pay you. I just don't think it's a very good idea for me."

She looks me over, and then her face lights up with comprehension. "Oh," she says, patting my stomach, which despite my six weeks of crunches still boasts a small pooch. "You no say you having baby! Your man think you sexy already, yes? Good for you!"

I don't even bother answering. I slip my jeans back on, then lie back on the table while she smoothes hot wax under my brows, firmly pressing a smooth strip of muslin against the brow bone before ripping it off.

When she's finished, my eyes are red and watering. Thank heavens I didn't let her do this to me anywhere else! As I reach for my wallet, she says, "You want lip wax too?"

I fight the urge to feel my upper lip, which until exactly ten seconds ago I've never been self-conscious about since the hair there is fine and blond.

"No, thanks," I manage before running out the door. I feel like I have just escaped an army of Vikings set on rape and pillage with my virginity intact. I make a mental note to look into some Post Traumatic Stress counseling.

"So," Angie says twenty minutes later when I arrive at her house to collect Daisy. "What did you think? Isn't it fabulous? Okay, it's a little weird when they wax in between your butt cheeks, but the good news is you shouldn't have to go back for at least a month."

I must look horrified because she rushes to add reassuringly, "It hurts less the more you go. Did you get a design?"

"Are you insane?" I practically shriek at her. "No, I didn't get a design! I didn't even get my underwear off. I totally got cold feet. You didn't tell me I was supposed to get completely naked and she wasn't even going to leave the room. I cannot believe you do that! You are a masochist. And possibly a sadist too."

Angie starts to laugh and before long, I am laughing with her. We laugh until there are tears running down our faces. When we finally stop to catch our breath I say, "You know Ang, I'm not going to sleep with him."

"I know, honey," she says. "Although you know I certainly won't judge you if you change your mind. He is gorgeous."

"I thought maybe that's why you thought I should get the Brazilian," I say.

"Liz, I thought you should get the Brazilian so you'd feel sexy and confident and like Liz the woman, not Liz the mom, while you're on this assignment. It's so easy for us to forget who we are as women when we're so busy taking care of everyone else."

"You're right," I say with a sigh. "I bet guys do think it's sexy, don't they?"

"Richard certainly does. But don't worry," Angie says, patting my back. "You know Scott thinks you're sexy no matter what. Now go home to your husband."

"He's in New York," I say with a sigh.

"Well then," Angie says with a wicked gleam in her eye, "go home to the bunny!"

Because I don't like to think of myself as a quitter, and Angie does have a point about feeling more confident and sexy, I stop off at Walgreens and buy some hair removal wax strips that I can do myself. By 9:00 p.m., the kids are all in bed, and with Scott in New York until tomorrow, I've dedicated the evening to Liz beautification to get me psyched up for the weekend. I've already given myself a mini pedicure, painting my toes a glamorous deep red, deep conditioned my hair, and applied a mud mask to my face. I figure I can wax my bikini line while the mud mask is working. Sitting in my bathroom in a cozy robe, I think how much better this is in the comfort of my own home. And so much less embarrassing. I open the box and read the directions. It sounds easy enough. I take one of the strips out, warm it in my hand, remove the double-sided strips, and press it along my bikini line. I rub the tape, and then grab the edge to rip it off. Maybe not just yet. I rub it again, then once more for good measure. I start to pull it off, but ouch. I can't do it. Maybe I'll just kind of ease it off. Ow! That's even worse!

Belatedly, I realize I should have had the foresight to know that if I can't rip a band-aid off myself, there's probably no way I will be able to pull my own hair off on a wax strip. Damn, damn, double damn. I dance around the bathroom, trying to work up the courage to pull the tape strip off. I try several more times, but chicken out. I just can't bring myself to do it. Suddenly, I have a flash of brilliance. Scissors! Of course! Why didn't I think of that sooner? I'll just get some scissors and cut the wax strip off from the hairs underneath. I find the tiniest scissors I can in Bella's art set and try to work them underneath the plastic strip. It's no use. The damn wax strip is firmly stuck to my hoo hoo. I debate just leaving it on and going about my life, waiting until the hair grows longer so I can fit the scissors underneath. Only I don't think

190

that's such a good plan. Not only are the sharp plastic edges the teensiest bit uncomfortable jabbing into my thigh every time I try to sit down, but I'm pretty sure the hair down there doesn't just keep growing. Otherwise, Jennifer might be into braiding instead. What I wouldn't give to have Jennifer now!

I pick up the phone and call Angie.

"Did I wake you up?" I say when she answers on the fifth ring.

"Are you kidding? I'm watching Desperate Housewives. It's the tornado episode."

"Ang, you've got to help me!" I implore.

The background noise on her end is suddenly silenced, which means she muted the TV. "You got it," Angie says. "Do you need me to kill anyone?"

"No, no, no," I say. "I thought about what you said earlier so I bought some of those at home cold wax strips, and well….one's stuck on my bikini line."

"What do mean it's stuck?"

"I mean I put it on, but I can't bring myself to pull it off. I tried to cut it off but it's too close."

There is a suspicious snorting sound on the other end of the line. "Thanks," I say dryly.

There's a muffled sound, and then Angie says in a strangled voice, "I'm not laughing!" Then in a more normal tone of voice, "Liz, did you or did you not give birth to three children, one of them without an epidural?"

"Well, yes," I hedge. "But that's different."

"Hell yeah, it's different! Waxing doesn't hurt nearly as bad. But it's the same premise. Just think of things Scott has done to make you mad, and then yell his name as you rip the wax strip off. Trust me, it works."

We say goodbye and I screw up my courage, thinking of all of the times Scott has snored on the couch while I, exhausted from chasing after three kids by myself all day, bathed them and put them all to bed single-handedly. I remember the countless times he has stood me up for dinner, or an at-home movie date, or not shown up in time when I had somewhere to be because he was working late or taking a client to dinner. I think of how many times he brushes me off or looks right through me, preoccupied with his own thoughts of work or going for a run or the Cowboys game. I remember how it feels to be cherished and loved and prioritized by a man whose face lights up when you walk into the room, and I realize it hasn't been that way with Scott for a long time. Thirty minutes later, I have a bikini line that could land a Boeing 737.

Chapter Twenty-Four

Wednesday, March 4th

This morning Scott calls from New York to tell me he has another meeting unexpectedly scheduled for this morning, so he won't be home until tonight.

"Really?" I moan. "Is there any way you can get home earlier? I have a ton to do before I leave tomorrow and I was counting on you helping out with the kids."

"What's there to do? You just throw some stuff in a bag."

"No Scott, guys just throw some stuff in a bag. Women do everything else. Remember when you just "threw some stuff in a bag" for New York? I did all the laundry beforehand, went to the cleaners, got your migraine prescription refill, and stocked up on travel-sized toothpaste so you'd have something to throw in the bag that *I* dug out of the back of the closet."

"Sorry, babe. I have to go, but I'll see you tonight. I'll get there as soon as I can."

Scott obviously doesn't understand. When he goes out of town, which he does fairly often, he leaves knowing that the kids and I will be doing exactly what we do when he walks out the door to go to the office or to the gym or to get a haircut. I know what they like for breakfast, who their friends are, where Will's favorite Power Ranger is, that Bella needs to wear her sneakers to school on Fridays for gym, and how to get Daisy to take a nap. Scott is a great dad, but he's not here enough to know their little idiosyncrasies, or even where Daisy's pajamas are.

Because I am feeling guilty enough about leaving them all for four days, I am determined to do everything I can to make it as easy on them all as possible. That means the kids and I spend the day rushing around like maniacs. I have cleaned the house, made sure that all the laundry is washed, folded, and put away, and stocked the frig and freezer with enough meals to last a month. I have purchased and wrapped a gift for the birthday party Bella is attending on Saturday, and arranged for a friend's mom to take her to the party so Scott doesn't have to juggle taking her to the party with Will and Daisy in tow. I have written out a schedule for Scott so he knows what time Daisy naps and which songs to sing to her so she will go to sleep and what she likes for snack, and I've pre-recorded a selection of everyone's favorite TV shows in case of emergency. And because this is the first time I have left them for more than one night, I have bought little gifts for all three of them to open each day, along with little notes to go with each gift telling them how much I love and miss them.

We have just gotten home from running a dozen errands when I realize that somewhere between the library, where we started our day, and the grocery store, where we ended it by purchasing enough chicken nuggets, peanut butter and jelly, and Cheerios to feed a third world country, we have lost Brown Bear. He's not in the car or anywhere in the house. There is no way Daisy can survive a single bedtime, much less an entire weekend without Mommy, without Brown Bear. There are nights that I wake up to the sound of Daisy screaming and I run upstairs, certain the house is on fire, only to find that Daisy just needs me to get Brown Bear for her. Most of the time, he is usually six inches away from her.

In a panic, I call every place we have been to see if anyone has turned in a well-loved (i.e. ratty) bear with tags sewn onto his ears. Unfortunately, no one has. It reminds me of the time when

Bella was little and lost one of her stuffed Teletubbies. We never found poor Tinky Winky, but since there were rumors at the time that the purple, fuzzy, purse-carrying Teletubby was gay, we figured he must have fallen victim to a hate crime.

When my phone calls yield nothing, I decide I will simply replace Brown Bear with a new one. I call the local toy store where Santa first found Brown Bear, but the girl who answers says they haven't carried any stuffed animals in the year that she has worked there. Not easily thwarted, I Google 'stuffed brown bears' on the internet. I get results for all kinds of stuffed bears, but none that look remotely like Brown Bear. Luckily, I still have E-Bay. You can buy anything on E-Bay. Anything, I soon find out, except a bear that looks like Brown Bear. Then I get the brilliant idea to call the manufacturer. This probably happens all the time. In fact, they probably keep an assortment of merchandise in some warehouse just for desperate parents like me. Twenty minutes later, I have talked to everyone up the chain of command at the Sarah Snell toy company.

"I will pay you $500 if you will overnight me another bear," I finally beg the president of the company.

"Look lady. I wish I could help you, but I can't. Contrary to what you seem to think, we don't keep a secret stock of every animal we've ever made in case a child loses his lovey five years later."

I screech, "What kind of heartless people are you? And for your information, she's not even two!" before slamming the phone down in frustration. Oh my gosh. I am totally losing it! But what, oh what, am I going to do? I am putting the finishing touches on a poster to hand out around town that I have made, complete with a picture of Brown Bear (there were plenty to choose from, as just about every picture I have of Daisy also includes Brown Bear) under the heading ""Have you seen me?" when I feel Daisy tugging at my shirt. "You find Brown Bear?" she asks hopefully.

"Not yet, honey. I'm sorry. But I know he'll turn up," I say with a confidence I don't feel. "Why don't you go see if Bella and Will can help you look?"

Bella, who has just wandered into the kitchen looks at me like I've finally lost it. "Why does she need help looking for Brown Bear? She's the one who put him under your sink."

"What?" I say incredulously, running to my bathroom. I open the cabinet and sure enough, there is Brown Bear, looking quite comfortable on a bed fashioned out of maxi pads.

"Good job, Mommy," Daisy says, clapping. She chortles with laughter and I sit down on the edge of the bathtub and cry.

"Mommy?" Daisy says with concern, putting her chubby hands on either side of my face and peering at me intently.

"It's okay baby," I say, swiping away my tears. "Mommy's just happy we found Brown Bear."

Scott arrives home at 9:30 with an armful of magazines and a movie theater size box of Hot Tamales, my favorite.

"For the plane ride," he says. "I'm sorry I'm late. I really couldn't help it."

Although I'm sure he's trying, I feel like I'm being bought off. A box of Tamales in exchange for a husband who really gives a crap. And just like that, I'm done. Done taking care of the kids and the house and Scott and getting nothing from him in return. Oh sure, he could argue I'm getting his paycheck in return, but life has never been about money for me. I don't want to be taken for granted anymore. I want to be loved. I want to be heard. I want to be important to someone. And I'm starting to think that someone is no longer Scott.

I could rage at him and spend the last night before I leave fighting with him, but I don't have the energy to try anymore. More importantly, I don't care anymore.

"Thanks," I say, flatly. Later, despite the detachment I feel towards Scott, I allow him to lead me into the bedroom because we have a well-established tradition of pre-trip sex whenever he is going out of town, and some part of me wants to give him one last chance to convince me he loves me, that he finds me worthy of his time and interest. But our lovemaking is like a visit to a fast food restaurant – brisk, efficient, and in and out in less than five minutes. He hesitates for just a moment when his hand brushes between my legs under the covers, but then he is inside me and we move together with the familiarity of years together. He keeps his eyes open, watching me as our bodies, unaware of the emotional distance between us, find a familiar rhythm, then sweet release. Afterwards, he pulls me close to his chest and kisses me gently behind the ear, smoothing my hair as I tuck my head under his chin.

"I'll miss you," he says softly. I am on the verge of sleep when I swear I hear him whisper, "Come back to me."

Chapter Twenty-Five

Thursday, March 5th

Scott hates to take all three kids anywhere by himself. In fact, I'm not certain he's even tried it since Daisy was born, so I have already made plans to drive myself to the airport. I tell him that it will be easier on the kids to see me off from home instead of the airport. He looks dubious, assuring me that he would be happy to drive me to the airport, but I can see the relief in his eyes. I briefly wonder what he will do if he runs out of milk or wants to rent a movie, but I quickly brush the thought aside. Not my problem this weekend!

It takes me thirty minutes to actually get out the door. Will keeps wanting "one more hug," telling me he doesn't want me to go, Bella is solemnly stoic, tucking notes and pictures and a favorite stuffed animal into my suitcase, while Daisy simply refuses to let me put her down. Scott finally takes pity on me and takes Daisy out of my arms, kisses me, and firmly tells the kids it's time for Mommy to go and that the tickle monster will soon be attacking so they should go make a fort to keep him out. It works like a charm, and they run off screaming with giggly anticipation while I let myself out the door. But instead of feeling free and excited, I just feel sad. I miss my kids already. I crank up the music in my car, real grown up music on a station I like to listen to, but my funk persists. I park in a self park lot, take a tram to the terminal, and go through the endless process of checking my bags and waiting in line after line before morosely arriving at my gate. And standing there like my own personal knight in shining armor is Charlie, casually dressed in jeans and a button down shirt.

Delighted to see him, I hug him tightly. There is nothing awkward about it this time. It seems completely natural, probably since we have been in touch with each other on Facebook for the last four months. We seem to have rebuilt our friendship, and I am so happy to see a friendly face I could kiss him. Of course, I don't.

"What are you doing here?" I ask, although there's no hiding how glad I am to see him.

"I had to fly in yesterday for a meeting and since I knew we would both be flying out of DWF to California today, I checked with the travel agency to see when your flight was and booked mine so we could fly together. Is that okay?"

"It's more than okay. I was feeling a little lonely. Pathetic, I know, but I've never left my kids for this long and I already miss them."

"It's not pathetic at all," Charlie says. "But they are going to be fine and you are going to have a fabulous weekend because Harbor Falls is truly amazing." He describes Harbor Falls to me, slipping in funny stories about mishaps that occurred during the construction, and before I know it the guilt and worry about the kids is gone and I realize I am actually enjoying myself.

Our boarding pass group is called (Charlie has managed to also book a seat next to mine) and we board the plane, settling into our seats next to a small man in his early twenties who is sitting next to the window. Charlie and I chat idly while the rest of the passengers board. Everyone is pretty much settled into their seats when a well dressed business woman comes striding down the aisle, a rolling overnight bag in tow. She opens overhead bin after overhead bin, slamming each shut with an explicative when she finds that each one is already full. She makes it all the way to the back of the plane before coming back to our section and loudly demanding, "Whose luggage is in here? It wouldn't be full if everyone just has one bag in here. Sir, is this your bag?" The object of her tirade puts his hands up defensively and shakes his head, while everyone else gets really interested in how to put on the oxygen mask.

"Bag Nazi," Charlie murmurs to me under his breath. I suppress a laugh.

The flight passes quickly, particularly since the guy sitting on the other side of me talks to us the entire time, telling us about his plan to convince the auto industry to resurrect the Yugo by getting media coverage documenting a huge cross country drive in one.

"And for the whole trip our mascot, the Yugo girl, is driving the car," he says excitedly. "Get it, the Yugo girl." He nudges my arm. "Like, 'You Go Girl!'" He snaps his fingers in a 'z' and chortles with laughter. My eyes meet Charlie's in perfect understanding, and I have to look away before I burst out laughing. "I've designed the whole look myself," he adds, handing me a piece of paper with a rough sketch of a girl wearing a bright yellow, form fitting jumpsuit.

"So who's the Yugo girl?" I ask, more to distract myself than because I really want to know.

"Probably me," he says glumly, "since I can't find anyone to do it." He looks up hopefully, "Unless you're interested…"

"No!" I say firmly, and I can feel Charlie shaking with silent laughter next to me.

Since the guy is obviously crazy, I pick up the magazine I brought and start to thumb through it, hoping he'll take the hint and shut up. All is quiet for a moment, and then Charlie says, "So dude, why a Yugo? I mean, those cars sucked. I think their tagline was 'Yugo, but they don't.'"

I turn to Charlie and give him an incredulous look that hopefully says 'what the hell did you do that for?' because sure enough the guy starts talking again, singing the praises of the underappreciated Yugo.

"They brought back the Mini Cooper and the Volkswagen Beatle," he says passionately. "Why not the Yugo?"

Charlie catches my eye, smiles wickedly, and winks at me, obviously enjoying himself.

Fifteen minutes later, as we begin our descent into San Francisco, Charlie reaches across me to shake hands with the guy who introduced himself as Dwayne something or other somewhere over Arizona. "Well, that's certainly the most interesting flight I've had in a long time," he says. "And who knows, maybe Liz here will change her mind and be your Yugo girl." He laughs as I elbow him in the stomach. "What? You'd look great in bright yellow spandex."

I try not to blush at the compliment.

"It's been nice to talk to you guys," Dwayne says. "The last few times I've been on a flight, the people next to me haven't spoken English. What a coincidence, huh?"

Charlie and I manage to ditch Dwayne at the baggage claim area, although he does insist on giving me his business card just in case I change my mind. We collect our bags, and then walk out into the balmy California sunshine where a limo is waiting to take us to Harbor Falls.

"Want me to tell you a little more about the development?" Charlie says, settling back into the plush seats.

"No hablo Ingles," I say, and we both start laughing again.

I feel like a little kid as we make the two hour drive along the Pacific Coast highway, marveling as the urban sprawl of the Bay area gives way to rugged cliffs, deserted beaches, and charming towns with whitewashed buildings and church steeples. About an hour outside of San Francisco, Charlie leans forward and says something to the driver, who stops the car. Charlie gets out, then turns and offers his hand to help me out of the limo. I take it, instantly feeling the electricity of his touch. He keeps my hand held lightly in his as we step away from the limo, and he points to a tall, classic looking lighthouse perched on a rock promontory.

"That's the Pigeon Point Lighthouse," he says. "It's one of the tallest lighthouses in the US."

"It's gorgeous," I say. "Can we climb it?"

"The lighthouse itself has been closed for repairs for years," he says, "but the surrounding area is a state park so we can walk around." As we make our way across the old boardwalk, he constantly turns to help me climb down the rocks or steady me, and the warm weight of his hand on my waist makes me feel like giddy school girl.

"Look," he says, pointing to a pod of gray whales.

I am speechless with delight. I have never seen whales before, and I reach for my camera, which I luckily thought to grab when we got out of the car. We stand on the beach as I shoot picture after picture of the whales, and then Charlie points out two sea lions at play several yards down the shoreline and I turn my lens on them. After I'm finished, I turn to Charlie. "Say cheese," I say. He smiles and I snap the picture.

We stay at the lighthouse for over an hour, taking our shoes off to wade in a nearby tide pool, laughing at the small hermit crabs that scuttle along the bottom. Eventually Charlie says, "I could stay here at the beach with you forever, but my boss will be wondering where we are if we don't get back on the road."

As we climb back into the limo, I realize I had almost forgotten that I was here to do a job, and I sternly remind myself that this trip is strictly professional. An hour later we roll through the security gates of the very elite development of Harbor Falls. We stop in front of the Harbor Falls condominiums, a group of charming whitewashed bungalows on the beach, and Charlie runs inside the front office, returning with two keys. He retrieves both of our bags from the car and then shows me to where I'm staying, a small (by Texas standards; it's a veritable mansion by California standards) one bedroom condominium decorated in sandy tones with accents of blue and green, and completely furnished with sheer draperies, wicker furniture, and a nice mix of old antiquey looking pieces alongside more modern ones.

"I'm in the condo next door," he says as he puts my bag inside the door where I am standing open mouthed in amazement, taking in the wall of windows and the attached covered porch that is a hop, skip and a jump from the dunes and the ocean with amazement. "Why don't you get settled? Come by in an hour or so and I'll take you to meet Steve."

After he leaves I pinch myself to make sure I'm not dreaming. Ouch. Okay, not dreaming. I unpack my bag and resist the urge to bounce on the bed like Bella would. That reminds me of Bella, which reminds me that I should check at home and see how everyone is doing. I call the house and get Scott, who sounds a bit harried. I realize that although it's four here, it's almost six o'clock at home-the witching hour when all the kids get grumpy and Daisy hangs onto your leg like a twenty-five pound shackle. I promise to call back later to say goodnight to the kids.

After I hang up, I wander around the apartment, appreciating the architectural details that coexist alongside the nods to convenience. I grab my camera and take a few more pictures. I take advantage of the waterfall shower and dress for dinner in a simple black sheath dress with a pair of kitten heals and a strand of pearls. Very professional and "old" Liz. I glance at the clock and see that I still have fifteen minutes. What the hell. I kick off my shoes and bounce on the bed.

Charlie is waiting for me on the front porch of his bungalow and whistles appreciatively when I walk up. Together we walk to the front of the condominiums, then cross a brick-cobbled street that frames a rolling grassy area flanked by a series of upscale shops and restaurants. Although this weekend marks the grand opening of the development, Charlie tells me that the soft opening was several weeks ago and many of the condominiums are already leased, which explains why there are other people milling around, shopping and dining in the beautiful resort-type community. We arrive at Dante's, a sumptuous looking, upscale restaurant that sits on the cove, and Charlie introduces me to his boss, Steve Castletree, the chairman and CEO of the development. We are joined for dinner by a cool California blonde named Ava who handles marketing for Castletree Developments, a man named Terry who is the Chief Design and Construction Officer, and a no-nonsense woman in a severe, tailored business suit who introduces herself as general counsel for the company.

The entire meal is spent, not surprisingly, discussing Harbor Falls. I make plans to meet with Ava in the morning to get up to speed on the overall marketing plan for the development and the scope of the job I'm going to be doing.

"Your work is really impressive," she says. "Very artistic, which is one of the reasons we went with you. We want Harbor Falls to appeal to the upper echelon of Californians, and our entire marketing plan is built around the artistry of the community."

I am secretly pleased. A small part of me had wondered if I'd only gotten this job because Charlie had insisted on it.

By the end of the meal, tomorrow is completely booked. After spending the morning with Ava, Terry is going to give me a tour of the entire property in the afternoon, and there is a huge party on the beach planned for tomorrow night. My head is spinning when we leave the restaurant, and I think it's only partly due to the three martinis I had. Steve wants to go over some things with Charlie, so I walk back to my condo alone. Once I'm inside, I call home.

"Hi," Scott's voice over the phone line sounds so far away. He tells me about his day with the kids and I tell him about the whales and how incredible Harbor Falls is. It strikes me how our roles have reversed this weekend. After I listen to him tell me about something cute that Daisy said and how he had to wait on hold for ten minutes for a sales representative to help him with a billing error for our newspaper subscription, I understand a little why his eyes sometimes glaze over when I tell him about my day. It's not that I don't care about what's going on at home; it's just that it seems so slow and mundane compared to the excitement of being here and being engaged in something stimulating and dynamic.

I talk to Bella, who tells me about her spelling test and the fight she had with Ellie over what they played at recess, and then I talk to Will, who in typical male fashion answers my questions about his day with one syllable answers, and then launches into a rambling explanation of the television show he is watching. Scott holds the phone up to Daisy's ear, and after a moment of heavy breathing, she says, "I lub you," then Scott is back on the phone.

"We're doing fine, don't worry," he says. "But I really miss you."

"I miss all of you too," I say.

After I hang up, I change into pajamas (crisp cotton capris and a tank top-a compromise between Angie's suggested sleazy lingerie and Kate's beekeeper suggestion) and get ready for my day tomorrow. I make a cup of tea in the kitchen that is infinitely nicer than my kitchen at home, decked out as it is with a sub-zero stainless refrigerator, marble countertops and white washed cabinets with lead glass windowpanes, and then I take my cup out onto the deck where I sit, mesmerized by the sound of the waves hitting the shore, infinite and unseen, until long after I see the lights go on and then off again in the bungalow next door. I finally go inside and climb into bed. Although it's after one in the morning Texas time, I don't feel that tired, so I check my phone for messages (there's a text from Scott saying goodnight), then log onto Facebook. I see that Angie has gone to bed early with a headache, which knowing Angie means she's having wild, jungle sex with Richard. I pull up Charlie's page and stare at his profile picture. It seems surreal that after months of looking at his photo,

I have spent the entire day today with him, very real and in the flesh. A status update pops up on his wall and I read his latest post: *"Charlie Bennett is….dreaming of the girl next door."*

Chapter Twenty-Six

Friday, March 6th

I wake up at 6:00 a.m., bleary eyed and still half-asleep, and stumble to the well appointed kitchen to make myself coffee. "No worries!" I tell myself encouragingly. I can do this. I am a mother; I am a sleep deprivation professional. There are three texts in my inbox. One from Angie (*"How's it going in LaLa land?"*), one from Scott (*"I missed waking up next to you this morning"*), and one from Charlie (*"Want to go grab breakfast this morning?"*).

I text Charlie back first. *"Definitely. My motto is never cook when you can go out. 7:00?"*

I text Angie back, giving her a quick summary of what Harbor Falls is like, then Scott, saying I miss everyone at home. A cup of coffee and fifteen minutes under the amazing waterfall shower that I'm quickly becoming attached to works wonders.

An hour later, I am dressed and ready, looking (I hope) like a professional photographer. Charlie is on the phone when I walk outside, pacing back and forth on the sidewalk that connects our bungalows. Seeing me, Charlie gives a little wave but continues his conversation. Five long minutes pass, and I'm starting to feel a little idiotic standing here like a star struck teenager when he mercifully finishes his call, shoving his phone in his pocket before turning his mega-watt smile on me.

"Sorry," he says. "That's a new job in the Catskills we're bidding on, and I'd heard a rumor they were going to go with someone else. I'm not about to let that happen." There's a steely glint in his eyes that I don't recognize, but in a flash it's gone and he is once again his charming self. "But enough about work. May I take the illustrious photographer out for coffee?" He holds out his arm, and he looks so unlike a courtly gentleman with his rakish smile that I have to laugh. We walk to a quaint café that is located on the main business square of Harbor Falls overlooking a pebbled stream that runs through the development, spanned here and there by cute little footbridges. The green lies to the left of the coffee shop, anchored by an old-fashioned bandstand that offers live music and entertainment on the weekends.

"Harbor Falls seems to have everything. Does anyone ever leave?" I ask as I take a small bite of the thick slab of banana bread the waitress in the café recommended.

"That's the whole idea," Charlie says. "We've tried to think of everything so that the people who live here feel like they're part of a community, and so they don't have to leave for anything. But of course California has too much to offer nearby to never leave, which is why I have volunteered to be your tour guide of the surrounding countryside tomorrow."

"Really?" I say, pleased.

"Yup, I am at your service for the entire day," he says. "The hard part is figuring out where to take you since we only have one day. Last night it sounded like your day today is pretty full."

"It is," I agree. I glance at my watch. "Crap, I've got to go. I promised Ava I'd be at her office at 8:00. I guess I'll see you at the beach party tonight?"

"I'll be the one in the Speedo," Charlie says, then laughs at the look of horror on my face. "Knock 'em dead, sweetheart."

As I walk the block and a half block to Ava's office, I inwardly thrill at Charlie's casually dropped endearment. The day passes in a blur of activity. I spend the morning discussing marketing, design and product branding with Ava, and I find it's kind of like riding a bike. I fall back into the lingo and dynamic atmosphere of the marketing world as if I have been out of the business for a day instead of seven years. It feels good, I realize, to talk about marketing strategies instead of potty training. I am on my own for lunch, so I walk around Harbor Falls exploring and taking photographs. I spend the afternoon with Terry, who gives me an in-depth tour of the entire development, pointing out all of the eco-friendly details they have incorporated into the design that have made Harbor Falls one of the premier examples of green construction. I don't get back to my condo until 6:00, which leaves me an hour to get ready for the official launch party on the beach.

Scott has sent me a half dozen text messages throughout the day and I can't help but wonder why he doesn't talk to me this much when I'm home. Even though I know I'll have to rush to get ready if I call home first, I do it anyway because I don't want to go a day without talking to the kids. Not only would they never forgive me for not calling (I have a mental image of Bella standing forlornly by the phone waiting for mommy to call), but I miss hearing their voices, hearing about their day, and telling them how much I love them. And in a weird way I need to talk to Scott; I need for the sound of his voice to ground me and remind me of my very real life with him, which seems more and more distant with me here in California. I need the reminder that this weekend is a nice break, but it's not real, no matter how much it feels like I have found myself here. However, not only is Bella not waiting by the phone, no one is even home, and I listen to myself cheerfully telling me to leave a message with all the kids chiming in to say goodbye.

"Hi, it's Mommy," I say. "I miss you guys and I was just calling to say goodnight because I'm about to go to a work thing and I won't be home 'til late. So, I guess I'll just talk to you tomorrow." I hang up the phone, feeling oddly sad. I try Scott's cell phone, but no one answers and this time I don't leave a message. As usual, Scott is not available. I mentally give myself a little shake. "Don't be ridiculous," I chastise myself. Why should I be sad? Here I am enjoying a fabulous vacation which I'm also getting paid for. I have nothing to do but enjoy myself and take pictures—there is no one expecting me to do something for them twenty-four hours a day. I should enjoy it!

I take my time getting dressed, for the first time in ages having time to slather myself with scented lotion, meticulously apply my makeup, blow dry and straighten my hair, and find just the right accessories. I admire myself in the full length mirror in the bathroom, and then type a quick text to Kate thanking her for helping me pack. The fact that I look totally great tonight is all thanks to her.

I walk down to the beach where the party is in full swing, despite the fact that it's only 7:15. The portion of private beach that is part of Harbor Falls has been transformed to look like the Orient. A pathway down to the beach is lined with red and yellow paper lanterns, and more Chinese lanterns are strung along the beach, casting a romantic glow over the sand. The tables and sand are strewn with cherry blossoms, with elaborate paper dragons here and there adding a festive touch. A pagoda is set up at one end of the beach where a band is playing and black skirted tables are laden with a delectable array of Asian cuisine.

As I know a total of about three people in the entire state of California, I'm not surprised I don't see anyone I know. I walk over to the bar and help myself to a festive pink cocktail the bartender tells me is called a Red Lotus. Mmm, it's so good! It's like drinking Kool-Aid. I spot Ava and go over to congratulate her on the success of the party. She introduces me to several people she knows and before I know it, it's an hour later and I have downed another drink. Surprised that I haven't seen Charlie, I excuse myself and head over to the food table, surreptitiously looking for him as I pile my plate with crisp spring rolls, dumplings, roast duck and noodles.

I find a seat and am just starting to tuck into the food when Mr. Castletree appears on the pagoda stage, welcoming everyone to the opening of Harbor Falls and giving a rah rah speech about how Harbor Falls will change the way Californians live. He introduces the rest of the team and my breath catches slightly when Charlie appears, talking about how privileged he feels to have been a part of the design of such an innovative development. Damn, he looks good in a pair of dark linen pants and a casual white shirt rolled up at the cuffs, accentuating his tanned wrists. It's not fair for a guy to look this good.

I'm feeling kind of warm, so I grab another Red Lotus from a waiter walking by with a silver tray. Several other people speak before Mr. Castletree urges everyone to enjoy the party, yielding the focus of attention to the evening's entertainment, which is a traditional Chinese Ribbon dance. I watch as the graceful dancers perform the centuries old dance, so mesmerized by the way they twirl and leap, the long ribbons echoing their moves that I barely notice as Charlie slips into the seat next to me.

We watch the remainder of the show in companionable silence. When it's over, Charlie leans over to me and says, "Want to take a walk on the beach?"

"Sure," I say. I slip off my sandals and we walk together down the beach, away from the lights and sounds of the party. A little ways down the beach, Charlie stops and holds out both of his hands which are closed into fists. "Fortune cookie? Choose your destiny."

"Okay," I say, lightly tapping his left hand. He opens his hand and I take the crispy cookie from his open palm. The warmth of his skin against my fingertips makes my spine tingle. Flustered, I open the cookie.

"What does it say?" Charlie says, obviously at ease and in his element at the culmination and celebration of the project he has worked on so hard. "You know all fortunes have to be followed with 'in bed,'" he teases, referring to the way we always used to read fortune cookie in high school and college, howling with laughter at how funny (and provocative) fortunes were when read that way. "Here, I'll read it," he says. He gently opens my hand, finger by finger, plucks the small strip of paper from my palm and plants a warm, sensual kiss in its place. Some secret place in my belly clenches.

"You will fall in love with someone from your past....in bed," he reads.

Dumbfounded, I stare at him. "It does not say that!" I exclaim.

"No, it doesn't," he agrees with a smile, but there is something serious in his voice that belies the teasing banter. "It really says, 'If you continually give, you will continually have...in bed.'"

I laugh, grateful for the return of our light hearted banter. I'm not sure I want to him to read my heart so accurately. "Now yours," I urge.

"Your talents will be recognized and suitably rewarded...in bed," he reads.

"C'mon, you're making that up," I say as I give him a playful push.

"I'm not!" he assures me, laughing as he shows me the fortune. We continue walking, the waves occasionally catching up with us and washing away our footprints as if we were never here.

"What a job," I say. "Wouldn't you love to be the guy who sits around thinking up this stuff? Although I think whoever writes these things knows the 'in bed' gig. Have you ever noticed that every fortune works when you read it that way?" I don't say that Scott and I also read our fortune cookies that way, or that I had forgotten that the ritual had originated with Charlie, one of those small things you carry over from one relationship to another until it becomes part of who you are and you don't even remember it ever belonged to you and someone else.

"Yeah, but it'd get boring after awhile. Wouldn't it be great if they had 'misfortune' cookies?"

"What?" I look at him quizzically.

"You know real life advice stuff like 'Give up now. You'll never get that promotion.' Or 'Sometimes secret admirers are really just stalkers.'

I laugh. "'He who laughs last probably didn't get the joke.'"

"'You're in over your head. Seek professional help,'" he shoots back.

"'When another man answers your phone, it's probably time to go home.'"

I look up expecting to see Charlie's infectious grin, but instead he has grown somber.

"Sorry," I say. "Not funny, huh?"

"No, it's okay," he says. "Just hits a little too close to home."

"Yeah?" I say. "Is that why you got divorced?" Although I normally would have never dreamed of asking him about his ex-wife, here on the beach, just the two of us, it seems like I can ask him anything.

He tells me about it then, about finding out his wife was seeing someone else, his son's baseball coach no less. "So what about you? Are you happy?" he asks.

"I'm thinking about leaving Scott," I say. Once I've said it out loud, I realize it's true, and that every moment that I have felt alone for the last year has been building up to this moment of truth, this acknowledgement that I am lonely in my marriage and I don't want to be lonely anymore. Something is missing from my life, and here before me is proof that there could be, and should be, something more. Talking to Charlie, being with Charlie, the way I feel so alive when I'm with him, has made me realize that I need to feel important, that I want a man who will love me and share his heart with me, not treat me as if I'm invisible.

"Whoa," says Charlie. "Seriously?"

"It's been a long time coming," I say with a sigh. "I'm just not...happy. We've grown apart. I guess it's not so different from you and Jennifer, it's just his job he's left me for instead of a woman."

"I'm sorry," Charlie says.

"Don't be," I say lightly. "It is what it is. But c'mon. I don't want to think about it anymore tonight. Tonight is about you and me. It's about celebrating your amazing work. And my amazing photography of course." Afraid he might think I'm suggesting ripping our clothes off and doing it on the beach right now I hastily add, "Let's head back to the party. I don't want to monopolize the star of the night."

As we turn back towards the party, which is a festive speck in the distance lit by glowing lanterns and a huge bonfire, Charlie casually grabs my hand and we walk silently back along the beach, my every nerve registering the warmth of his hand around mine, a warmth that wastes no time going straight to my stomach again, where the muscles in my belly are doing a fantastic little jig of sexual anticipation. It's as if me saying aloud that I am unhappy in my marriage has opened a world of possibilities to my traitorous body.

Once we get back to the party, we are instantly reabsorbed by the energy of the night's festivities. Charlie is pulled away by first one person and then another and I find myself whirled into the mad melee of the impromptu dance floor, only stopping from time to time to cool off with another Red Lotus drink. It's almost an hour and a half later when Charlie reappears, just in time to pull me into his arms for a slow dance. The music is unfamiliar but haunting, and I lay my head against Charlie's chest, willing myself to live in this perfect moment. I try hard to memorize the details-the moon shining brightly in the sky, it's reflection on the ocean almost as bright, the sound of the waves, the feel of the sand beneath my feet, and most of all, the feel of Charlie's arms around me-- holding me, loving me, cherishing me. The feel of his chin, scratchy with a day's growth of beard, resting on the top of my head, the catch of his breath as he runs his hand along my back, the feeling that I never want this moment to end.

But of course it does end, and the band breaks into a wild song for the remaining revelers who are hanging around ready to cut loose and have fun. Charlie grabs my hand and pulls me away from the still dancing crowd. I spy a chess board set up at a table nearby and clap with delight.

"Oooh, chess!" I say. "Want to play?" I love chess.

"Okay," Charlie says, sliding onto a bench alongside the chess board and pulling me down beside him, his arm still protectively wrapped around my shoulders. "What are we playing for?" he asks teasingly.

"Hmmm," I consider the question flirtatiously. "We can't play strip chess. Too many people. Any suggestions?"

"Whoever wins decides whose place we go to afterwards," Charlie says.

"Deal," I say. I am an ace chess player, so I have no doubt that I will be choosing whether to go to my place, where I will say goodnight to Charlie, or his, where I have a feeling we won't be saying goodnight. I don't know how I feel about this, so I grab another drink from a passing waiter and make my first move.

Several moves later, Charlie says, "You are an amazing woman of contrasts, Elizabeth Moore."

"Oh yeah?" I say, preoccupied with planning my next move. "How so?"

"Well, you're all woman. I mean you're gorgeous and sexy as hell. Yet you have no compunction with sitting down to play, and excel at I might add, a man's game like chess."

"Aha," I say. "But that's where you're wrong, Mr. Bennett. Chess isn't a man's game, it's a woman's game. Think about it. The king's on a short leash. He can only move one space at a time, but the queen can go wherever she wants. The woman has all the power in chess."

Charlie laughs, but his eyes are hooded with sensuality and the look in them is anything but innocent.

"Point well taken," he says. "I concede. You can go wherever you want, Liz. Where do you want to go?"

I have lost count of how many drinks I have had, but there have been enough to drown the responsible part of my brain that is telling me that I should go back to my place and firmly say goodnight to Charlie at the door. I have had enough to make me feel reckless and young and beautiful, with an ache to grab this chance to actually *feel* something again.

"Your place," I say. "Let's go to your place."

We walk hand in hand back to Charlie's bungalow. He opens the door and without turning on the lights, leads me out to the deck in the back which overlooks the ocean. It's huge, taking up the entire back of the house.

"Wow, what a huge dick!" I exclaim. Yikes! Freudian slip. Flustered I add, "I mean deck."

Charlie cups my chin with his hand, rubbing his thumb across my lower lip in a sensual caress. His eyes are dark and hooded with desire, and when I put my hand on his chest, I can feel his heart beating faster. I think my own heart has stopped. He leans down and our lips meet. With a sigh, I close my eyes and give in to the moment.

Despite all the times I imagined how this would feel in the months following our breakup, and all the times my subconscious has conjured it up in my dreams in the subsequent years, nothing does justice to the reality of kissing Charlie. I lose track of time as our tongues meet and flit around each other in a slow, erotic dance they have never forgotten. His hands move to hold my head as our kiss deepens, then travel down my back where they hold me pressed close to him. When we finally break apart, we are both

216

breathless. He runs his hands down the length of my arms and catches my hands in his, linking his fingers with mine. I stare into his brown eyes, just inches from my own, and see my own desire reflected back in his gaze. I look down at our fingers, which are still intertwined. This is the moment. Except that I have to pee.

"Give me five minutes," I say, reluctantly pulling my hand from his. As I turn to go inside, I can feel his eyes following me.

Chapter Twenty-Seven

I wake up feeling like a bus ran over me, then turned around, came back, and ran over me again. The house is way too quiet, and I look at the blue hued furnishings around me with a sense of disorientation. Who redecorated my bedroom? Why is no one jumping on my head? And why are the windows open? Scott doesn't like to leave them open at night since he's afraid a band of wild-eyed, escaped convicts will hide out in stuffy Westfield, stumble upon our one open window and kill us all. I remember with a rush that I'm in California, which would explain the roar of the surf coming from said open windows, and immediately on the heels of that revelation is the one that this is not the bedroom I remember falling asleep in on Thursday. I look around, trying to get my bearings, and see Charlie sitting in an upholstered easy chair in the corner, intently working on his laptop. He feels my gaze and looks up, a slow smile lighting up his face.

"Good morning sunshine," he says.

"Ummphh," I say, burying my head back in the pillows. I'm sure I look like hell, and what's worse, I have no recollection of what happened last night. I remember kissing Charlie, in fact, I'll probably never forget kissing Charlie, even when I'm ninety and have Alzheimer's, but after that, zilch.

I turn back to Charlie. "Umm, so, did we….." I begin, uncertain how to ask the question I'm dying to know the answer to.

"Sweetheart, if you have to ask, nothing happened," he says, amused. "If we'd done anything, I guarantee I would have made sure you remembered it."

"Oh," I say, both relieved and disappointed. "I remember wanting to," I say softly, and God help me but it's true.

Charlie gets up and comes over to sit next to me on the side of the bed. "We kissed," he says. "Like this." He leans forward and his lips softy touch mine. Even though my mind, unencumbered by Red Lotus drinks, is trying to convince me otherwise, I want this. I lean into him and we kiss, a slow, languid, soul searing, toe curling kiss.

He pulls back a little, his face inches from mine.

"Oh yeah, I kind of remember that!" I say with a smile.

"Then you got up to come inside. I thought you were going to slip into something more comfortable, but I didn't think it would be my bed," he adds wryly. "I came in five minutes later, following the trail of discarded clothes, and found you dead asleep right here, so I tucked you in and here we are nine hours later."

"Mmm," I say. I don't want to ask exactly how naked I was when he tucked me in, so instead I try to focus on the rest of what he's saying. I bolt up in the bed, the sheets clutched to my chest since it hasn't escaped my notice that I'm still a little compromised in the clothing department. "Nine hours? What time is it?"

"It's a little after nine," says Charlie. "But relax, it's Saturday. Your only obligation today is to be entertained by me, remember?"

"Oh, right," I say, falling back against the pillows. "Where are we going again?"

"I'm going to show you California," he says. "So up and at 'em. Coffee's made and I picked up some egg and sausage bagels when I went out for a run."

"Coffee?" I say, salivating at the mere thought of it. "Have I told you that you are totally hot?"

219

"Yeah, yeah," Charlie says. "You only love me for my coffee. See you in a few."

Once he's gone, I get out of bed, grab the clothes he has thoughtfully folded and placed on the nearby dresser, and go into the bathroom to inspect the damage. Other than looking like I slept on my head, and of course the fact that I'm butt naked, I don't look so bad. I put my clothes back on, borrow Charlie's brush and run it through my hair until it lies flat, then snitch a swig of mouthwash from his toiletry bag. When I come out of the bedroom, he has breakfast set up on the deck and we eat together, talking about the party and carefully avoiding talking about The Kiss after the party. After breakfast, I surreptitiously tiptoe back to my cottage for a shower and to change clothes. I call home again and get the answering machine. Although I'm disappointed to not talk to the kids, I'm a little relieved that I don't have to talk to Scott. I remember that Bella has a birthday party to go to today. Maybe Scott ended up taking her.

Dressed casually in a pair of jeans, I pack my camera and walk back over to Charlie's house. Today is going to be perfect, I can just feel it. It is the most beautiful day imaginable, sunny and bright with the promise of spring, with a sky so blue it hurts. While I was in the shower, I thought a lot about where this is whole thing with Charlie is going, but I don't have any answers. What I want is to seduce him and to be seduced by him. I want to give him my heart and my body like a gift to be slowly unwrapped and savored. But I'm married. What constitutes cheating? A touch, a kiss, an emotional connection, the act of making love with someone else? Have I already cheated on Scott? Did I cheat on him when I turned to Charlie that night that I needed to talk and Scott wasn't there, either physically or emotionally? When I held Charlie's hand? When we kissed? Am I betraying Scott if he betrayed me first? And he has betrayed me, in ways recognized by the heart if not by the law. I think of the book I bought at that awful party seven months ago, of all the things I have done to try

220

to seduce him, to connect with him and make him love me like he used to, like he really *sees* me and wants to be with me. And I think how none of it—the panty-less tennis game, the crotchless thong, the suggested game of strip Scrabble—has worked. It's time I accept the fact that my husband doesn't love me anymore, at least not the way I want to be loved, wholly and completely, like I'm the most beautiful and desirable woman in the world. And yet here like a gift is Charlie, who does.

He's waiting for me in front of his cottage when I walk over, two motorcycle helmets tucked under his arm.

"What are those?" I ask suspiciously.

"Exactly what you think they are," he says. "I didn't forget how much you used to love to ride on the back of my bike, so I thought I'd rent one to show you around. There's nothing like the Pacific Coast Highway on a motorcycle. That is, if you want to. If not, we can take a car."

"Want to?" I shout, throwing my arms around him exuberantly. "I haven't ridden a motorcycle in years. I'd love to!"

I have never felt freer, or more alive, than I do cruising down the Pacific Coast highway on the back of Charlie's bike, the wind in my hair and my arms wrapped around the solidness of his waist. We stop from time to time to play tourist, sipping wine at the vineyards that dot the countryside, enjoying steaming bowls of clam chowder at Old Fisherman's Wharf, and laughing at the otters at the Monterey Bay Aquarium. At 4:00, we are walking around Cannery Row, exploring the shops where I am looking for little gifts to take home to the kids when my phone rings. It's Scott. I think about letting it go to voicemail, but decide I'd better not.

"Sorry," I say to Charlie before answering with an overly cheerful, "Hey! How are you guys?"

"Liz, I think you should come home. It's Bella," Scott says, and my heart stops. I hear 'horseback riding accident,' 'emergency room,' 'don't know the extent of her injuries yet' and I realize I was wrong before. My deepest darkest fear isn't something happening to me, it's something happening to one of my children.

The next two hours pass in a blur. I'm vaguely aware of Charlie pushing the limits of the law as we ride back to Harbor Falls, but it seems as if it's someone else hastily packing my bag, then riding in silence to the airport with Charlie, not me. He is wonderful, insisting on walking me to my gate, silencing me with a finger to my lips when I finally think of something besides Bella for two minutes and start fretting about finishing the photo assignment.

"I'm sure you have everything you need," he says. "Just e-mail me what you've got when things settle down. I'll explain everything to Steve. Don't worry. Everything's going to be okay."

As I sit on the runway, I cling to his words, hoping he's right. Scott's texts have arrived fast and furious since the phone call, keeping me abreast of what's happening with my little girl as I work my way across the country back to her. Apparently she was at her friend's birthday party at a horseback riding stable (I have learned that children in Texas have Texas sized birthday parties-the more elaborate the better) and was on a trail ride when something spooked her horse. The horse took off running and Bella hung on for a few minutes, but was ultimately thrown from the horse. By the time Scott got to the stables, she was dizzy, asking when she was going to the birthday party, and had vomited once, so Scott had taken her to the nearest hospital. After taking a look at her, they'd decided to Care Flight her to Children's Hospital, worried that she had a lacerated spleen. By the time I have to turn off my phone for takeoff, Scott's sister has arrived at our house to stay with Will and Daisy, and Scott is at the hospital with Bella, waiting for a CT scan.

Although my terror has taken precedence over every other emotion, guilt is running a close second. Intellectually, I know I could not have prevented the accident from happening had I not been in California, but at least I would have been there with her when she went to the hospital. I castigate myself, telling myself that I am a bad mother, selfish for pursuing my dream when I should have been home taking care of my children. Distractedly, I watch as the flight attendant shows us how to use the oxygen masks "in the unlikely event we lose cabin pressure." I listen numbly as she instructs parents of small children to put their own oxygen mask on first before assisting their child.

"If you put your child's on first, you might pass out, and then you'd be no help to anyone," she says. I close my eyes, shutting out the world around me and willing myself home. I spend the flight alternating between praying to God that Bella will be okay and thinking about my firstborn, the one who in a heartbeat transformed me from a regular person into a mommy, part of the club of women who live life with their hearts outside their bodies. When Bella was born, I loved her so intensely that I felt like I could never love anyone else more. I looked into her infant face and my soul recognized hers-she completed a part of me I hadn't even known was missing. When I got pregnant again, I was secretly afraid that I wouldn't be able to love this second baby as much as the first, that it would be a deep, dark secret I would have to keep forever. Of course, nothing could have been further from the truth. The tenderness I felt for the new life inside me grew as surely as the baby itself, exploding into full blown love when the nurse put Will into my arms for the first time. When I looked into his adorable, tiny face, my soul recognized his just as surely as it had Bella's, although instead of seeing my soul's compliment, his was more a reflection of my own. I knew him already because he was just like me. By the time Daisy was born, I didn't worry that I wouldn't love her enough because I knew my heart would grow a little bigger just for her. I knew that my love for each of my children might be slightly different, but no greater or less. I would love them equally but in different ways, kind of like I love wine, shoes and Hot Tamales. Sure enough, when her tiny fingers closed around mine and her blue eyes met mine, I loved her with all my being, my soul once again recognizing hers, the last child of my heart and my soul's future. She completed the circle.

Of course, love is a dynamic thing, always growing and changing, and your heart has to break sometimes so it can be filled with more love. I now know nothing breaks a mother's heart more than knowing her child is hurt.

Once my flight lands, I waste no time getting my bag and disembarking, switching my phone on as soon as I can to check for updates. "CT scan confirmed Bella has a concussion, but the doctor says it's not severe. No spleen injury. X-rays show she broke her collarbone and he's put her in a sling, but that's the extent of her injuries. She's going to be fine. We're in room 325. Can't wait to see you," I read.

Thankful that I drove myself to the airport, I find my car and drive as quickly as I can to the hospital. When I walk into Bella's hospital room, she is lying on the bed fast asleep, looking tiny and frail in the big bed, her left arm folded next to her body in a hot pink sling that makes me smile. Scott looks up when I walk in and within seconds, I am enfolded in his arms, as familiar and comfortable as my favorite pair of broken in jeans.

"Ah, Liz. Thank God you're here," he says, laying his cheek against my hair. We stay like that, our arms locked around each other, for several long, healing minutes, until Scott pulls back a little to look into my face.

"I'm so sorry," he says, and there is a world of emotion behind his remark.

"For what?" I say. "It wasn't your fault Scott, you weren't even there. You couldn't have prevented it, and even though I feel guilty for not being here, I couldn't have either."

"I know," he says with a sigh. "Not just that, although I wish like hell I could have stopped her from getting hurt. I'm sorry for everything. For you having to come back from California early. For getting so wrapped up in my job that I forgot that the most important job in the world is being a husband to you and a dad to our kids. For possibly losing you forever because I've been such an ass."

"What makes you think…." I begin, sitting down heavily in a chair. This is all going way too fast for me.

"Liz, I may have been a self absorbed idiot lately, but I haven't been so preoccupied that I haven't noticed what's going on. I may be a little slow noticing things but I'm not blind, particularly when it comes to you. I know this job was important to you from a professional standpoint, but the night before you left I suddenly realized this guy Charlie probably had some interest in you. Who could blame him? You're gorgeous and funny and smart. And I realized I had left the door wide open. When you walked out the door on Thursday, I knew exactly what I stood to lose, which is everything that matters the most to me."

I stare at him, speechless for possibly the first time in my life.

"I don't know what happened in California, and I don't want to know. I hope you will choose me, and our kids, and the life we have built together, but the last thing I wanted was to force you to make that decision for something like this. I want you to choose me because you still love me. I know I haven't shown you as much as I should have, but Elizabeth, I love you with all of my heart and all of my soul. I have loved you since the day you climbed into my car with a box of magnum sized condoms, and I will love you until the day that I die. I want you to be happy. If you're not happy staying at home, then we'll figure out a way for you to go back to work, or I'll cut back my hours so we can share the parenting duties more."

"You'd do that?" I ask.

"Sweetheart, I'd do anything for you," he says. "I just want us to be together."

Bella moans and thrashes about a bit, and I look over at her in alarm. More than anything I want to rush over to her and hold her in my arms, but I don't want to wake her, or hurt her.

"She's been doing that since we've been here," Scott says. "She's okay. The doctor says she'll probably sleep through the night, although nurses come in every hour to check on her." He gently straightens the oxygen mask that covers her mouth and nose.

The oxygen mask makes me remember the flight attendant's instructions and suddenly it's all crystal clear. Parenting in life isn't that different from parenting on an airplane. If you're so intent on giving your children everything they need that you forget about yourself, you won't be able to help anyone. You've got to give yourself the oxygen first. You have to pursue your dreams and be your own person and do what gives your life joy and meaning, or you will be an empty shell. I realize that's what I've been doing for the past seven years. I've been so focused on getting the oxygen to my kids that I have totally forgotten to breathe myself.

Scott takes my chin in his hand and tilts my face up until I'm looking directly into his eyes. "I hate like hell knowing that I have not been the man you deserve. I hate knowing I haven't been the dad my kids deserve. But I promise you, right here and right now that I am never, ever going to make that mistake again."

Just then, Bella opens her eyes. "Mommy?" she says raspily.

In a second I am by her side, carefully climbing into the small bed beside her. "I'm here baby," I whisper. I take her small hand into mine, and she lays her head against my shoulder.

"Mommy," she says again, this time as a sigh of comfort, her whole body relaxing as if she has been waiting all this time for me to come. This, I think, is my true happiness. Because even though I know I need my own fresh air, I would give my last breath to any of my children. As nice as it was to rediscover myself in

226

California, as rewarding as it was to take pictures and feel like I was doing something important, nothing could possibly be as important as holding my daughter while she sleeps, knowing that she will sleep easier knowing I am here to watch over her. Scott comes and sits in the chair next to the bed, lacing his fingers through mine, and we stay that way as Bella sleeps, the three of us inextricably linked.

Chapter Twenty-Eight

Sunday, March 8th

Miraculously, by mid-afternoon Bella is cleared to leave the hospital provided we keep a close eye on her and she takes it easy, so we take her home, me driving Bella and Scott following in his car. We are greeted by squeals of joy and exuberant hugs from both Will and Daisy (not to mention Elise, who is undoubtedly thrilled to be going home to her quiet, orderly house), and it's hard to tell if they're more excited to see Bella, me, or Scott. Daisy in particular seems to have become more of a Daddy's girl in my absence. Bella dramatically and with great relish recounts her entire adventure to her fascinated little brother, who wants blow by blow details of the helicopter ride, and her horrified mom, who cringes at the details of the helicopter ride. I unpack and hand out the gifts I got for them in California, much to the delight of Will, who has been looking jealously at the array of flowers and stuffed animals that have arrived for Bella. Hugging the stuffed otter I brought him, he snuggles up to me and wants to hear all about California, so I tell them about seeing the pod of whales, the antics of the otters, and the beautiful beach that was just outside my door.

Not to be left out, Daisy climbs into my lap, bouncing up and down as she says, "My see whales too!"

"Really!" I exclaim, used to her vivid imagination.

"No Daisy, those were penguins we saw," Will says, and I look questioningly at Scott.

"I took them to the zoo on Friday," he explains.

"Wow," I say. "I'm impressed."

"I was serious, Liz," Scott says.

Confused, I turn back to Daisy, who is still babbling about the whales she saw. I want to believe him, but how can I be sure he's really changed, and that he won't go back to his old ways, tomorrow or in a month, or in a year?

Over the next few days, as I try to settle back into my life I feel like a slightly off-kilter wooden puzzle pieces that Daisy is trying to push into place. I'm in the right spot, but I haven't quite slipped into place. I watch Bella for headaches, listlessness, balance problems, or other signs of complications from her concussion, and I watch Scott for signs that he will once again stop being the man I fell in love with. And I keep thinking about Charlie, what could have happened, and what could still happen.

By Wednesday I'm slowly going stir crazy, so I'm thrilled when Angie calls to see if I want to meet for drinks after dinner. Although she's come by several times since I've been home to see Bella, we haven't been able to really talk with the kids around. I know she's dying to hear about my weekend almost as much as I'm dying to talk to her about it.

We meet at Tia Carmen's, a local Mexican restaurant that's our favorite place to chat over margaritas and chips and hot sauce.

"Hey," I say, hugging her before sliding into the booth opposite her. "I am so glad you called! I really needed to get out. Are Meg and Kate coming?"

"Yes, but not until eight. Kate is at a meeting and Meg's husband was doing something, so it's just us for awhile, which is good because I wanted a chance for just us to talk first. So, what happened? I can see in your face that you are not the same as when you left. Did you do it? Did you join the Ex Sex Club?"

"Oh Ang," I say with a sigh. "I don't even know where to begin. It seems like it's been a year since I went to the airport last

Thursday, and it hasn't even been a whole week." I tell her about my weekend with Charlie, how close I came to making love with him, how alive and like my old self I felt when I was with him, about Scott's speech at the hospital, and how totally confused I am now.

I know it's bad when Angie has nothing to say. I wait patiently as she methodically scoops hot sauce onto her chip, and then pops it into her mouth, chewing thoughtfully.

"Have I told you about Shawn?" she says.

"Your ex? Sure," I say. "You were engaged to him when you met Richard."

"Well, I kept having these dreams about him. In one of them, we were on some fantasy mission and together we had to take a crystal ball through the forest. In other dreams, I'd just be with him doing regular things, sometimes with Tyler and Hannah, and sometimes just us, and it just felt so right in my dream. It made me start wondering if maybe I'd picked the wrong guy. Things aren't always that perfect with Richard, and I thought maybe I screwed up, maybe I was supposed to have married Shawn. The last dream I had about him he was living next door and we were taking the kids somewhere together, as naturally as anything, and it seemed so real it made me wonder how true my dreams were. Like maybe we were soul mates and were really meeting in some parallel universe. In my dream, I still recognized him but he looked older and his curly blond hair had been closely shaved into that hot "older man losing his hair" look. It was so freaking real! I had to know for sure, so I looked him up."

"And?" I say. "Did you find him?"

"I found him, but I barely recognized him. He didn't look anything like he did in my dreams. He looked middle-aged, with thinning blond hair, two chins and a pocket protector."

"Seriously?" I exclaim.

"Yes," she says glumly. "I felt so betrayed. It's very demoralizing when your hot ex turns into a middle aged used car salesman. But I haven't dreamed about him again since then. It made me realize he was just a fantasy my mind had invented to get me through the rough spots in my own marriage. I think time and our memory give our exes a luster they probably can't live up to in real life. Now, unfortunately for you, your Charlie is still as hot..."

"Hotter," I interject.

"Okay, hotter than you remember, but you two broke up for a reason. He may have been wonderful for a weekend, but what would he be like as a partner for the long haul? He wasn't there when you were pregnant and gained fifty pounds and threw up every day. He didn't talk you through post partum depression and rub your feet when you couldn't reach them yourself. He hasn't sat by your daughter lying in a hospital bed all night. Would he offer to change jobs so you could stay home with your kids? I'm just saying, be honest with yourself. Are you in love with Charlie, or are you in love with the memory of some super guy you've created in your mind to fall back on when reality doesn't measure up?"

"I don't know, Ang," I say. "You're right. I do, or I did love Scott, and he and I have this whole history together. He's the father of my children, for crying out loud. But I don't know if it's enough anymore. I don't know what Charlie would be like for the long haul. I mean, we did break up because he couldn't do a long distance relationship, but that was a lifetime ago. We're adults now. And since we've reconnected, Charlie really listens to me. He makes me feel like I am important, like I matter. Besides, I thought you were all for me having a fling with Charlie."

"Liz, you are in the enviable position of having two men in love with you. But I have never thought this was about Charlie, or even Scott, loving you. It's about you loving you. You need to reconcile who you used to be with the woman you are now and the

231

woman you want to be, and then you need to be that woman and love that woman."

"You know, you can really be a bitch sometimes," I say to Angie.

She smiles. "I know," she says. "And I take great pride in that. But you know I'm a bitch because I love you. Now take Auntie Angie's advice and have a margarita. A margarita, or even better, five margaritas, can fix just about anything. "

Just then, Meg and Kate arrive with a fanfare of hugs and finding spots for purses and ordering drinks and the seriousness of the moment is over.

"How's Bella?" Kate asks.

"She's going to be fine," I say. "But I think it took about six years off my life. Now she's bored and ready to go back to school."

"That was so scary," Meg says.

"Tell me about it," I agree. "But she was pretty nonchalant about the whole thing. She asked me last night if I was worried that she might have gone to heaven and I said yes because I wanted to be with her for a long, long time and she said, 'Don't worry mommy, even when we're in heaven we'll always be in each other's hearts.'" I tear up just thinking about it.

"Aw," Meg and Kate say in unison, and Kate leans over to hug me. Then she adds, "But honey, you can't think about the 'what ifs'. The important thing is what is."

"So tell us about your weekend," Meg says. "What happened with Charlie?"

"Well, we know she looked good," teases Kate.

I give them the edited version, telling them about Harbor Falls, my sightseeing trip with Charlie and the beach party, but leaving out the parts where I kissed Charlie and fell asleep at his house naked, and thinking he might be my destiny.

"Wow," says Meg. "It sounds wonderful. It makes me want to go on vacation."

"The best part is I got paid for it, or I will," I say.

"I think you need a writer to accompany you on your next fantastic assignment," Kate says. "Or perhaps an on-site wardrobe consultant?"

"I'll be your assistant," Meg volunteers.

"I'll bring the drinks," Angie says, and we all laugh.

"Seriously," Kate says. "We should all go somewhere together. Wouldn't that be fun? We can leave the kids with the daddies and have a girl's weekend."

"I'm in," I say. I might have been hesitant to do this before, but I now know Scott can handle the kids. "But no one is allowed to go to any birthday parties while we're gone."

"Here, here," Angie says, lifting her glass. "To girls' weekends."

"I'm in," Meg says, touching her glass to Angie's, "as long as we don't go on a Monday, Wednesday or Friday."

We all look at her quizzically. "That's why I'm late. When I told John we were going out tonight, he informed me that he ALWAYS he works out on Mondays, Wednesdays and Fridays and they are 'non-negotiable.' Let's hope I don't die on a Monday, Wednesday or Friday because they're non-negotiable." She imitates her husband so well that we all bust out laughing.

The conversation and margaritas flow, and the evening flies by. Before we know it, we are the last people in the restaurant and the waiters are stacking up the chairs around us. We are still laughing at Angie's story about confiscating her son's dive torpedoes ("Have you seen those things? They're downright sexual. They're much better off in my bedroom.") when Meg says, "Oh my gosh, I'm about to pee my pants." We all laugh again, and then she gives Angie a little shove. "No really. Move! I'm about to pee my pants."

Once we're all up, we go to the restroom together like we're teenagers and then leave, much to the relief of the restaurant workers. As I drive home, I find myself thinking about my friends and their marriages. There's Angie, who is so confident in every area of her life but feels like she has to work so hard to keep Richard in love with her. And Kate, who stays with her husband despite his constant infidelity because despite it all, she still loves him and wants to keep her family intact for Chloe. Then there's Meg and John, who act like two CEOs who have figured out how to divide running the company based on each other's strengths and live separate lives organized around getting their kids from one activity to the next. I realize no marriage is perfect, but mine is pretty good. Even though Scott's not perfect, he wants to be, and maybe that's enough.

He may go back to taking me for granted, but it's really up to me to make sure that doesn't happen again. I've got to have enough respect and love for myself to demand more. In that instant, I make peace with the fact that it's okay for me to have a life, to have aspirations for myself, and that my children will actually be better off for it. Not only will I be able to give them more of myself when I'm personally fulfilled, but I also need to set a good example. I want my girls to dream big and chase those dreams, and I want Will to one day find and love a woman who thinks for herself and has her own ideas and wants and needs. I realize Angie is right. This whole thing with Charlie has been more about me finding and loving me than about someone else loving me.

When I get home, Scott is asleep in bed with the lamp on. Smiling over his apparent attempt to wait up for me, I gently remove the book he was reading that is laying across his chest, intending to put it on the night table before climbing into bed. But as I glance at the book, I realize he has been reading *52 Weeks of Spice*. Where on earth did he find this? I look to see what page he's on and find that in typical Scott fashion, he has marked certain pages with sticky notes. I glance around, half expecting to find a highlighter. Curious, I climb into bed and thumb through the book, checking out what he's marked.

'Cook a candlelight dinner and serve it naked.' Hmm, has some potential, but memories of Will pointing to Scott's guy parts when they were in the shower, saying, "Daddy, when I grow up I'm going to be big like you!" make me think this isn't a good idea unless all the kids are sleeping over somewhere else. 'Experiment with chocolate syrup, whipped cream and bananas.' Bananas? Really? 'Send your lover on a scavenger hunt, with suggestive photographs as clues.' That has blackmail written all over it. Definite potential!

I am smiling at the entry that suggests having sex in a public place when I feel Scott's hand on my thigh. I look over at him and he is smiling at me, that wonderful, easy smile I fell in love with that makes me feel like the only woman in the world, the one he is inviting to accompany him on a great adventure.

"Sex in a public place?" I say. "Was my humiliation on the tennis courts not enough?"

"I'm just trying to think of everything I can to make you stay," he says simply.

"Oh, Scott," I say with a sigh. "You have been a total ass, but I still love you. And nothing happened in California. We kissed, but that's all. Charlie is my past, but you are my present. You are my future. I'm not going anywhere. And I don't think we need this anymore," I add, tossing the book onto the floor.

He scoots closer to me, wrapping his arm around me and pulling me tight against his chest so we are spooning.

"No," he agrees in a low, sexy voice. "All we need is each other."

Chapter Twenty-Nine

Six weeks later (Friday)

"C'mon, Bella, we're going to be late," I yell up the stairs. I swear, I don't remember caring as much about what I wore when I was Bella's age, but then again, she is getting ready for her grandfather's wedding so I guess I should be a little more understanding. Not that I didn't agonize a bit over what I was going to wear myself. In fact, I had a nice little black dress picked out for myself, but Scott nixed it.

"You wear black to a funeral," he said.

"And your point is?" I had said questioningly.

He had sighed and wrapped his arms around me, rubbing my back, and I had leaned into him, still thrilled with our newly rediscovered habit of connecting physically whenever possible--a hug here, a brush of the hand there. "We should at least pretend we're happy about it," he said.

Although I won't really admit it to anyone but myself, the truth is I've finally made a sort of peace with Harry marrying Ruthless. After all, but for the grace of God, too many Red Lotus cocktails, and a rogue horse, I might have followed in his orthopedic shoe wearing footsteps. I never thought I would say this, but I even kind of understand him; life is too short to not be happy. I still miss my mother-in-law and life as we knew it before they got divorced, but I no longer wonder if Scott or I will end up like them and one day wake up and not love each other anymore.

That's not to say that we won't ever have marital trouble again, but at least I know if we go down, we'll go down fighting.

The last six weeks have reminded me of the first few years Scott and I were dating, although back then I'm pretty sure I never grabbed his hand on a date and said excitedly, "Look honey, a red fire truck!" Will delightedly moans "Gross" every time he catches us kissing in the kitchen, and I once again feel loved and cherished, both by Scott and by myself.

I haven't talked to Charlie again since I called him the week after Bella got out of the hospital to tell him I was over-nighting the photos to him.

"I'm going to be in Dallas next week," he'd said. "Why don't you give them to me in person? Then I can see you again." I could hear the smile in his voice, and I dreaded the inevitable conversation we had to have.

"I don't think that's a good idea Charlie," I'd started.

"Decided to stick with what you've got, huh?" he'd asked lightly, and for a split second I fancied I was still the one who could see through his bravado and chase away the hurt he wouldn't show. But that wasn't my place anymore.

"Charlie, I will always love you. I will always love who we used to be together, and I value the friendship we have now. But I am right where I'm supposed to be…where I want to be."

"I hope he loves you," he'd said. "I mean, really loves you. You deserve it Liz."

"Thank you," I'd said. "I do deserve it. And so do you. Goodbye Charlie. Thanks for everything."

"Goodbye, Lizzie Moore, more, more," he'd said softly, and after he hung up, I sat there for a long time, realizing that we had both finally said goodbye to Lizzie Moore, but that Lizzie Cartwright was turning out to be alright. A few seconds later, my phone had beeped, alerting me that I had a text. It was from Scott.

"The leftover Chinese food is good, but it's spicy," I'd read. I'd smiled at the familiar domesticity of it which was surprisingly welcome.

"Just like the chef," I had texted back, grateful yet again for Scott's innate ability to ground me and remind me of just how fantastic he, and my life with him, was when I needed it most.

Three minutes later, he'd sent another text that said,

"Dear Mrs. Cartwright, Please be advised that Struthers, Compton and Williams has strict policies regarding sexual innuendo and your recent texts are inappropriate and in violation of our sexual harassment work ethics. Please note that all texts and phone calls received during business hours will be monitored for compliance. If your behavior persists, you will be required to attend a sensitivity training class, which will be led by counselor Cartwright."

Sensitivity training, huh? Sounded kind of kinky. Smiling, I had texted my response. *"Kiss my spicy ass."*

Scott's response arrived a heartbeat later. *"Believe me, I will."*

I shake off the pleasant memory of him doing just that last night after the kids went to bed and try to focus on the weekend before us, which is certain to be filled with wedding festivities. At the last minute, Harry and Ruth decided to get married at Ruth's house where she and Harry have been living together since he gave up his bachelor pad in November, instead of the church as they had originally planned. We are going there tonight for the rehearsal and a family dinner with Harry's family, which consists of us, Mike and Elise, plus Ruth's family, a horde of half a dozen siblings and their families, none of whom we have ever met, as well as Ruth's son. Tomorrow the wedding will take place in their backyard, followed by a reception/pig roast. Only in Texas!

Scott has been at the house with his dad since this morning, and now that Bella is home from school, we are driving to Fort Worth to meet up with them. I check once more to make sure I haven't forgotten the wedding gift, the girls' white dresses, Will's miniature suit, and the just above the knee ruched silk lime green sheath with one sequined shoulder strap that I finally chose for myself , which I think says I'm happy it's spring but I'm definitely not part of the geezer wedding party. Satisfied I haven't forgotten anything, we make the one hour trek to Ruth and Harry's.

Scott is already half drunk when we arrive, which I suppose is to be expected given that he's about to get a step mother at the tender age of thirty-six.

"You doing okay?" I ask when we get there.

"I am now," he says, hugging me and the kids.

I get us settled into the adjoining guest rooms Ruth has assigned us to, then go outside to meet Ruth's family while the kids run around with the assortment of other children racing around the folding chairs that are set up outside. After being introduced to a dizzying number of family members ("Hi, I'm Rory, Ruth's son and these are my four kids," "I'm Ruth's sister Anne, and these are my kids, Thing One and Thing Two"), I realize I am never going to be able to keep them all straight. I head to the kitchen to look for a bottle of wine. At least if I start drinking I'll have an excuse for not remembering anyone's name.

The women are bustling about the kitchen, along with a team of caterers who have brought in huge pans of lasagna, giant bowls of salad, and jugs of sweet tea for the odd friend or relative who shuns the two cases of wine sitting on the granite bar. I help out wherever I'm needed until we are summoned for the rehearsal. I sit next to Scott on the front row watching as the various children of both families walk up the aisle-Ruth's teenaged granddaughters methodical and self-conscious as junior bridesmaids, Bella and Daisy precious and adorable (at least until Daisy takes a fistful of rose petals and hurls them at her sister, giggling), and Will, who sprints up the aisle with pillow holding the rings clutched under his arm like a running back intent upon making it across the goal line without being tackled.

239

When the rehearsal is over, we all gather for dinner around the tables that have been set up under the trees. The kids sit at their own table nearby, while Scott and I are seated with Harry and Ruth, Elise and Mike, Ruth's son and daughter-in-law and her sister Anne, who is the matron of honor, and her husband. We are just about finished with our lasagna when Ruth clears her throat and says, "I have a few small gifts for everyone."

She turns to me and Scott first, and says, "I got the kids some little toys to give them after the wedding tomorrow, but I wanted you to have these." She hands me three flat, square packages, wrapped in glossy white paper and topped with silver bows. Inside I am touched by the gift. I'm also a little pissed because it's getting harder and harder to dislike her, and now it will be virtually impossible since she has given me such a perfect and thoughtful gift. "Thank you," I say genuinely. "These are wonderful."

She gives her son Rory drawings of each of his girls as well, and her sister Anne and Elise each get a beautiful painting of flowers – roses for Anne and violets for Elise.

"Ruth is quite the artist," Harry says proudly, giving his bride to be a hearty slap on the back as if she is one of his fishing buddies, leaving me to wonder again what could possibly have drawn them together. I find out soon enough, when Ruth hands Harry a larger version of the packages she has given us. "For the love of my life," she says.

He tears open the paper and we all stare, stunned, at the 11x14 self-portrait she has drawn of herself completely nude.

"Wow," Harry says, leaning over to kiss her. "This is without a doubt the best present I have ever received. I love it! And we were looking for something to hang over the couch. This will be perfect."

"I thought so too," Ruth agrees.

I am frantically looking about for the kids to make sure they aren't watching their grandfather open his "gift," when Harry says, "Thank you all for being here to share our big day. It's going to be great. And we have a little surprise planned for everyone tomorrow."

"Heaven help us," Elise mutters to me, and we both dissolve into giggles.

After dinner and dessert, I round up the kids and take them to get ready for bed. Once they are tucked in, Scott comes in to kiss them goodnight.

"The guys are staying up playing poker. Kind of like a bachelor party for dad. You okay with me hanging out for awhile?" he asks.

"Sure," I say, giving him a kiss. "I'm just going to lie here and stare at the light until the image of your step mom naked is burned out of my memory."

I fall asleep quickly despite the noise and celebration outside, waking up once around three when Daisy cries out. Bleary eyed, I tiptoe over to the pack and play and rub her back, and she quickly falls back to sleep. I gratefully climb back into bed, scooting over to wrap myself around Scott's naked and warm body.

When I wake up again, the sun is streaming in through the slats of the blinds and Scott and I are spooning.

"Good morning," I say seductively, reaching back and squeezing his butt. "How did you do last night? I have two of a kind if you want to see." I roll over to give him a kiss and "AAAAAARRGGGGHHH!" There's a naked man in my bed, a man whose butt I just squeezed. A man who is not Scott!

The man, who is roughly Scott's size but about fifteen years younger and decidedly more shaggy and unshaven, opens one eye and drawls, "Well, hello, angel face."

By now I have jumped out of bed and gotten a hold of myself just enough to start blabbering nonsensically. "Oh my gosh.

I am so sorry. I thought you were someone else. What the hell are you doing in my bed? Look, you'd better leave."

He languidly climbs out of bed, stark naked, and starts gathering his clothes off the floor.

"Oh, my head," he moans. "Too much tequila." He starts to go into the bathroom.

"Wait! You can't go in there!" I say. "My kids might see you."

"Kids?" he looks horrified. "You have kids? Geez lady, who are you?"

"I'm Liz, Harry's daughter-in-law," I say. "Who are you?"

"Seth. My dad is Ruth's brother."

"Okay, okay," I say, just wanting to get this young, naked man out of my bedroom before one of the kids wander in. "Just go."

"Can I put my clothes on first?"

"If you have to," I say, turning around. It's getting awkward having a conversation with a naked guy.

Unfortunately, at that moment Scott walks in. "What the hell is going on?" he asks in bewilderment.

The next few minutes would be comical if they weren't happening to me. Actually, they're pretty comical anyway, especially since Scott and I keep catching each other's eye, trying not to laugh, as Seth, still naked, looking terrified, and obviously uncertain what happened last night, starts trying to explain how he apparently stumbled into my room.

Scott finally takes pity on him and says, "Let's just forget about it. Nothing happened; it was an accident. No foul, no harm. Just go in there," he gestures towards the adjoining bathroom, "put some clothes on and find your own room. And your own woman."

"Dude, she has kids!" he warns as he scurries into the bathroom.

When we hear the door to the bathroom close, Scott and I finally lose it. Once we stop laughing long enough to catch our breath I say, "Oh my gosh, that was horrible. When I first woke up I thought he was you! I actually felt him up!"

This sends Scott into another fit of laughter, and I am grateful that he is not a man who is prone to jealousy, that even given everything we have been through over the last few months he is confident enough in me and our marriage to laugh at finding another man in my bed. I finally get a hold of myself enough to say, "So where were you?"

"I fell asleep on a lawn chair with Dad talking to me. Didn't wake up until the sprinklers came on." I look at him more closely and notice that his shirt and pants are spotted with water.

"Please tell me we will survive this weekend," I groan, falling back into his comfortable embrace.

"We will survive this weekend," Scott assures me. "Wait here. I've got a present for you."

He gets up and comes back with a brown handled shopping bag, which he hands to me. "For today," he says.

I open the bag and pull out a shoe box. I lift the lid and squeal with delight as I pull out a pair of lime green, Jimmy Choo sling back pumps, just like the ones that were confiscated during the handbag store fiasco, although these look startlingly like the real thing.

"How did you get these?" I ask. "I thought the police kept them."

"They did," he says. "But you liked them so much and you were so disappointed, I went out the next week and bought you the real thing."

I realize that he has had them all this time. All that time I had been thinking he didn't pay attention to what I wanted, that he didn't really know me anymore, and he'd had these wonderful, fabulous shoes. I throw my arms around him and say, "Thank

243

you! Thank you! Thank you! Thank you! I love them. And I love you for being you and for loving me and for buying me shoes." I am crying now because I realize how close we both came to totally screwing up something so right.

"No crying," Scott says tenderly. "It's my dad's wedding day." He pauses for a second and then says, "You're right. Totally appropriate. Carry on!" Of course that makes me laugh and the moment passes.

Marriage, I think, is like a quilt fashioned out of squares made up of all the little moments stitched together, until one day you look back and can finally see the pattern that is the life you have woven together. If you look closely you might see some crooked stitches, but it's still beautiful because it's yours. I know when I look back on the quilt of the life Scott and I have made together, somewhere there will be a lime green shoe, the symbol of one imperfect man's love for one imperfect woman.

Chapter Thirty

Saturday, 3:00 p.m.

It's three o'clock and all of the wedding guests are seated. I am in the front row designated for family, flirting with the best man who is standing next to his dad looking like he might throw up. He looks so cute in the dark suit he usually saves for court appearances, and I notice that he needs a haircut since his blond hair is curling around his collar. On second thought, he looks kind of rugged and hot and movie star-ish this way, so maybe I won't mention it.

The music starts and Ruth's four granddaughters appear, followed by Bella and Daisy, who throw fistfuls of rose petals along the red carpet that has been laid out over the grass to create an aisle as they make their way to the front. They both look so beautiful and precious in their identical cream colored dresses with little sequins sewn at the bodice and a huge organza bow tied at the back, wreaths of flowers in their blond hair, that my heart literally catches in my throat. Daisy stops to wave to her daddy before depositing her basket at the alter, and then they both run over to join me. I settle Bella in a tulle covered folding chair between me and Elise, Daisy snuggled in my lap, and we watch Will hurtle up the aisle again, practically tossing the pillow at Harry before rushing over to me and whispering loudly, "How was that?"

"Touchdown!" I say, tousling his sandy blond hair.

After that, Ruth's sister walks down the aisle followed by Ruth herself, looking elegant in a cream colored suit, and I can't help but notice how Harry's eyes light up when he sees her. The ceremony itself is over quickly, uneventful except for the moment right after Harry says "I do," when Daisy drops one of the fruit snacks I have given her in an attempt to keep her quiet and loudly says, "Uh oh!"

The small crowd erupts into applause as Harry dramatically dips Ruth and kisses her, and I idly wonder if he will throw his back out again. Then everyone is congratulating the happy couple, and we are making our way across the lawn to where a band and dance floor has been set up alongside long tables loaded with food and the poor pig.

Harry taps on his glass and addresses us all. "Thank you all for sharing this wonderful day with us. Ruth has made me so happy, and I am looking forward to a lot of good times together. We want you all to have a good time, so please eat, drink and dance. For our first dance together, we decided to do something that means something special to us, so here goes."

He grabs Ruth's hand and the band starts to play. Except oddly, instead of something by Nat King Cole or Neil Diamond that Kate could sing along to, it sounds a lot like Michael Jackson's "Thriller."

"Oh no," I say, nudging Scott. "You should go tell the band they're playing the wrong song." Harry and Ruth are kind of lamely bobbing their heads in time to the opening sequence. I wonder if they even know what song this is.

Just as Scott is striding across the lawn to the bandstand, Harry and Ruth plant themselves in the middle of the dance floor and start stepping in time to the music, their heads jerking to the side in complete tandem.

"Oh no," I breathe to no one in particular as they both start zombie dancing. "They did not pick "Thriller" as their wedding song!" Harry is gyrating his hips, and I feel certain I will need some kind of formal therapy after this weekend.

"C'mon," Harry yells, motioning for us to join them. I am shaking my head in horror, but Bella is laughing and grasping both Scott's and my hands, pulling us out onto the dance floor, and before I know it I am line dancing and making zombie hands. "Thriller" ends, and then we are doing the "Twist" and "YMCA" and a bunch of other songs I don't even know, but I am dancing along to them anyway.

An hour later I collapse in a chair, exhausted. My kids, with their infinite energy, are still out there dancing.

Scott sits down next to me. "Want a slow comfortable screw?"

"Right now?" I say, a bit taken aback.

It's a drink dad's made for the pig roast," he explains. "Sloe gin, Southern Comfort and orange juice."

"I'll pass," I say regretfully with a nod towards the kids. He pulls me to him and whispers in my ear, "I love that you even considered that!"

"You should've offered her a Slow Comfortable Screw against the Wall!" says Harry with a guffaw. I didn't hear him coming.

"Dad!" Scott says, exasperated. To me he says, "It's the same recipe with vodka and Galliano. Sorry." He gets up to go help his dad retrieve more wine from the house, and I take a glass of champagne that Mike offers me before he sweeps Elise out onto the dance floor.

Rory wanders over, sits down next to me, and says, "Welcome to the family. Although I have to warn you, we put the fun in dysfunctional."

I smile. "Then we should all get along fine," I say. "But I should tell you, I'm the normal one on our side."

"Of course," he says with a conspiratorial wink. "So am I!" We laugh, and the first piece of the bridge connecting my family with this new one is laid.

"Mom said Scott is a lawyer. What about you?"

Seven years ago, this was an easy question to answer-I was a media consultant and could support that claim by conversing intelligently about marketing strategies, insider gossip on hotels and travel talk. One year ago, I would have likely given a flippant answer to hide my own insecurity and belief, buried somewhere in my subconscious, that "stay at home mom" was not a respectable or important enough job. Three months ago, with a death grip on a new found sense of purpose, I would have quickly said "photographer" to assure the asker that I actually did something worthwhile, as if raising three children to be well-adjusted and productive adults wasn't. I could still claim that title, since Ava called me last week, going on about how happy they were with my photographs and asking if I would be interested in doing more freelance work, and since my portrait business is steadily growing. But today, with the wisdom of knowing that a woman is defined by the way she lives rather than by any title you can try to label her with, I give the most honest answer I can.

"I'm someone," I say simply. "Someone who wishes on stars and turns kisses into magic. Someone who dances in the living room and doesn't care how ridiculous it looks because it's worth anything to hear my kids laugh. Someone who enjoys a glass of wine once a week with my three best friends, and who loses and gains the same five pounds over and over. Someone who lays her head on her husband's chest each night and falls asleep to the sound of his heartbeat. Someone who takes the occasional picture that stops time, if only for a moment. Someone who makes memories-for myself, for my husband, for my kids, and sometimes for people I don't know."

"Wow," he says. "I'm just an engineer."

We sit there in companionable silence until I say, "So what did you get them for a wedding gift?" I had been truly challenged by this, since between the two of them they already have everything, and they hadn't registered for so much as a fork.

"An electric drill," he says sheepishly. "What can I say? I'm a guy. What did you give them?"

"A book," I say with a grin, thinking of the *52 Weeks of Spice* book wrapped in silver paper sitting on the gift table. "Oh, and a really fantastic eggbeater. So where are your girls? They were all so poised and beautiful in the wedding."

"I think they've snuck off with their cell phones," he says with exasperation. "Just wait," he warns. His eyes drift to the dance floor, where Bella and Daisy are twirling around until they get so dizzy they fall down and Will is doing a really jacked up rendition of the chicken dance. "Believe it or not, I actually miss the days when they were little," he says wistfully.

I look at my children and realize that although there are days I long for silence and me time, nights when I could sit down and cry with fatigue and exasperation, I'm going to miss these days too. I watch as Scott comes onto the dance floor and hoists Daisy onto his shoulders, then takes both Bella and Will by the hand and leads them in an impromptu waltz. They are all flushed cheeked and laughing, and my heart feels full. I try to take a mental snapshot, knowing this is one of those moments I will want to keep forever as a reminder of what sheer happiness feels like. This moment, right here, right now, has never felt so perfect, and I know without a doubt this is where I'm supposed to be. I'm not lost anymore, wondering who I am. I am Elizabeth Cartwright- wife, mother, daughter, daughter-in-law, and friend. I am an individual, but Scott, Bella, Will and Daisy are part of me too. They complete me and make me a better version of myself.

Out of the blue, it starts to rain. It's just a spring shower, not a heavy downpour, so the band carries on and I watch my husband and kids on the dance floor, twirling with delight in the rain. Bella looks over and sees me watching them and yells, "Mommy, come dance with us." For just a moment, I tilt my face back to feel the rain, soft and cleansing, washing away the old and making way for something new. Then, with a smile, I get up and go join my family.

Made in the USA
Middletown, DE
12 November 2017